UNEXPECTED THREAT

GERI KROTOW

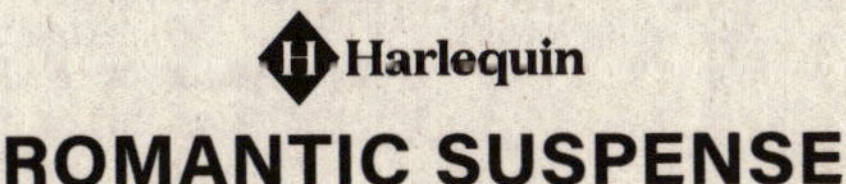

Harlequin

ROMANTIC SUSPENSE

ISBN-13: 978-1-335-47198-7

Unexpected Threat

Copyright © 2026 by Geri Krotow

Recycling programs for this product may not exist in your area.

 Harlequin Enterprises ULC
22 Adelaide St. West, 41st Floor
Toronto, Ontario M5H 4E3, Canada
www.Harlequin.com

HarperCollins Publishers
Macken House, 39/40 Mayor Street Upper,
Dublin 1, D01 C9W8, Ireland
www.HarperCollins.com

Printed in Lithuania

1 2 3 4 5 6 7 8 9 10 LIT 28 27 26 25

"Friends?" He held out a hand. The same hand that had comforted her, twice, in the last five minutes.

Her body tensed, though, as if he'd wielded a knife. Except the taut coil in her stomach wasn't from fear or impending danger.

Get him out of here.

"Friends." She allowed her hand to be swallowed by his, expecting—hoping for?—a quick, short-lived gesture.

And shocked both of them when she reached her other hand up to his nape and pulled his face down to hers.

"Toni?" His query was even, and his neutral expression hadn't changed, but she saw his pupils dilate, heard his sharp inhalation. Most telling? He didn't take a step backward.

She closed the distance between them.

Their lips met in chaste surprise, probably the most platonic contact they'd ever shared with their mouths. Until the pressure that had been ratcheting the tension deep inside her took over, insisting upon release.

Dear Reader,

Welcome back to the Cascade Confidential miniseries and the Pacific Northwest!

Book 2 finds Toni O'Malley, the oldest O'Malley sibling, stunned when her ex and co-parent with twelve-year-old Sierra, Brandon Anderson, moves back to the Seattle area after over a decade living half a world apart. Toni liked their co-parenting arrangement when Brandon was stationed at diplomatic posts throughout Asia. Now that he's become her next-door neighbor—really!—she's not happy about all of the emotions his nearness is bringing up, including their very potent sexual chemistry.

But there's a killer on the loose who targets Toni because of the success of the family security agency, and worse, the killer decides the best way to send a sinister message to Toni is by harming her daughter.

I had so much fun writing Toni and Brandon's story, and seeing them work together to save their (very smart) twelve-year-old daughter as well as their relationship. Plus, writing about the Pacific Northwest is always fun since my Navy family lived there for several years, and it's where I set my first Harlequin miniseries, Whidbey Island.

Do you know that besides romantic suspense, I write mystery novels, too? Keep up with my latest by subscribing to my newsletter via my website at www.gerikrotow.com.

I'd love for you to follow me, too!

Facebook: www.Facebook.com/gerikrotow

Instagram: www.Instagram.com/geri_krotow/

Enjoy Toni and Brandon's journey!

Peace,

Geri

Former naval intelligence officer and US Naval Academy graduate **Geri Krotow** draws inspiration from the global situations she's experienced. Geri loves to hear from her readers. You can email her via her website and blog, gerikrotow.com.

Books by Geri Krotow

Harlequin Romantic Suspense

Cascade Confidential

Agent Under Wraps
Unexpected Threat

Silver Valley P.D.

Her Christmas Protector
Wedding Takedown
Her Secret Christmas Agent
Secret Agent Under Fire
The Fugitive's Secret Child
Reunion Under Fire
Snowbound with the Secret Agent
Incognito Ex
Stalked in Silver Valley

The Coltons of Grave Gulch

Colton Bullseye

The Coltons of Colorado

Stalking Colton's Family

Visit the Author Profile page
at Harlequin.com for more titles.

For Lisa, Paul, Jordan and Josh, with love

Chapter 1

O'Malley Homestead, Montana

"That was intense, Mom."

Toni O'Malley's stomach twisted at the expression on her daughter Sierra's twelve-year-old face. It resembled an aged woman more than a preteen.

"I know, honey. Come here." She hugged her daughter close and kissed the top of her head. For once Sierra didn't fight the physical affection, something she'd been doing more and more as official teenagedom approached. They were both on their knees after having hit the floor in a hail of bullets. The shooting had ceased and the wide-planked wooden floor of her parents' brand-new Montana home was hard yet reassuring under her knees. Sierra's heartbeat pounded against hers, her breathing still coming in shallow pants after surviving the gunfire attack. Toni held back sobs. Sierra was in one piece. Alive.

This is all that matters.

"My whole body's shaking!" Sierra's muffled observation vibrated against Toni's bare shoulder as Sierra clutched Toni's halter-top dress. On a whim, she'd bought a new dress for the occasion, something very much out of her usual professional attire of white buttoned blouse, fitted ponte knit pants or leggings, and either a cardigan or a jacket. The hem of the fuchsia chiffon A-line with spaghetti straps was crushed under both their knees. One of Sierra's kitten-heel shoes lay on its side next to one of Toni's pink stilettos, another impulse purchase. The mismatched pair seemed to mock the celebratory mood she'd been in when she'd taken them dress shopping for the O'Malley family event.

So much for a dance party.

"I'm so sorry, baby." Toni's apology came out automatically as she rested her chin on top of Sierra's head, soaking in the relief—she wasn't above using the awful situation to take advantage of being able to express her mama bear love in the way Sierra no longer asked for—even though she wasn't at fault for a rogue crime syndicate member's attack on the entire O'Malley family only moments earlier. The shootout had occurred in the middle of her parents' fiftieth wedding anniversary celebration, no less.

Toni had thrown her body over Sierra's, taking cover from the gunfire. Fortunately the showdown had been short-lived, thanks to her mother Donna's steady hand with an automatic rifle and both her parents' foresight to install bulletproof glass instead of plain for the huge picture windows that lined the far wall of their great room. Donna had retired several months ago from the family's private security firm that she'd founded decades earlier, but her skills remained intact. *Thank goodness.*

"Okay, everyone, I think it's safe to say we can resume our celebration." Kirk O'Malley, Toni's father and

Sierra's beloved grandad, stood in front of the fireplace that boasted a custom cedar mantel he'd hewn from a fallen tree on their over two hundred acres. Local river rock adorned the fireplace and ran up to the ceiling, where the outer side of the enormous chimney was visible through a skylight. "The authorities have the suspect in custody and there's no further threat." The unique timbre of Dad's voice hadn't changed, no matter how gravelly his voice had become, and it rolled across the great room like a comfy blanket. Toni's shoulders let go of the invisible yet tangible weight they'd been holding and she rubbed Sierra's upper arms.

As long as Toni could remember, Dad had always been the one to bring the family back to "planet earth," as he was wont to describe their life away from the intensity of Mom's private security business, Cascade Confidential, or CC, as the family referred to the agency.

Donna had launched the business after she left her operative position at the CIA, thinking it was a better fit for the requirements of the family she desired. Over the last few decades, CC had grown from a small, rented office space near SeaTac International Airport to the restored Victorian Seattle home that now served as its administrative headquarters. They had satellite offices sprinkled throughout the Pacific Northwest, including Portland, Oregon, and Coeur d'Alene, Idaho.

"Give us a minute, will you, Dad?" Aubrey, Toni's younger sister by two years, stood at the kitchen sink and spoke between gulps of water.

Kirk shook his head. "We're all okay, honeybunch. I'll be damned if some son of a pup is going to ruin our—"

"Everybody come out here on the deck, quick!"

Mom's cry from the open deck door interrupted Kirk's declaration.

"What now?" Kevin, thirty and the older of their two brothers, let out a long sigh. "Wasn't the *High Noon* remake enough for one day?"

"Maybe she wants us to do some target practice. You know, since she's already all fired up." Jake, twenty-eight, loved using Kevin as his straight man. Toni would have groaned if she wasn't still shaking off the scary episode. She wasn't the tough person her other siblings were, and it never bothered her that she was their "admin warrior." She knew her strengths as well as her weaknesses. But the reality that she'd not reached for a weapon scared her as much as the bullets had. If the shooter had come nearer, or worse, invaded the multilevel home, she would have been helpless to protect Sierra.

"Come on, Mom!" Sierra urged, unaware of Toni's emotional distress as she tugged on Toni's wrist. *Stay present.* When was the last time Sierra had wanted her to do anything with her?

Regret sucker punched Toni in the gut. While still possessing moments of childlike wonder and enthusiasm, Sierra wasn't walking into adolescence, she was sprinting. Along with the expected physical changes, she'd recently started shutting her bedroom door for privacy and spent hours talking to her best friend instead of Toni. While Toni would do anything to erase the scene they'd just survived, to have it have been one of her frequent anxiety nightmares instead of reality, she was grateful to have her daughter so close she could smell her citrusy shampoo.

"Mom!" Sierra turned the word multisyllabic, adding in the eye roll she'd perfected since starting seventh grade last month.

"Lead the way." Reluctant to let the moment pass, Toni followed Sierra outside. As they joined the rest of the family lined up at the expansive deck's railing, Toni comprehended the urgency of Mom's request.

Her youngest sister, Willow, CC's most recent hire and a former US Marine, was in an intimate embrace with a very attractive man who Toni assumed was none other than FBI Special Agent Jay Lambert.

Jay was the man Willow had been assigned to protect last month on short notice. Toni had given her mere hours to report for duty in eastern Washington, not too far from the satellite office Willow managed for CC in Coeur d'Alene. No one in CC had known Jay was an undercover FBI agent, and in fact, Toni had warned Willow that she believed Jay was part of the crime syndicate that was using the logging company he worked for as a front.

Her stomach churned with compounding regret and not a little guilt. Toni had been wrong about Jay, and Mack Logging and Manufacturing. On so many levels, too, not simply their actual identities.

Willow had handled it. It was over. But Toni kept fighting waves of nausea as acid swirled in her belly. She'd sent her little sister, Marine or no, out to what could have been a lethal assignment. Toni hadn't performed the proper research and vetting of a new client, or she would have found out sooner that the company that had reached out to CC for security was in fact a front for one of the Pacific Northwest's most powerful crime syndicates.

You don't have to do this all alone. Her mother's words

to her as she'd retired from the business ricocheted in her mind.

If she'd only reached out, Donna could have used her numerous contacts to figure out that Jay wasn't an employee of some random logging company, under threat from possible environmental terrorists, but an FBI agent working under deep cover that he'd cultivated over a twenty-four-month period. Jay had planned to stop his supposed boss from completing a bloody takedown of rival syndicates.

Maybe it was fate.

Willow had privately admitted to Toni that she'd fallen in love with Jay, no doubt fearing Toni's ire for getting involved with someone she was paid to protect. Surprising herself, Toni had felt nothing but compassion for her younger sister, and now, happiness. Joy. Not because Jay had literally saved the day, either. He'd been incommunicado with Willow since they'd worked together to bring down the crime syndicate, and the reason was now clear. Two remaining syndicate operatives had escaped apprehension during the main takedown event in the mountains of eastern Washington and had vowed vengeance for losing their entire base of operations. One of them had been stalking Willow over the last weeks and had planned to kill her, along with her family, today. His plans were blown apart when Jay showed up along with an entire team of elite law enforcement officers, who had ensured this was indeed the syndicate's last stand.

Except for the one remaining criminal, still at large. Thankfully he was last pinpointed in Buenos Aires. Far, far away.

Let work go. Everyone's safe.

Watching Willow and Jay openly express their affection was an unusual but most welcome way to cleanse the trauma from her mental palate.

"Cringe much? They need to get a room." Sierra's exclamation broke the thrall the romantic scene held over the family, with Toni's younger brothers being the first to add to the humor.

"Hey, Willow, did you hear your niece? You're burning her eyeballs out over here! Keep it PG, will ya!" Jake yelled, eliciting a guffaw from Kevin.

"Are you going to propose to her?" Kevin added.

The entire family laughed, then drew in a collective gasp as Jay stepped back from Willow and got to one knee.

"Dope," Sierra said, but more quietly. Apparently it was okay to vocalize her disgust at her aunt's PDA, but approval of the situation required more decorum.

"This is something special." Toni spoke without thinking and inwardly winced at how wistful her tone sounded. She didn't want what Willow appeared to now have, and she certainly didn't want her daughter thinking that a man would be her ticket to happily-ever-after.

In fact, Toni had never wanted anything but a career like her mom's, without the spouse and kids. But then Sierra happened, and her only child had become the center of her life as if she'd always been part of the plan. Being a single parent wasn't easy, but Toni considered it a small price for the privilege of raising her sweet girl. The sweet child who was quickly blossoming into a woman.

"Mom, are you crying?" Sierra asked with…awe.

Toni wiped at her cheeks. "I'm so happy for Aunt Willow, honey."

"Huh." The reply was par for the course these days as Sierra seemed as dumbfounded by her mother's behavior as Toni was by her preteen's. Sierra was leaving behind her need for parental approval as she entered her teens. Which meant that she wouldn't need Toni for much of anything before too long. She bit down on her bottom lip, hard.

Maybe you're lonely. And a little jealous of Willow?

She mentally shook off the unbidden thoughts. No, she wasn't lonely. How could the mother of a preteen and CEO of the PNW's largest private security firm ever be lonely? And she had no reason to be jealous of Willow, either. Okay, maybe she was a little envious of her younger sister's ability to throw herself into a love affair, to not have to worry about anyone except herself. But Willow had yet to experience the sheer joy, the incredible gift, that having and raising a child entailed. Toni wouldn't trade being a single mom for anything.

She'd had her shot at a "one and only" years ago, and had passed it up.

Willow and Jay had made their way back up onto the deck, and she stood back, waiting for everyone else to congratulate them. Willow was hugging Jake when her gaze landed on Toni. Within seconds she was giving her younger sister a hug while Jay kept talking to Jake. Tears welled again, but these weren't from fear or relief. Toni was genuinely happy for Willow, if a little surprised at the rapid escalation of her relationship with a man she'd known for little more than a month.

"I'm so glad we caught this bastard," Willow whispered in her ear as they hugged, referring to Fred Clayton. "But we still need to catch his brother, Toby." Typical of Willow, she was still more focused on her assignment than her newly acquired engaged status.

"*We* aren't going to be doing anything of the sort, and you definitely aren't." She pulled back and grasped Willow's shoulders as she smiled at her sister. "Your assignment is complete. We've helped catch all the bad guys. Enjoy this special time with your husband-to-be."

Willow returned the smile, but her expression remained grave. "Listen to me, Toni. Fred came after me because of what Jay and I did, bringing in Veronica and Cal Clayton. He was screaming at us down there—" she pointed at the woods where Fred had tried to kidnap and kill both Willow and Jay "—that the Claytons weren't done with Cascade Confidential. We have to be prepared." Willow's eyes were full of steely conviction. "They're going to try to hurt one of us."

Toni ignored the fear knifing through her and quickly pulled Willow close again. "I hear you, and you have to trust me that I'm on it. Now, go enjoy your fiancé."

Willow walked back to the main group and slid her arm around Jay's waist, lifting her face for a quick kiss. It was a heartwarming scene, no question. But there wasn't enough warmth to melt the ice that had frozen Toni's heart. And her resolve.

No one was going to come after her family and get away with it.

"What have I missed?" A deep male baritone broke through her thoughts and struck a primal chord deep inside. "Jeez, you look so serious, Toni." The man's voice resembled the one person she meticulously kept from her thoughts. *Brandon.*

No. Brandon was in south eastern China, on a consulate trip, unless he'd returned to the embassy, in Beijing, by now? She mentally shook the thoughts away.

Maybe this recent drama really was messing with her mind. Toni turned toward the person who'd asked the question, expecting one of her brothers.

Instead, her long-ago lover, the father of her child and longest-lasting emotional nemesis, stood behind her.

Brandon gazed at her from his stance a few feet away.

Nope, not a dream. More like harsh reality. She opened her mouth, but no words formed as she stared at what she wanted to believe was an apparition.

Chapter 2

"Daddy!" Sierra's shriek had everyone's attention on Brandon, leaving Willow and Jay to finish their PDA without several pairs of eyes on them.

Shock tinged with bemusement elicited tiny goose bumps across her forearms as she watched Sierra launch herself into her father's arms, winding both her arms and legs around the man she worshipped from afar, save for holidays and the month she spent with him every summer. This summer was an exception. Brandon had informed Toni last spring that he wouldn't be able to be available to Sierra until early fall, when he'd come through Seattle. He was a week early.

Just great. The day hadn't escaped becoming a disaster after all. Not when Sierra's biological father—aka Toni's worst yet best mistake—stood on her parents' new deck, in the flesh. He'd crashed a very private *family* event, appearing every bit the most beloved parent in the world. Why hadn't he let her know he'd be here? And who had invited him, anyway?

Mom and Dad, that's who. Her family had always welcomed Jay as one of their own, no matter that he and Toni were 'estranged.' The 'estranged' was something only she and Jay knew about. Her family didn't know that they were in fact, still legally married. Or that they'd been married at all.

She should have pressed for a divorce after they'd secured Sierra's State Department benefits as Brandon's dependent child, right after it was clear that Toni was never going to need a diplomatic spousal status. Because she'd decided making anything but coparenting work was going to be too much, that her family of origin needed her more than Brandon did. Not for the first time, regret at the decision she'd made in the throes of being overwhelmed as a new mom—while Brandon was already at a far distant post, expecting her to follow—raised its ugly specter.

Don't go there. You're just shook up from the gunfire.

Looking for a quick distraction from the self-recrimination that continued to haunt her, she walked to the hammered-tin bucket full of ice and an assortment of beverages, grabbing a split of champagne and a crystal flute from the matching tray. Neither item had suffered any damage from the brief shootout. "Miracles never cease," she murmured to herself as she sat on a cushioned bench and proceeded to open the carbonated beverage.

It took several minutes for Sierra and the rest of the O'Malleys to greet Brandon. He stood with his back near the wall of the house, far from the balcony railing. He'd never been a fan of heights. The image of popping a different bottle of bubbly in a Las Vegas hotel room loomed in her mind, and she remembered she'd been the one to enjoy the sun-drenched balcony of their room while he preferred a poolside chaise lounge.

Toni slowly sipped her bubbly, loath to speak to the

man she much preferred discussing Sierra's needs with on the phone or in emails. They'd both limited their in-person interactions over the years, more so during the last two years. Sierra was old enough to fly on her own and visit Brandon at whatever godforsaken post the State Department sent him to, so they didn't have a whole lot to discuss these days, save for annual video calls to address how they each felt about Sierra's formal education and extracurricular activities. It was the perfect arrangement, as she didn't have to deal with Brandon more than nec-essary and her daughter still had a relationship with her father. In many ways, the quality time Sierra spent with Brandon provided her with more paternal attention than Toni felt she'd ever received from her own father. From as early as she recalled, she'd been the one in charge of all her siblings. She forced herself to relax, crossing her legs and sitting back into the cushions. Yes, she and Bran-don were actually the epitome of a coparenting team.

If your arrangement with Brandon is so perfect, why do you resent him showing up here?

Because Brandon remained a reminder of the impetu-ous woman she'd once been. And the incredible procras-tinator she could still be, exhibit A being the divorce that still hadn't happened.

As though he'd read her mind, he abruptly looked up from his conversation with Sierra. Their gazes met, and the unwelcome—but usual—lightning-bolt awareness shot through her. It was natural, purely hormonal. She didn't date, and her body reminded her that she needed to start considering her physical needs more. Then there was the simple fact that she and Brandon had shared amazing chemistry. The circumstances of Sierra's conception had been incredibly sexy. As her mind ran through its usual thought process that Brandon ignited, however, years of resentment and judgment of the man who'd broken her heart so long ago quickly smothered any sexy thoughts.

Brandon ended his conversation and strode toward her. She sucked in a deep breath and dismissed the loitering moths in her belly. No way in hell would she ever credit Brandon with setting butterflies aflutter. Standing, she squared her shoulders and faced him. The man who'd made her crazy with lust—what she'd briefly believed was love—had aged into an even more attractive middle-aged dad. *So what?* She wasn't the woman who'd fallen for his charms any longer.

He stopped a good two feet away, leaving room for their mutual animosity, no doubt. Perhaps sensing her discomfort.

"Brandon." She gave a curt nod.

"Toni." His gaze sparkled, his mouth curved upward in a polite smile. His silence made her want to squirm.

"What?" She shifted on her feet, crossed her arms over her chest. Brandon didn't reply but took her in as though he were a sponge and she was spilled milk. How long had it been since they'd seen one another in person? *Five years.* At his continued observation, she lost the sliver of patience she'd scraped up. "You've got something on your mind. And I'm guessing you're afraid of my reaction? For the record, yes, I'm not happy at the moment, and yes, your lack of communication is the cause. But enough about me. Just say whatever you need to, Brandon."

"Am I that transparent?" The shutters were closed

on the interest that had glinted in his damnable brown irises only seconds ago, and his smile no longer reached his eyes.

"You look like you have tea you can't wait to spill." She looked past his shoulder, unable to maintain the eye contact. It was always like this with him. Too intense.

He laughed, and the ever-present Montana mountain breeze ruffled his brown hair. Hair that was streaked with silver at his temples—far more than the last time she'd seen him in person—and on the forelock that refused to be tamed. "You sound like Sierra, using such up-to-date lingo. No, I'm not keeping any secrets, and I didn't bring you anything remotely resembling gossip." He had the nerve to grin, and his expression looked more genuine this time as the skin around his eyes folded into deep lines. He took a half step closer. "How are you, Toni?"

She fought to stand her ground, because the bench she'd stood from was right behind her and falling onto it would be most undignified. A sign of weakness. "I'm fine, thank you."

"Really?" His brow raised, he motioned at the remaining cruisers visible in the long drive. "It looks like a combat zone here. I had to show my ID to more officials than I do to enter China." *Zing.* Her family's line of work had never impressed him. He'd expressed concern for his daughter's safety myriad times since they'd began their coparenting custody arrangement.

"It doesn't ever take you long to disparage my choices, does it?" she asked.

"It's a simple observation, Toni. You know I've never taken issue with your family. I love your family—they're part of my daughter. Our daughter. It's their job descriptions I've never been too keen on." Brandon speak for "you chose a job that could put Sierra in danger over me."

Always the diplomat.

"I'm not getting into it with you today, Brandon." Toni bent and took her drink, intent on walking away. She'd thought he'd finally given up on trying to convince her that Sierra would be safer if Toni had a different line of work, or at least distanced herself from any visible involvement with CC. Thankfully he'd stopped asking her to bring Sierra with her and relocate to a foreign service post in the middle of nowhere. As if.

He gently grasped her wrist, stopping her. Again, their eyes met. Brandon actually looked apologetic as they hovered over the coffee table, their faces inches apart. "I don't want to spar with you, either." He'd lowered his voice, his expression grave.

"Too late." She sighed. "Why, exactly, are you here a full week early?"

An amused expression flitted across his features. "Your parents' housewarming and big anniversary party isn't enough?"

"You had no business telling Sierra without my knowing, Brandon." She hated how her voice shook but hopefully he'd take her passion for anger and not disappointment.

He sighed. "Point taken. I didn't have a lot of time what with checking out of my post… I've got something to tell you, and it can't wait. It has to be done in person, too."

Her stomach dipped. Brandon was supposed to be in China for another two years. He'd never leave, not voluntarily. Unless…was he sick? He looked the epitome of healthy American male, but there were so many diseases… She mentally clawed at her composure. "Let me guess. You've decided to marry, and you need my signature on the annulment papers?" She kept her voice low.

He straightened, his gaze narrowed. She shoved her hands into the pockets of her full skirt. The satin cocktail dress seemed too fun, too frivolous in the midst of their dialogue, which had turned scary in a heartbeat.

"We both know that can't happen…without some forethought." The knowing glance he shot her lit embers of anger deep in her belly. Memories of that Vegas weekend, exactly nine months before Sierra was born, assaulted her attempts to ignore them. And what they'd done in the aftermath, while in a lust hangover…

"Right. So what is it, Brandon? If you're not here to tell me you're starting another family, that is. By the way, how long are you in town for this time? Long enough to remind Sierra that you're still the perfect parent? While I'm the big bad disciplinarian?" Her barbs weren't fair but she was still angry that he'd kept his visit from her.

"That's just it. I'm not 'in town,' Toni." He emphasized her phrase. "I'm not here on a visit, or for leave, or for anything temporary. I'm here…for good." He looked around. "Well, not *here* here." He motioned at the surrounding property. "Not Montana."

"What do you mean, 'for good'?" The embers started to flicker into flames, making her face grow hot. Was her pale skin betraying her by turning fire-engine red? Did he notice it? "You're leaving China for a new post?"

He shook his head. "No. I've resigned from the foreign service, Toni. I'm opening my own consulting firm, in Washington."

"Okay. Well, at least DC is a lot closer than Asia. That works better for Sierra." Washington, DC, was where State Department headquarters was, and a natural fit for Brandon since he'd had almost every job an FSO could, except for ambassador. She knew Sierra would love the change, too. She'd accompanied her father to the nation's capital several times, whenever he'd been assigned back there to complete additional diplomatic training.

"Not Washington, DC, Toni. Washington State. I've purchased a home here." His neutral expression showed no indication of the verbal bombshell he'd dropped into their conversation. The implosion these words…if she'd heard him correctly…would make on her life. Her until-now damned near perfect life with Sierra.

She blinked against the stinging sensation striking her eyeballs. And blinked again. The roiling anger in her center turned to brittle ice. She couldn't move. Her breath hitched, but it sounded as though it was someone else's lungs struggling to expand.

What. The. Hell.

He briefly touched her again, this time just above her elbow. "This isn't the place to discuss it—not all the details, anyhow. Let me take you and Sierra out to breakfast when we're all back in the city. You're heading back tomorrow morning?" He spoke as calmly as someone discussing their retirement plans. Not as if he'd just flipped her life on its head.

Sierra jogged over to them, leaned against her father. "Did you tell her yet, Dad?"

"Yes, honey. I've just let your mom know I'm moving to Seattle. Permanently." He looked at Toni as he spoke, his words beginning to sink in as fury ignited deep in her center.

"Your father certainly surprised me." She choked on the words but had to show enthusiasm for Sierra's sake, didn't she? "This will be…so nice for you, sweetie."

"Are you kidding me? It's sick!" She grinned with zero self-consciousness, unusual since she'd had the full set of braces put on six months ago.

"Sick?" Brandon asked. "Who's sick?"

"It means 'cool.'" She spoke as her mind whirred with the consequences of his statement. "You're moving to Seattle."

"I am. I have, in fact, already moved in."

At least Seattle was a forty-minute to one-hour commute from the Craftsman-style home she'd purchased for herself and Sierra less than two years ago. It wasn't as though she'd have to see him all the time. Plenty of co-parents did this, right? And truth was, she'd had it easy until now. As hard as it had been to place Sierra on an international flight alone, she hadn't had to deal with an in-person confrontation with Brandon.

Calm down. She needed to talk to her confidante, Willow. Except her sister was going through her own life-changing phase at the moment.

"Tell her the best part, Dad!" Sierra rocked forward on her brightly painted toes, bursting with excitement. Had it only been yesterday that she and Sierra had gone together for precelebratory mani-pedis? Had that been their last mother-daughter outing without concern for Brandon's schedule?

"Later might be best, sweetheart." He hugged Sierra to him. "Let's enjoy the party for now."

"Tell me what, Brandon?" Toni struggled to mask her confusion, her least favorite emotion.

"Go on, Dad." Sierra encouraged, then placed a hand on Toni's forearm, unconsciously mimicking her father's gesture. "It'll be good for you, too, Mom. You won't have to worry about me as much, because you'll have more time to yourself."

The ice coating in her gut turned glacial. Toni looked to Brandon for a clue. If he thought he was going to take full custody—

He let out a quiet swear word meant for her ears only. "I wanted to wait to tell you, but here goes. I'm not moving to the Seattle *area*. I've decided to be closer. As in, Everett. I bought the house next door to yours."

Toni's stomach stopped churning and plummeted to her pale-pink toenails.

"Wait, what? You…" *Get a grip, girl!* "You bought the…the Flowerses' house?" The midcentury home had been on sale for months, longer than any other in their area, probably because it had had few upgrades since being built, until recently. There had been workers in and out of the house all summer, and she'd assumed they were completing upgrades to expedite a sale. She knew this because the house next door to hers was no farther than the fifteen-foot gravel path that ran between the houses.

"That's the one," Brandon said. His scrutiny was unavoidable as she met his gaze. And wasn't fooled by the wariness in it—he had nothing to fear from her. There was nothing she could do about this very uncozy arrangement.

"I'll have my own bedroom there, too!" Sierra added. Toni looked from her daughter to Brandon and back again. They'd been talking about this behind her back? *For how freaking long?*

"Don't worry, Mom. I'll still use our house as my sleeping house. Dad's house will be my homework place, and where my friends can hang with me when you're downtown. Dad's working entirely from home from here on out." Sierra was clearly parroting what Brandon must have already shared with her. "Dad will be there when I get off the bus every day, too!" Sierra's enthusiastic chatter probably had more to do with her discomfort at her mother's surprise, but Toni wasn't in a space to absorb it.

She couldn't get past the "I bought the house next door" part.

Toni handled top-level security operations and supervised the most delicate assignments for Cascade Confidential. She kept her cool under the direst circumstances, prided herself on her ability to clearly communicate her company's needs and desires no matter the pressure from unexpected and, at times, dangerous, sources.

Brandon's big news had not only left her speechless, but unable to break out of the sense of impending doom that her mind was so good at going to. This was also part of her job at Cascade Confidential: figure out a worst-case scenario and prepare for it. Defeat the enemy before they struck.

But Brandon had not only made a significant move, he'd occupied her and Sierra's until-now perfectly constructed life.

"You okay, Mom?" Sierra spoke as if she were the parent, not Toni.

"Of course I'm fine. We'll talk about this later. I need to go check on your Aunt Willow." Before her anger morphed into a rage she didn't want to express in front of Sierra. "I'll be right back."

It wasn't her best excuse to get out of an uncomfortable spot, but at least it was true. She wanted to see for herself how Willow was doing. Plus, Willow knew her best, and would help her make sense of this mess.

Because there was no better descriptor for what Brandon's presence would make of her life. A total mess.

Chapter 3

Toni walked into the main suite of her parents' new home and found the spa bathroom door was slightly ajar, so she sat on the king-size bed and waited for Willow to finish up. She gave herself a minute to take in the contemporary yet cozy decor, even though her gut still churned from Brandon's announcement.

Mom and Dad had scrimped and saved for years while they raised all of them. As CC's clout and earning power grew, Mom had convinced Dad they needed to move from their modest suburb to a larger home in an excellent school district in Seattle. This had afforded Donna a very short commute to the CC headquarters, then the only office in the agency. But their large family soon filled, then grew out of, the modest Victorian.

Finally, her parents had what they'd deserved all along and it reflected in the main bedroom suite. The high-ceilinged room was set off by exposed beams stained a washed honey, and the polished hardwood floors were softened by plush handwoven area rugs in neutral tones of taupe and blue.

Toni checked her phone for the time. She didn't want to be away from Sierra for too long. And she didn't want

Brandon to think for one second that she'd run from dealing with him.

Even though she had.

Fortunately Willow was once a Marine and almost insanely quick in the shower. She walked out of the bathroom clad in a thick robe that Toni assumed was Mom's. Willow's eyes sparked with enthusiasm when she saw Toni.

"Hey! Have you been waiting for long? The hot water was what my body needed after all that drama!" Willow bent over and wrapped a towel turban-style around her long hair as she spoke. "Did you know Mom and Dad installed steam valves, too? It's a true sauna in there. If this was my place, I'd live in the bathroom."

"After what you've been through, a cold soak might have been smarter. You're going to hurt tomorrow. Ice is your friend right now."

Willow waved her concern away. "I know I look like I took a beating, but this is nothing, trust me. You should have seen how bruised I used to get every time I ran the Marine PT course." She grinned. She plopped down on the bed next to Toni and curled one leg under, facing her. "I promise, you'll have the final report from me before Monday. Let me soak in my new status as an engaged woman, will ya?"

Toni shook her head. "I'm not here to talk about work." Sure, she needed Willow's report to wrap up the case Willow had worked on. The police and FBI would need the report, too, as Willow had stumbled onto a much bigger case when she'd taken on security for an eastern Washington State logging company. But she was more concerned about Willow's very fast—too fast?—

romance with Jay. "I wanted to make sure you're physically okay, of course. But more importantly, I need to know you're really happy, is all." Toni watched Willow as she spoke, grateful for the reprieve from the ongoing housewarming party at the other end of the house. She treasured alone time with her sister and BFF.

"*Happy* doesn't touch how I feel about Jay, Toni." Willow's joy shone through with luminous intensity, contrasting with the shadows under her eyes, the recent scrapes and bruises on her cheekbones, and a particularly ugly gash on her forehead that the EMTs had treated with narrow strips of adhesive bandages.

"Hey, I didn't notice those outside. Aren't you supposed to keep those dry?" Toni gently touched the skin next to the cut.

"I didn't soak them, and my hair had to be shampooed after rolling around in the woods. This is the happiest day of my life, Toni. Do you think I care about bandages? I can't even feel the cut, to be honest." She laughed.

"I'm over the moon for you, really, I am. But are you certain? You and Jay worked together in such intense circumstances. I'm not saying your feelings aren't real, but you have to see how, from my standpoint, it seems a bit rushed. Maybe not the romance or relationship part, but committing to marriage so soon…" She didn't want to say it aloud: that it was so easy to mistake hot sex and a good working partnership for more. For something that would last a lifetime.

Like you did with Brandon.

"I've never been more sure of anything in my life, Toni. This reminds me of when I became a Marine. It feels as though I've stepped into the life I'm meant to live. Jay's the one for me, have no doubts. Who cares how we met? The fact that we did is all that matters in the end." Willow leaned back on her elbows and winced. "Oh man, I think there's a bruise on my butt, too."

"I wouldn't doubt it. Fred Clayton is a big guy, and you're a heck of a fighter." A twinge of envy thrummed her conscience. Willow had fighting instincts and physical prowess Toni never dreamed of having. Toni was the brains of their family and glad to utilize her gifts to run CC—when being Sierra's mom wasn't using all her mental faculties.

And now Brandon was going to drain more of her energy...

"I don't want to talk about the case anymore, or about the Claytons. No offense, sis, but I've got a fiancé waiting for me." Willow paused. "So let's figure out the bigger reason you came in here. What's going on with you?"

Rut-roh.

"Me?" Willow always saw through her older sister or CC boss façades. They weren't always masks, but she knew she didn't share as easily with her other siblings. She and Willow enjoyed a special bond.

"Spill it. Is it about Brandon showing up here? Why is he here, by the way?" Willow wasn't going to stop until Toni came clean.

"How the heck am I supposed to know what motivates that man? He was invited by Mom and Dad, of course."

"Of course. They've never stopped hoping you'd work things out with him." Willow and she agreed that both of their parents were hopeless romantics. After five kids and so many years together, they'd earned the right to the belief Toni knew didn't apply to her life.

"No, they never have. You know, as much as they're good about letting us live our lives, they have a way—"

"Of manipulating?" Willow grinned.

Toni sighed, her smile weak. "Yeah."

"So let me summarize." Willow held up her hand. "They invited Brandon, he shows up, and it's when he planned to spend his time with Sierra." She lowered each finger as she ticked off her observations. "I'm not seeing the problem, sis."

Toni inwardly cringed at Willow's gentle tone. It signified she was concerned about Toni's judgement, maybe her grasp on reality. It was worse than if she'd come out and told Toni to 'get over it,' because it reminded Willow of what her family most feared. That she was burying her head in CC and not living her life to the fullest. But none of them had ever been a single parent.

"Well, first off, he's a whole week early. And second, remember when he said he had to push his usual summertime vacation with Sierra into the fall?"

"Because of his diplomatic workload, yes. You told me during one of my long drives when I moved back home." Willow had recently transferred from Northern Virginia to Coeur d'Alene when she'd left the Marine Corps.

"It wasn't diplomacy he was talking about, Wil. He was really in the midst of moving."

"Okay—where's his next post?" Willow didn't think twice about anyone having to move, as she'd transferred duty stations herself.

"There is no 'next' post. He's retired from the State Department and moving back Stateside, for good," Toni said.

"That will be better for Sierra, right? She'll get to see him a lot more."

"He's going to see her every day, Wil. Every. Single. Damn. Day." She watched Willow's eyes widen. "He's moving back to Everett. He's going to be our next door neighbor. And Sierra already knew about it. He didn't have the balls to tell me first."

"Ah, so that's what's got you ticked off. The 'next-door' part. And you should be angry—you're right, he had no right to blindside you, no question." She paused, tilted her head as she looked at Toni. A spark shone from Willow's eyes that Toni suspected didn't have anything to do with Jay, and it made her hackles raise. "It might not be so bad, you know. Lot of parents handle their divorces this way, and live together or nearby, to raise their kids, while living separate lives."

"You always take the positive side."

"Not everything is a threat to your carefully built, um, routine, Toni."

Guilt clawed at her, and the temptation to spill the beans on her still-legal marriage to Brandon was greater than ever.

But she couldn't do it. It was bad enough she'd backed out of her relationship with Brandon all those years ago. To admit she'd done something so stupid as to marry him in a lust haze wasn't on her to-do list.

"Our arrangement was fine the way it was." But she heard the selfishness in her tone and stopped. "Why change it now?"

"Hey, I'm on your side. Brandon should have owned up to his plans sooner, no question. But think about all the extra time you're going to have to yourself, sis. No more running ragged between work and Sierra, no more driving Sierra by yourself to all of the afterschool activities. You'll have a partner available to share more than the financial load, Toni. And this is so good for Sierra, especially as she's getting older."

"I don't run myself rag—" The warmth of Willow's hand on her wrist stopped her.

"You do. If I hadn't gotten so distracted with the Clayton case and the love of my life I was going to tell you that you need to slow down. Focus on you more. Since I got back from the Marine Corps, you haven't taken a single day off for yourself. Your routine is all-work or all-Sierra, all the time. We all need regular breaks. I was in the Corps, for heaven's sake, and even I know enough to take down time."

"Like going the extra mile to bring down the Claytons?" But her mention of the drug front Willow had stumbled upon didn't change the stubborn expression on her sister's face. Toni's rebuttal died. "Maybe you're right, Wil, but I don't know what I'll do with extra time. CC is growing business like never before." In the last year, Toni had signed twice as many contracts for their agency as in the five years previously. "We need to hire more agents, and that takes time." She appreciated Willow's concern but also knew it was an impractical request, for her to slow down.

"If you won't take your foot off the gas for yourself, then do it for Sierra. You know, give yourself the oxygen first?" Willow stood and unwrapped the towel from her head, finger combed her long locks.

Toni stood next to her. Their sister bonding moment had passed.

"Tell you what—this is your big weekend and you're the one who needs a break right now. You've already sent your notes up through yesterday, so I'm pretty certain I have all I need from you to write the final report. I'll write the after-action report when I'm back in the office on Monday, and send it to you for a last look before I forward to the LEs." It was a point of pride for their family agency that they were well respected in law enforcement, locally and nationally. Which made the fact that she'd not done her due diligence with vetting the Claytons all the more painful. She'd failed the team, let down her sister.

"Sounds good." Willow motioned with her thumb at their parents' adjacent spa bathroom. "I'm going to dry my hair and borrow some of Mom's fancy makeup before I go back out there. I'd love some nicer photos of this day than the ones you all took from the deck."

"You mean the ones where you're surrounded by LE agents?" They both laughed. "Come here." Toni opened her arms wide and Willow mirrored the action. They hugged tightly. Tears burned her eyes as she stepped back. "Now, let me go find a clean outfit for you. Is your bag in your car?"

Willow nodded, then looked Toni up and down, taking in the sexy dress and her brightly painted toes. "Just don't be disappointed that I didn't pack anything sparkly." Willow leaned toward neutral tones and crisp lines with her clothing, whereas while Toni also wore more streamlined outfits for work, she adored all the feminine trimmings. They were so close in spirit but worlds apart in life experience and style preference.

"I'd never think that."

"Liar." Willow smiled, but then her expression sobered. "We haven't escaped the Claytons, have we? They're infamous for their revenge. Cascade Confidential is a softer target than going after the FBI or any other LEs."

"Stop worrying about Toby Clayton." Toni dismissed Willow's concern. "He was last seen in South America. I appreciate your assessment, I get that you're used dealing with more global problems in cyber security. Trust me, a regional security firm like ours isn't worth anyone's time to target. It would only draw LE attention to them if they did. Besides, we'll be notified if Toby Clayton ever steps foot in the U.S. again." She turned and walked to the door. "I'll get your outfit, princess," she shot over her shoulder, and the sound of Willow's laughter followed her down the hallway.

A shiver ran between her shoulder blades as she replayed what she'd told Willow about Toby Clayton. Could Willow be right? Was Toby going to come back to the States and threaten Cascade Confidential, or worse, Willow?

No. Toni knew she was second guessing her every work decision because she'd dropped the ball on doing the appropriate research for the Clayton case, and it almost cost Willow her life. But she'd dug deep into the Clayton's these last days and from all she'd gleaned Toby Clayton wasn't a major concern. They'd have a heads-up from LE if he tried to enter the country via any legal means, and besides, the recent apprehension of his stepmother Veronica Clayton would be enough to keep Toby Clayton hiding under a rock if he was halfway intelligent. All the O'Malleys kept low social media profiles, if any, and were careful to not disclose personal information to clients. Public records of mortgages and property sales couldn't always be kept private, but it would take a lot of effort on any stalker's part to track any one of them down.

Toni mentally shook her head. She had a bigger threat to worry about with her newest neighbor.

Brandon. She needed to brace herself to see him more than their coparenting arrangement had ever required. Which made him the number-one threat to her peace of mind.

She hadn't begun to examine what his presence was going to mean to her heart.

Chapter 4

"**Y**ou're the only one left to finish this. I'm never giving you what you want until you do what I tell you." Toby Clayton watched his stepmother's spittle hit the bulletproof glass that separated them, her eyes cold. He'd never understood what Daddy had seen in her. Sure, she had those big tits and legs up to her ears, but Veronica wasn't worth the trouble she'd rained on their family. They'd all been just fine after Momma died—him, Fred and Daddy.

But then Veronica ruined it.

Her appearance in prison drab was a far cry from the gold digger's usual haute couture. He only knew the term for her fancy outfits because she'd been quick to correct an employee who'd complimented one of her bags early on.

No question, Veronica was a spoiled brat who thought she was going to inherit what was rightfully his and Fred's. Daddy had said as much.

"It's not my fault that Fred messed up," he said, referring to his older brother and the apple of his father's eye, "and you owe me. You tried to kill our father, and all the while you were stealing from him. I'm not the only one who sees you for the conniver that you are. Do I need to remind you of the charges against you? You need me more than I need you, Veronica. It's going to take a high-priced lawyer a lot of slick talking to keep you from getting the death penalty. You're nothing but a washed-up bitch." His brother had been caught by feds when he'd mentally gone off campus and tried to kill that private investigator, some chick working for Cascade Confidential. Hell, Toby hadn't ever heard of the security firm until everything Veronica touched at Mack Logging had gone tits up last year.

"I wasn't trying to kill Cal. I've kept him fit as a fiddle! You know it. Compare how he looks now to back when we got hitched. His pot belly is gone and there's color back in his cheeks." She sniffed loudly enough that he heard it through the headset. "I didn't want him to have one of his anxiety attacks, is all, that's why I ordered he be kept sedated."

"Sedated? According to the nurse you hired, he'd been given enough to knock a horse out." But Daddy had been smarter, convincing the nurse to pretend to give him the meds so he could catch Veronica at her game. Problem was, the law had caught them both before Veronica's scheme worked out to her advantage.

"I don't see what the big deal is. It was just a bit of sleeping medication added to his IV. Listen to me, Toby Clayton. Do what I'm telling you, and it'll mean more money for you when I get out. Otherwise, you're on your own, you son—"

"Time!" The prison guard stood next to Veronica, having warned her to leave moments earlier.

"I'll never be your son." He purposefully misinterpreted her unfinished words.

She kept her stare on him, and as much as he wanted to look away from her hatred, he stood his ground. For Daddy. For the Claytons and all that they'd worked for.

"Don't forget, Toby. I have what you want. I keep my word. You'll get what I have when you do your job."

He didn't keep himself from flipping her the bird the minute her back was turned.

"See you later, Mom." Sierra's firm peck against Toni's cheek forced her to look up from her laptop.

"Hang on, sweetie pie." Toni stood and gave Sierra a tight hug, forcing herself to keep it short. She'd learned to keep her affectionate gestures quick and to the point. Having Sierra squirm out of her embrace was too painful. Too much of a reminder that her little girl was turning into a young woman and needed her less and less.

Especially with her father living right next door. Sierra and Brandon's bond had always been strong, and while Brandon might not believe it, Toni's heart filled with gratitude that, like her, Sierra had a strong father figure in her life even if their large family had necessitated her doing more than the average older sister. But it had been easier to be happy about Brandon's and Sierra's father-daughter relationship when it didn't interfere with the carefully laid-out routine and life plan Toni had in place for Sierra.

Stop being a control freak.

"You're doing it again, Mom. You know, the hovering

thing." Sierra must have sensed her jumbled thoughts, because she pulled back and shrugged out of Toni's hug.

"Sorry. It's one of the hazards of motherhood."

"Remember, Mom, Dad's getting me after orchestra practice today, so you can relax this afternoon." Sierra didn't wait for a reply as she slammed the solid oak door behind her. Three quick pounding steps later—she'd jumped the last two steps again—and she was off to the bus stop in front of Brandon's house. His driveway ended at the tip of their cul-de-sac.

Toni hurried to the door and stepped outside, keeping her line of sight on Sierra until the bus pulled up and her daughter, along with three other neighborhood kids, piled onto the big yellow vehicle. As the bus pulled away, she scanned the neighborhood, her gaze landing on Brandon's front door. Inadvertently, of course. She'd noticed that Brandon didn't come out onto his porch when Sierra left his house to make sure she got safely to Toni's. Nor did he come out to wait for her when the school bus dropped her off on the days she didn't stay after school for orchestra practice.

"You're hovering too much, Mom."

Sierra's refrain tugged at Toni's heart, because she wasn't ready to let go of her daughter's younger self yet. Would she ever be able to let go? She knew she was the epitome of a helicopter parent. At least she wasn't a lawnmower parent, plowing down every obstacle and conflict Sierra encountered. Her own childhood had been chock-full of issues from bullying to peer pressure, and she'd grown all the stronger for surviving them. But if Mom had been a bit more available, not so deep into her career, Toni couldn't help thinking that maybe her childhood would have gone smoother. Maybe she'd have explored other options for a career than being a part of CC.

In her heart, she knew she'd never let go of her parental privilege to care about her daughter's welfare. There were too many people with nefarious motives in the world. Sure, she'd earned advanced degrees in psychology after she'd had Sierra, with night and weekend classes. Her PhD program had concluded only months before Mom retired—perfect timing for Toni to assume the Cascade Confidential mantle. Being a lifelong student had been a good example for Sierra.

Except Sierra didn't seem as interested in what Toni was up to these days. As if their mother-daughter relationship was no longer as important to her.

Toni knew the statistics, knew that the odds of anyone hurting Sierra in the neighborhood she'd chosen along with its stellar school district were minimal. But no amount of intellectual knowledge ever eased her mother heart.

As the bus turned the corner and left the cul-de-sac, a battered pickup truck drove in, circled slowly around the curb, and seemingly followed the school bus. She caught a glimpse of the passenger side door. A logo that displayed a row of tall pines was embossed on the door. Her breath caught as she immediately thought of Mack Logging and Manufacturing, the crime-riddled firm that Willow had infiltrated last year.

Calm down. Every random vehicle in their neighborhood wasn't driven by a kidnapper. The memory of last year's case that Toni felt responsible for almost bungling, along with the cold case involving three missing preteen girls that Willow was working on, was playing with her mama heart. That's all her uneasiness was about.

"It's another tree service." The Pacific Northwest had endured three high-wind events after the last heavy downpour. Weather events like these always led to a spate of uprooted trees and threatened wooded lots. Their entire neighborhood was dotted with swaths of woods. She loved the ubiquitous scents of cedar and pine that permeated the area. The only issue was that they were in a residential area. Trees were like dominoes—when one fell, several more were ready to. It was up to each homeowner to have trees that threatened any homes, including their own, taken down, and it required an expert with the correct equipment. DIY tree removal wasn't only frowned upon but downright dangerous.

This morning's truck was one of many that had driven through the neighborhood recently. But still…one could never be too careful when it came to unfamiliar vehicles on her street. She shivered in the morning wind. The next time she saw an unknown truck or car in their cul-de-sac, she was going to write down the license plate, just in case.

You're letting fear run the show.

Maybe. She wasn't the warrior agents her siblings were, so she had to rely on her brain. Logic was how she managed everything from CC operations to her parental worries. It would assuage the anxiety stalking her lately.

If only logic could help her with her emotions when it came to Brandon.

Sierra loved computer class, and today was the one she'd been waiting for. Her classmate's mother was a real

FBI agent, and she was going to talk about cybersecurity and how to catch the bad guys. At least, that's what Sierra had hoped for.

Instead she'd sat in the front row for nothing. The FBI agent had asked them to log into their laptops and instructed them to practice figuring out which apps had weak passwords and to set up three-factor identification on at least two. They'd been given twenty minutes to complete the assignment. She'd finished after two.

So pathetic.

With nothing else to do—phones were not allowed in class during the official school day—she pulled up the website for Cascade Confidential and read the description of services offered. She had to do it on the down low, as Mom would flip if she knew Sierra didn't dream of becoming a scientist or classical musician. She wanted to run the business her grandmother had begun a long time ago. Cascade Confidential was a living piece of history as far as Sierra was concerned.

"Huh." She quickly threw a glance at the teacher and the FBI mom, but they hadn't heard her, thank goodness. She had good reason to voice her surprise. There was a new service offered by CC—cyber–cold case investigation. That was because of Aunt Willow, who'd left the Marine Corps last year to join CC. She loved Aunt Willow, and all her aunts and uncles. They'd spoiled her since forever and had given her breaks from Mom when she was getting too stressed out over work. Which was a lot. Stress was her mother's middle name.

Although, since Dad had moved next door, Mom had actually backed off of her constant hovering. At least she didn't have a snowplow mom like so many of her classmates. Their parents made sure that they helped with their homework and even spoke to other kids if they thought their own kid was being picked on. Both Mom and Dad were very clear that Sierra needed to do her schoolwork, practice her oboe and never lie. She had no problem with any of those rules, but lately she felt guilty because she wasn't telling them everything she was doing.

Sierra wanted to work at CC when she grew up, like her mom. But Mom had ignored her when she said just that, and told her, "You're too smart to automatically roll into the family biz, honey. Give yourself a chance to find out who you are before you set your sights on one kind of career."

She'd mentioned her interest in security and even law enforcement to her father, who had been a little more encouraging but quickly began talking about how good she was at the oboe, and didn't she want to explore her interest in the arts more?

Both parents seemed to enjoy their jobs well enough but didn't want her to do anything remotely like them. So that part of her life was annoying. It would be easier for all three of them if they'd accept her thoughts on what she should be when she grew up. Besides, growing up was still going on. She had a long time before college.

But… Dad had moved to Washington State to be near her, and she had to admit, having both parents so close was really nice. Almost like a normal kid with a family living in the same house. It was great, and she loved it. But she couldn't help thinking it would be nice if her parents actually got together. She didn't want to think about all that would entail—just, ick—but having Dad in the room with Mom, across from hers, seemed…natural. Especially when she thought about how Mom blushed whenever Dad was around, and how Dad stood up a little straighter.

She looked up to make sure the teacher and FBI parent weren't watching her and did a little more online research about coding and creating apps. There was no time like now to start working on her cyber skills.

Chapter 5

Toni sat back down at the dining room table just as the CC VP of operations, her younger sister Aubrey, texted.

All fine in the office. You're clear to work from home today, again [rolling eyes emoji] [laughing emoji]. Willow wants to talk to you ASAP.

No sooner had she read Aubrey's text than her laptop pinged with a video call from Willow, the manager of their Coeur d'Alene satellite office.

"Hey, sis. Aubrey said you wanted to talk. What's going on?" Willow's face filled Toni's laptop screen, the rosy glow on her cheeks no doubt from her in-love status with Jay Lambert.

"What gave it away?" Willow grinned.

"You don't call a whole lot lately unless it's for work. I'm not complaining, you know. Just stating reality." Toni was grateful they'd all spent Christmas together on their parents' estate in Montana last month.

Willow let out a throaty laugh. "Sorry. I know I've been absent as far as being a good sister is concerned. Let's do a girls' night soon, with Aubrey and Sierra, too, okay?"

"Sure thing." The three O'Malley sisters had taken to including Sierra in their girls outings since she'd turned twelve. Toni focused back on business. "Any new information on the missing girls cold case?"

"In fact, yes. But before I go into details, there's something that needs to be addressed."

"What's wrong?" Her gut tightened at her sister's words. Willow was not an alarmist, so this must be serious.

"I have a bad feeling about this cold case, Toni. The witnesses I've interviewed are getting edgier, more easily spooked, the more questions I ask. Everyone so far has been willing to meet with me and answer my questions, as long as I keep to the script they're used to."

"Explain," she prompted.

"For example, the brother of one of the missing girls had no problem talking to me at first. Until he understood I wasn't looking for a rehash of events that happened thirty-five years ago, but that I intend to get to the bottom of the case and find out what happened to these girls. He actually told me I should 'let sleeping dogs lie.' Can you believe that? You'd think any of the affected family members would do whatever it took to have their girl back, or, more likely with this case, their remains. Some kind of closure, at least."

"Do you think you're closer to figuring it out, then? I mean, if they sense you're digging too deep?"

"Well, yes, there's that, but more. Why do you suppose he'd warn me off? Especially since local LE determined it was an accidental tragedy, that the girls had fallen into an abandoned mine shaft that was too dangerous to risk investigation?"

"The brother knows the kidnapper is still alive. Could he have been the kidnapper?" Toni asked the question as her interest warred with dread. This was her favorite part of her job—collaboration with her siblings, sometimes with LE, too. But her enthusiasm wasn't enough to douse the bile that churned at the thought of ever having the same thing happen to Sierra.

"Exactly. No, he was two years younger than the girls, and definitely not a suspect. I gave him my Cascade Confidential business card, as I do every interviewee. Which means CC could become a target of whoever took those girls. No one likes a snoop."

"It's a lucrative contract from one of the girls' grandmothers, but that doesn't mean we can't cancel it. If you think it's getting too hot, maybe we need to turn it back over to cold case LE unit." Toni almost wished they'd never agreed to take the case. But since their mother retired, she'd wanted to expand CC's capabilities across the PNW. And since Willow had arrived home from the Marines with expertise in both cybersecurity and cold case investigation techniques, she was a perfect fit to accept the contract.

Willow laughed. "Are you kidding? I love this work. Well, I mean, I love the job, hate that we have to do it. I'm only keeping it real with you as to what I'm picking up in the field. Heck, I'm probably stressing over nothing. It's only been, what, six months that I've been working for you? The Marine in me pays attention to details, to a fault at times. It'll take me some time to become a full-fledged civilian."

"You'll never lose the Marine, sis." They both laughed,

a nice break from the heavy subject. "Details matter in our business. That's why you're a perfect fit for CC."

"Thanks. Okay, to get to my current belief, I don't think the girls were abducted by force or coercion. I believe they knew their abductor, and I think the kidnapper is still alive."

"Okay. Go on."

"The girls all hung out together, a kind of band of misfits, if you will, and I believe their spot to meet was at the abandoned mine shaft, where one of their bracelets was discovered shortly after their disappearance."

"Maybe, but you're assuming a lot with this. They were only eleven years old at the time, Veronica was six year old. Wasn't the mine shaft an hour's hike from the closest family? That seems awfully far for a schoolgirl meet-up. I still think someone took them there." Toni couldn't imagine letting Sierra out of her sight long enough to first hike to a mine shaft, much less spend hours in the woods, and she was a year older than the missing girls had been.

"I hear you, and I knew you'd say that. You'd never allow Sierra to be off leash like we were left to play on our own, or the generation before that, either." Willow echoed her thoughts. "But these were different times, and the three girls had parents who were distracted with their own failings." Willow went on to list brief descriptions of each of the missing girls' families, all three of which had their share of tragic dysfunction. "I don't have as much information on two of the girls as I do on the one who was Veronica's sister."

"Right," Toni agreed.

Willow had accidentally discovered Veronica's connection to the cold case when she and Jay were inside the Clayton mansion in eastern Washington during the take-down. It was reasonable to assume the trauma of losing her sister at such a young age had helped turn Veronica into a criminal, but more likely the family's dysfunctional dynamics had been the true culprit. Veronica had never had a chance. Her sister, less so, as all three girls, who'd be in their forties today, were presumed dead.

"Any chance of interviewing Veronica now?" Veronica was expected to serve a life sentence for her crimes, providing the trial went the way they all hoped.

"I've got a request in, and Aubrey would have to conduct the actual interview, if we're ever granted one." Their sister had practiced law before joining CC.

"So it's up to Veronica's lawyer whether or not we'll get an interview?"

"Let's be real, Toni. They're not going to allow Veronica to talk to anyone from CC. Definitely not before the trial." Willow frowned.

"Okay, so that's a dead end for now. Back to the case. Three eleven-year-olds, all in the same elementary school—"

"It was middle school, and they were in the same class and shared the same schedules. According to the police interviews from the time, their classmates were interviewed and observed that each of the girls spent a lot of time at home when not together as a threesome. None of the three ever accepted birthday party invitations, for example, or joined scouting groups, or participated in extracurricular activities like dancing. This fits with their sad family dynamics, that they wouldn't invite classmates over or have parents to take them to play with other kids at their homes."

"What else did you get from the classmates now?" The words came out automatically, and Toni knew she'd ticked off Willow when she saw her sister's brows slam together.

"You didn't read any of the files I sent last week, did you?" Willow's frown was loud and clear on Toni's laptop screen.

"I looked them over, but you have an awful lot of detail in them that I didn't have time to sink into." Nor should she; Toni tried to keep healthy boundaries about being the CEO and not micromanaging her siblings' assignments. Collaborative brainstorming was where her role ended. "I completely trust you to weave the threads together, though. You're the cold case expert, not me."

"Hey, it wasn't an accusation." Willow was sincere. "I don't expect you to hang on to every word, that's why I included a summary page of bullet points. Which you would have seen if you'd opened the file." *Zing.*

"Sorry. My bad."

Willow shook her head. "No frets. I'd never want your job, Toni. I don't know how you manage keeping all of our cases straight, plus bring in new contracts. It's a lot."

"I think you've figured out by now that Aubrey handles the day-to-day operations at headquarters, leaving me free to monitor both our strategic goals and contract benchmarks. I'm lucky that our support staff at headquarters and the satellites is tops." She referred to the over two hundred employees who served Cascade Confidential, from security agents for high-profile events to PIs for private investigative work and agents for personal security. The Seattle headquarters, where her desk was when she wasn't working from home, boasted the largest employee group at one hundred. "With Kevin handling forensics and Jake running the Portland office, there's not as much on my plate these days. Honestly, most days I'm a glorified babysitter to our cases. Nothing more than a conductor."

Willow's sigh grated through Toni's earbuds. "Please don't do the low self-esteem thing with me, sis. For heaven's sake, weren't we all at your capping ceremony last year?"

"You know what I mean. And my degree is something I did for me, not for CC." Toni smiled at the memory of her entire family showing up to cheer her on as she received her PhD in forensic psychology.

Willow wasn't hearing it. "Again, stop with the false humility." *Ouch*. "Your psychological insight is invaluable to me, to all of us. You identified Veronica Clayton as a probable criminal when I was willing to accept her as nothing more than a nasty gold digger."

"I messed up with your case and we both know it." Guilt pierced her coffee buzz and she shook her head. "If you weren't as good as you are with a weapon—"

"Stop, Toni." Willow held her palm up to the laptop camera. "We all lived, it's all good. And we have three of four very bad people in jail." Willow's reminder that there was still a Clayton son at large in South America grounded Toni in the present.

"Has Jay heard anything more about the missing brother, Toby?" Toni hadn't heard anything about Toby since she and Willow had spoken at her parents' at Christmas, and before that, the day of the takedown.

Jay might hear sooner than Toni about Toby Clayton. He'd recently transferred to the FBI's Pacific Northwest region, with the intention of leaving the bureau sometime in the next couple of years. He'd expressed an interest in working with CC.

"Not that he can officially tell me anything about the Clayton family syndicate anymore, but 'unofficially'—" she made air quotes with her fingers "—no. Last known location of Toby Clayton remains Buenos Aires."

"Hopefully we'll never hear of him again, or we'll read about it when he eventually gets arrested trying to reenter the country." She wasn't concerned about a criminal happened to be the brother of the Clayton who had been apprehended at her parents' housewarming last year. When Brandon had made a bad day worse.

Stop. She forced her focus on the cold case.

"Right. So with Veronica Clayton unavailable, I'm still tracking down living relatives of all three girls. It's just a matter of time before I crack the case open." Willow's positive attitude was infectious, but not enough to persuade Toni that their client was going to get the answers she wanted about her granddaughter.

"I hope I'm wrong, Willow, but I honestly think you're going to find what the police concluded three decades ago: Three middle school friends—misfits, as you described—wandered too far off their beaten track and fell down an unmarked mine shaft." Her voice caught ever so slightly, but Willow's brow rose.

"Hey, sis, if this is too much with Sierra being so close to the same age and all, I can talk about the specifics with Aubrey until I solve it."

"No!" She took a breath. *Calm down.* "I'm fine. Sierra's fine. She'd never think of herself as a misfit, and thank goodness she doesn't wander off without her phone, or me knowing exactly where she's going, which nowadays is mostly next door." Always with Brandon, which was both a relief and a heartbreak.

"Speaking of Brandon, how's it going?" Willow read her mind with ease.

"All right. Great, in fact. Sierra's the happiest I've ever seen her."

"What about you? How are you and Brandon getting along?" Willow's real reason for asking the question couldn't be more obvious.

"Look, I've got to go. So do you." Avoidance usually worked with her sister. Willow would come back to the subject of Brandon later, of course, but it would give Toni a reprieve this morning.

"Remember, Mom, Dad's getting me after orchestra practice today..."

The intrusive reminder stopped her racing thoughts. She took a sip of coffee, waiting for Willow to end the call.

"No, I'm not finished." Willow's words made Toni sit up. She put her mug down on the electric warmer next to her keypad.

"What?"

"I saw how you and Brandon were at Christmas. Before you get all defensive, I know and appreciate that parents share a special bond, since they've had a kid together. But be real, Toni. It's just me. Are you sure there isn't something more...kindling between you two?"

"You're in your rosy frame of mind about your own love life. It's naturally that you'd project your emotions onto my completely platonic relationship with a barely ex. We weren't together long enough for me to call him an ex, and since we're coparenting Sierra we don't want to use that term, anyhow." Guilt at telling the half-truth to Willow sent heat to her face and she hoped her laptop camera wasn't picking it up.

"That's just your fancy-speak for you're not going to tell me anything. You know, being a control freak doesn't work when it comes to the heart, dear sister."

"What, me, a control freak?" Toni laughed as she replied.

"Just remember, I saw the sparks between you first!" Willow grinned.

"Gotta go, sis!" She waggled her fingers in front of the camera. "Keep me posted on the Coeur d'Alene office. Say hi to Jay for me. Love you!"

"Will do. Talk to you soon." Willow blew her a kiss.

They disconnected and Toni stood up to head for the kitchen and more coffee. Work was the answer to turning down the volume on her concern over the cold case. It triggered her because Sierra was so close in age to the girls when they'd gone missing. Losing her child was her worst fear, always.

Which reminded her: Brandon was not being as careful with Sierra's personal security as he should be. She'd have to mention it the next time she saw him without Sierra to overhear.

She wasn't being a control freak about it. Just a concerned mother—who happened to have a job in security.

Chapter 6

Brandon stood at his kitchen sink and looked through the window, across the common area his house shared with Toni, into her side dining room window. Her murky silhouette on the other side of the sheer curtains proved she was home. He watched her for a few moments, as he had more days than not since he'd been back. Not as a creeper—heck no—but he had to admit, he felt like a jerk for doing so. Each time he saw her alone and knew Sierra was out, he tried to muster the courage to talk to her. Not about Sierra, but about them.

So far he'd been unable to gird his emotional loins to his satisfaction. He'd backed down from a more direct approach each morning, convincing himself that patience and perseverance were the sure way to earn Toni's trust. Because it was going to take her trusting him completely for them to ever be more than the coparents they currently were. It'd be nice to be friends, too.

Who are you kidding? You want more. You've always wanted more.

He knew it had been a shock to her that he'd quit the State Department. It had shaken her that he'd decided to settle down from his nomadic lifestyle, no doubt. But the worst for her had been that he'd moved in next door. Toni valued her space and privacy. And he'd totally overstepped.

They'd tiptoed through the last few months, avoiding any intimate discussions or conversation in general unless it had to do with Sierra. Nothing different than when he'd lived on the other side of the globe, in fact. These last few weeks since Christmas he'd realized it was getting old, this pretense that being civil when Sierra was present was enough.

Sierra deserved more. They all did.

No time like now.

Before he talked himself out of it, he grabbed two of the oatmeal–chocolate chip muffins he and Sierra had baked this past weekend and made the quick trip outside, across his back lawn and side yard, through the gate to Toni's back door.

He rapped lightly on the window pane, not wanting to scare the heck out of her. He could have texted first but didn't want to give her a way to wiggle out of talking to him alone. Plus, his lifetime of diplomacy work had taught him that sometimes a pleasant surprise was a good tool when dealing with a particularly spiky adversary.

After a moment, said prickly coparent opened the door.

"Yeah?" Toni's monosyllabic greeting and deadpan expression would make the most hardened intruder reconsider. His hands gripped the plate tighter. She remained the epitome of feminine beauty to him and her sheer presence had only strengthened over the years. Did she know she exuded such a sense of power, of complete control over everything?

"Good morning! Did you see how bright the water

is today?" *Crap.* He always talked too much when he was nervous.

"Um, can I do something for you, Brandon?" She stood a step above him, giving her a slight height advantage, as she was only half a foot shorter than him when they were both barefoot. Not that he thought about her bare feet, or how she liked to keep her toes polished in bright colors no matter the time of year. Not that often, anyway. "Brandon?" A look of concern washed over her features.

"Ah, jeez, yes, sorry. Not enough coffee yet." He shook his head, grinned. "No, wait, let me start over. Good morning, Toni." He held out the plate of muffins. "I've brought a peace offering. Interested?"

Her gaze left his for the treats, and a tiny line appeared between her brows. He remembered smoothing that line out many years ago, on one of their short but intense meet-ups in whatever hotel in whatever city they could mutually travel to as quickly as possible. Over a four-month period after they met, they would do anything to be together no matter how long the flights were, how short their time making love was. Before she'd decided to stay here and not follow him.

Don't go there.

"There's no need for a peace offering unless you need to apologize for something. We're enjoying a decent détente, aren't we?" Toni's neutral expression was back in place, her emotional guardrails firmly up. He detested this. Being treated as if he were no more than another client. An acquaintance.

"Yes, about that…can I come in?" He wanted, no, *needed* to talk to her, to explain his side of their current living arrangement. And not on her back stoop.

She paused, then stepped aside and turned her back to him as she walked away. At least she left the door wide-open. "Come on in. I'm getting coffee, but then I have to get back to work. Shortly."

"Same." He walked into the kitchen, knowing an olive branch when he saw one. From Toni, the peace offering had thorns, but he'd take what he could get.

"Really?" She turned back, eyed him. "I thought you retired."

"From government service, yes. But you don't expect me to retire in my forties, do you?" Before she could say something acerbic about his silver-spoon family, he pressed on. "I recently agreed to take on some contract work." There was the teaching offer from a local university, but he didn't want to spring that on her, too. It took months, sometimes years to get the coveted position and he wasn't about to confess he'd been planning this for years. He'd always hoped to live closer to his daughter.

And make more of your relationship with Toni.

He held back a grunt. *So not happening.*

Yet.

"That's nice, I suppose, that after years of overseas jobs you now have the option of going into business for yourself and working remotely. I love being able to do remote work when I can." She hesitated, as if vacillating on letting her guard down. "I have to say, Brandon, it's hard to imagine you doing desk work, or staying in one place. You've been moving around every couple of years and working in the field for so long. I guess I thought you'd always want to be on the move." She lifted the towel off the plate of muffins. "Do you want your muffin heated?"

"Sure." He didn't see an iota of humor in her expression, so he passed on reminding her about how she'd once had a lot to say about how heated he made her muffin.

Stop. Going. There.

Geesh. Maybe he really was a creeper. *No.* He was nothing more than a man who'd lived solo practically his entire adult life. Minus casual dating here and there, no one had ever been enough to turn his head, to become a third parent for Sierra.

"The microwave is over the stove." She pointed and he suppressed a grin. Toni definitely didn't want him to confuse her with someone who'd provide any more hospitality than necessary. "Would you like coffee?"

"That would be great, but you don't have to. Neither of us has a lot of time to spare." He didn't want to overstay. It was a miracle enough that Toni had invited him in. And maybe this wasn't such a great idea, after all. Her shampoo's scent permeated the small kitchen, and they stood close enough that he saw how her blue eyes reflected the morning light that streamed through the window above the sink. Without her customary Mariners baseball cap's brim pulled low he was able to take in her entire face, see where the years had added the lines that only deepened her beauty.

Had she always appealed this much to him, even when clearly annoyed with him?

Yes.

"It's actually good that you came over. I have something I've been meaning to talk to you about, too." She weighed coffee beans as she spoke, put them in a grinder and filled an electric kettle with water. Her tone and actions seemed casual enough, but he knew her better. Toni had never been one for small talk.

"You do?" His stomach, already tight with awareness, dipped. "What is it?"

"You go first." The microwave beeped and she took the muffins out, sliding the plate across the island toward him. "Napkins are there." She nodded toward the end of the surface.

"Thanks." He paused, did his best to remain nonthreatening. If he put her on the defensive, any meaningful conversation would more than likely digress into a verbal spat. "Toni, I didn't come over for casual coffee talk. I want to explain in more detail why I moved here. Without worrying about Sierra misinterpreting anything I say."

She batted his words away with a single blink of her eyes. "You already have. You wanted to be closer to your daughter. A very good reason—the only good reason, am I right?" Her query was rhetorical, and it struck his annoyance chord. Proof positive that she didn't trust him with anything resembling her innermost thoughts. The mask she wore as a front against him was far from what he remembered as the genuine Toni. *A lifetime from.* "Unless there's something more you need to get off your chest?" Her head tilted ever so slightly.

Yeah, she looked at him as if he was a criminal. Persona non grata in the diplomatic world.

"I owe you an apology. I should have told you I was buying the house next door way before you found out." Her unwavering gaze would shoot laser zaps at him if she could, he determined. He shifted on his seat. "I could have at least let you in on my thought process when I originally considered leaving the foreign service."

"Hmm. Or after you made your decision but before you signed the sales contract, maybe you could have let me know you were leaving the foreign service for good? That your income might take a dive, resulting in me becoming the sole breadwinner for Sierra's sake until you got on your feet? How about the small detail that you were intending to move here, as in *right* here? Yes, you're damn right you should have cut me in on your 'process'—" she made air quotes, then shrugged "—but you didn't." She turned away as if she didn't expect anything more than subpar from him. He ignored the defensive stance his mind shouted for him to take. Getting his hackles up would threaten this entire dialogue, worsen the too-polite relationship they currently shared.

Man up.

"No excuses on my part, Toni. I put you in an awful position with Sierra. You and I need to be a united front with her, and I let her know my plans before I spoke with you. I messed up. I'm sorry, Toni." Now wasn't the time to remind her that he had a modest pension to go with his retirement from State and plenty of savings. She'd always assumed he accepted funding from his wealthy family and yet, other than for his undergraduate degree, he'd never taken another penny from his parents.

He'd lined up employment to ensure Sierra's well-being wouldn't be adversely affected by the economic pitfalls of such a big move, too. But neglected to let Toni in on his work positioning.

"I appreciate the gesture, Brandon. But you didn't need to make such a big deal of apologizing. If I was still angry about it I'd let you know."

"Would you?" He contemplated her refusal to admit how selfish he'd been. Was it her way of staying calm, not letting him in? "I gave you no choice but to accept what I'd done."

She startled him with a short bark of laughter. "It's just like you, Brandon, to think that there's a diplomatic answer for everything. Have you ever considered that just because you have diplomatic training that you yourself are anything but a peacemaker? A nice smile and smooth talking aren't always the answer." They faced off, she with a glare and he with what he prayed was a neutral, calm demeanor.

He had no reply.

"And for God's sake, Brandon, sit down already. You look like you're waiting for me to use the butcher knife on you." She turned away, refocused on the brew.

Her camel-colored sweater—was it cashmere, he wondered?—hugged her upper body, emphasizing the indentation for her waist, and her slacks or whatever women called them stretched enticingly over her full hips. A warm ball of awareness swirled under his rib cage, pushed against his logic. He looked away, out the kitchen window at the wooded area behind their homes. Anywhere but at the incredibly attractive woman standing mere feet away. The bond they shared was no longer romantic, but tell that to his libido. He mentally shut down his physical response to her as best he could. It was a tall order. His body reacted involuntarily whenever he saw her. His physical desire for her was in the way of the new friendship he hoped to mark today as the beginning of.

Didn't she see that the impulsive man he'd been when they'd met all those years ago was dead? Long hours, mostly overseas, hashing out agreements that made the difference between nations going to war or not had tempered his spontaneity. He'd learned to think before he spoke, and definitely before he acted.

Except for surprising her with the muffins this morning. But he'd been planning to talk to her for weeks, months. Self-recrimination scraped on his esteem at his hubris for believing he'd get her to see his side, to forgive him for invading her until-now safe haven with Sierra.

He sat down at the island. She must have seen him in her peripheral vision because this side of her profile revealed the curve of her lips—still so full—in a small smile. "There. You look a bit more relaxed."

"I didn't know I looked tense." He white-lied fluently, another diplomatic skill. "And for the record, I don't think you're going to murder me. You want to, sure. I get it. But I trust that you won't." His words sounded ridiculous and so did how quickly he spoke. Disapproval radiated off Toni's presence and he had to figure out how to forge ahead regardless of the fire-breathing dragon in front of him. He let out a quick breath. "You're right. I'm used to keeping things positive instead of facing the hard truth."

"We call that people pleasing here in the real world." She paused, her hand on the kettle as she looked at him. Her sapphire eyes sparkled with regret. "I shouldn't have said that. What you do, what you did, is more real than anything. I'm sorry, too. I know it must sound as if I have issues with your line of work. I have tremendous respect for what you've accomplished, Brandon. I guess that's what threw me when you moved here. I never pictured you doing anything but international diplomacy. And traveling for the rest of your life."

Glancing away from him, she poured hot water over the grounds and hit the timer on her watch. Was she timing his visit, too? But then he saw the slight shake in her hand, the quick, nervous lick of her lips. *Keep your eyes off her mouth, damn it.* Toni was unsettled by his presence, too.

Glimmers of the cracks in her relationship with Sierra came to mind. It was natural for a mother and daughter to be close, but also to reestablish their relationship during early adolescence, sometimes only after huge meltdown fights. He remembered his mother and sister going at it, how he and his father would get the heck out of the room during the preteen angst tumult.

They remained in thoughtful silence until her watch pinged and she tapped it, silencing the alarm.

He waited for her to pour the coffee. She slid his, black, across the table, not offering milk or sugar. She'd remembered how he liked it.

"It's odd that we haven't had a coffee together since I moved in." Before the words left his mouth he regretted them.

"Hmm, probably. But we've never been like other… coparents." She added half-and-half to her mug.

"No." He gulped his brew and almost coughed. It was very hot. Needing a distraction from her nearness, he concentrated on their surroundings.

They sat opposite one another on stools, the butcher-block island in between them cluttered with detritus of family life. Two apples, one getting wrinkly, and a half-eaten banana rested in a wooden bowl that also held an unopened protein bar and a pack of gum.

"I need to put in a grocery order." She'd mistaken his observation for judgment.

"I meant to ask you about that. The supermarkets have

changed since I was last back. The aisles used to seem too big, and now they're crowded with store clerks or gig workers, shopping for delivery orders. Does anyone do their own food shopping anymore?" There were supermarkets in China, but he'd relied on the local markets for all his fresh produce, proteins, spices and honey. "I'm not a Luddite, by the way. I've downloaded the local grocer's app."

She grinned, and it was the first time he'd seen her genuinely smile at him since…forever. Familiar warmth shot through his chest. And went straight to—

Don't go there.

"Tell me if I'm wrong, Brandon, but I imagine you're used to a much slower pace. Lifestyle-wise, that is, not work-wise." He sensed she was trying hard to maintain a level of calm, and it reminded him of how they'd once been, during their brief but insanely passionate relationship. The push and pull of the constant tension between them, the way they'd matched wits. And then resolved any differences with a round of deeply satisfying sex. One round of which had created Sierra.

Toni's cheeks reddened and she continued when he didn't say anything. Had she seen the lusty memories in his gaze? "You had your apology, now it's my turn. I'm sorry that I haven't personally reached out to see if you need anything while you've been readjusting to life back in the States. Sierra keeps me informed of your day-to-day, of course. I'm sure she does the same with you about my daily goings-on." Another grin, a shared glance of understanding. "Every time I think to touch base with you on my own, there's a distraction. To be honest, it's almost always Sierra. I don't want her eavesdropping on our more adult conversations, for obvious reasons."

"No apologies or explanations necessary. We both want the same thing—what's best for Sierra. I hope I haven't turned your routine upside down these past several months. Not too much, anyway."

"You haven't." She took a sip of her coffee. "Well, not as much as I originally thought you would. I've tried to give you space so you could get used to having Sierra around regularly, and give her space to adjust to you, too. Not that she seems to ever need any space—that child is a wonder. She didn't need any adjustment period with you here 24-7, in case you didn't notice. And she is so happy you're here, Brandon. Please don't take my standoffishness as a reflection of anything she's said or done. I don't want to criticize how you do things. Each of us bring something different to the table for Sierra."

"True," he agreed.

"It was easier dealing with one another when we were in different countries, I have to be honest." She grimaced, and he wondered if it was at having to say something unpleasant, or if the things she believed he'd messed up on were really that bad.

"What do you mean?" He'd found it so much simpler to be able to look Sierra in the face, hear about her day-to-day happenings in person instead of on a twice-weekly video call.

She took a long sip of her coffee, as if bracing herself for his reaction. "I don't know how to say this, but when you were overseas, I was able to email you with any concerns I had, which gave me a buffer, so to speak. From your reactions, good or bad. From worrying about

Sierra's reactions, too, once she was with you. Do you remember when Sierra visited you and I knew your parents were going to be with you, too?"

He nodded. "I do. You were worried that they were going to take her off on a deep in-country tour she'd never come back from." His own frustration had been that Toni didn't trust him enough to know he'd never send Sierra on any kind of travel that wasn't sanctioned by the embassy or consulate, depending on where he was assigned.

"Right. And you set me straight. You told me the tours were done by employees of the embassy. You were in Beijing then."

"Yes."

Their gazes met, and the conflict in her eyes raised his mental red flags. The warm glow of affection—it had to be no more than that, after all this time—was smothered by a sense of dread.

"So go ahead, dive in. Tell me what's been bothering you." He put on his best neutral expression, the one he'd employed when the cooperation of an adversary nation's representative had been paramount. He had to, because the last thing he wanted was for Toni to catch on to his greatest fear as Sierra's dad.

That he'd made the move back to Sierra too late to make a difference in the young adult she was quickly growing up to be.

Chapter 7

"Go ahead, dive in."

This was her big chance. Toni could finally unload on Brandon, let him know how she saw the world Sierra was growing up in. A world he hadn't lived in for literally decades, minus a short tour of eighteen months in Washington, DC. A Chinese studies major in college, Brandon had always been determined to serve as an FSO in China, and he'd been successful on his first take of the State Department entrance exam, which was very unusual. It usually took five or more tries to be hired. Brandon was an exceptional human being and a skilled diplomat, but Toni knew none of that meant anything if he wasn't aware of the threats Sierra faced each and every day, simply because she was a preteen with Internet access.

She needed him to understand that they weren't living in the safety bubble of a US embassy overseas, protected by the close-knit network of expats, far away from many of the temptations thrown at kids each and every day in the States.

So why did she think she needed to pause, to take it

slow with Brandon, her parenting partner and the father of her daughter?

He was once a hell of a lot more than your coparent.

She blocked off the unwelcome thought, along with the tingles of awareness he'd set off the minute she'd opened the back door to him. It didn't help that Brandon was sitting across from her, filling up her kitchen with his quiet yet very powerful presence. Brandon had always been a force of nature, and not just sexually. And damn it, that was still there, too. The thrum of tension between them.

Maybe it's just on your part. It was unrealistic to think that he'd not had a partner over the last thirteen years, wasn't it? He might have someone special now—maybe a woman who was another reason he'd moved back here.

Sierra had never once mentioned meeting anyone on her trips to visit him. The only people Sierra had ever talked about after her trips abroad, besides her father, had been Brandon's work colleagues, or his brother—Sierra's favorite uncle—Christopher. But he was a good dad; he wouldn't parade lovers in front of his daughter, not unless they were going to become more.

"It's that bad, huh? Whatever it is you need to say?" Brandon broke the silence as he swiped a napkin from the pile atop the bread basket and helped himself to one of his muffins.

"No, it's just that…" She took a deep breath. "This isn't some bucolic village in the middle of nowhere. Neighbors aren't family, and most don't know one another past saying hello when walking their dog or going for a run."

"But you only moved here almost two years ago. You

vetted the area, did you not? That's one reason I bought in this neighborhood on such short notice. I completely trust your judgment."

"You bought here to be near Sierra, period." And maybe a little bit to annoy her? She immediately ignored the petty idea. Why was she allowing him to make her feel cornered?

"True, but for the record, I'd originally put an offer on a houseboat." He mentioned the pier that was less than a mile away. "But the sale fell through and I had little time left to find a place before I came back. I could have rented, and that would probably have been smarter, in case this didn't work out." He made a swirling motion with his hand between them.

"The houseboat might have been a better arrangement." It would have allowed for more…boundaries. And keep her from wondering what he was doing in his house next door. "And you saved a lot of rent by buying immediately."

"I took it as a good omen when the houseboat sale fell through, and this house was still for sale." His earnestness tugged at her heart. He'd always been the most positive man she'd ever been around—still was, in fact. A man who still believed in signs about day-to-day events, for example?

"Yeah, it was a sad situation next door—ah, um, at your house. Jane had taken such good care of the property for decades, I'm told." She referred to the previous owner of Brandon's home. "But then her husband passed, and after taking care of him for many years, it was all too much for her. Their kids wanted to maximize her assets for her health-care expenses as she ages, so selling was the best option."

His eyebrow, the same one she used to trace with her fingertips, quirked over his dark brown eye. "Seems to me you know enough about a neighbor you only had for what, a year?"

Chagrin forced her to begin again. "Touché." She looked away as she inhaled deeply, exhaled. When she faced him again, his expression was open, kind. Not the antagonistic stance she'd have if he were criticizing her. But then, Brandon had always been the less volatile of the two of them. He'd been a gentle yet incredibly proficient lover—

Stop thinking of yourself as part of anything with Brandon other than Sierra's parenting partner.

She leaned back from the island, making a few more inches of space between them. "You don't seem to comprehend the potential danger that lurks at every step of Sierra's life, Brandon. From walking to the bus stop to riding the bus to when she comes home and I'm— we're—not here. My commute to CC headquarters downtown is less than an hour on a good day. Most evenings, it's up to ninety minutes. And I can't work remotely all the time like I did during the pandemic." Wistfulness crept around her heart as she remembered how tiny Sierra had been, how much their days had intertwined.

"With me here, you don't have to worry about how late you get home. I've told you this at least a dozen times since I moved in. I mean it, Toni. We're in this together and Sierra's best interests are our priority. No question. But I can't give you what you won't take, like my support with parental supervision and presence."

"I guess I'm not used to having backup. I used to be able to count on my mom to pick up the slack for me, but now that they moved to Montana…"

"Sounds like I moved back at just the right time, then." Brandon's words, though soothing, weren't enough to calm her, not yet.

"Maybe. There's more, Brandon. It's not only Sierra's physical security I'm worried about. She's a target online, no matter how well I lock down her social media. All kids are. She's always trying to push it, by the way. It's part of being a preteen, but it doesn't make it any easier to handle. Do you know what the statistics are of children who become troubled at her age? It's such a pivotal time for mental illness, addiction, criminal behavior, sexual activity—you name it."

"Wow, Toni." He appeared sincerely surprised. "Do you carry all this on your shoulders every minute of every day?"

Her shoulders tightened in response to his observation. "I don't understand how you don't think about these things all the time. It's what any good parent does, Brandon. It's reality." As soon as she said it, she realized how awful it sounded. But it was too late.

"Oh, okay. I get it. This is about my lack of parenting skills." His open expression had vanished, replaced by stern lines between his brows. "So what exactly am I doing, or not doing, that you think I need to change? Be specific here, please." His gaze homed in on her. The strength in his quiet tone seemed calm enough, but she heard the intent. He wasn't going to back down.

Always the diplomat.

The steely glint in his eyes, the way they'd narrowed

at her tirade, made her spine stiffen. She fought against squirming on the island bench. This was how his counterparts from other nations must have felt opposite him at a boardroom table. The same way a salmon felt as a bald eagle swoops in for lunch, its bright yellow talons extended for the kill.

"I'm sorry. That came out wrong."

"Darn right it did." But his expression had softened from granite to limestone.

"Let me try to start over. What I need from you is that you walk outside, onto your front porch, when Sierra leaves in the morning. And the same when she's due to return on the bus. There was a case a few years back where a kid got nabbed from the bus stop—and it was right in front of their house!"

The lines on his face deepened and included his frown. "I had no idea, Toni. Right here, in this neighborhood?"

"Ah, no, not this neighborhood…" She looked away. Blew out a puff of air. "It…it was in Cincinnati. But it could have been here." She risked a quick glance at him. He'd never take her seriously now.

Brandon's eyes widened for a split second, but to his credit he didn't laugh, or even smile. "I can see the bus stop from my front window, Toni, which I'm able to look through from my kitchen island." It was true; Brandon's home had been modernized—to a ridiculous extent in her opinion—first by the Flowerses' children in minimal pre-sale preparations, and then by Brandon in the flurry of upgrades he'd made. His living spaces were no longer walled-in as with her Craftsman home, and his lot was actually at a slightly higher elevation than hers.

Not a lot, but enough to afford him a sparkling glimpse of Puget Sound several blocks away. Treetops obscured her home's view of the water, except from the rooftop, which was only accessible through an attic window that she had expressly forbidden Sierra from ever using without a parent nearby.

"You do have a beautiful view on clear days."

"I'm a lucky guy. I love seeing the water."

Where his houseboat would have been. Where she wouldn't have to brace herself against seeing him every day. Or worry when she didn't think he was home yet and Sierra was, when Toni had to stay longer in her office downtown.

"But do you look up from whatever you're doing on your computer, Brandon?" The man she'd known, albeit briefly and over a decade ago, had disappeared into his work, writing point papers, doing cultural and political research.

"You mean to tell me that you go out to meet Sierra each and every time she gets on or off the bus? She's not in kindergarten, Toni," he deflected, triggering a curl of distrust in her gut.

"But she's still a target." It stung that the tables had turned and he was looking at her with an expression similar to how she felt toward him. As if she were the negligent parent.

"Of course there's always a risk, no matter what either of us do. But I have to disagree with you on how much you hover over Sierra. We're doing her a disservice if we don't empower her to be independent. She can't learn street smarts if we're always layering her in bubble wrap."

Guilt poked at her parental self-righteousness. She'd heard this before, from each of her siblings and her mother. She sighed. "Maybe I am being overprotective, but I'd rather be this way than lose my daughter." She braced herself for his disagreement, a probable disappointment in her stance.

And was completely stunned when his hands reached across the island and engulfed hers. Warmth that she'd missed for too long radiated from his palms, and she stared at their hands. Together.

"I'm not judging your parenting, Toni. Without you, Sierra wouldn't have had a solid sense of herself, of her family, of unconditional love. God knows I've been absent enough."

"Oh no, you—"

He squeezed her hands, gave a quick head shake.

"No, let me finish. You're dealing with the bad guys in your day job all the time, right? I've met my share of them over the years and countries I've lived in. I know there are risks, trust me. But statistically—" he emphasized the phrase she'd used "—the reality is that the vast majority of kids grow up without being kidnapped."

"It only takes one time. And there are a lot of crimes besides kidnapping." Her jaw clenched and she felt her breathing go shallow.

Their gazes fused. His eyes, that damnable shade of whiskey, remained steady. "We're in this together, Toni. You and me. And Sierra."

She swallowed and nodded but didn't take her hands from under his. Not yet. This was okay, right? Friends held hands all the time, didn't they? "I supposed this is how coparenting is really meant to work?"

"Mmm." His affirmation gave her time to keep observing, to see the gray that was silvering his eyebrows. To see that the same silver shade coming in heavier in the lock of hair that still insisted on falling over his forehead.

What did he see in her face after all the years apart? The wrinkles that bookended her eyes, the deep smile lines, for certain, but did he see her mental exhaustion? The interminable worry over Sierra having the best childhood possible? Having a mother who was present, involved in her life? While Toni and her siblings had always known they were loved, the fact was that Donna had been an absentee mom a lot of the time and Dad, while loving and present as much as he could be, had scrambled to make his own living separate from CC. He was a farmer and unhappy in the city, so he'd tended a dairy herd that required him to leave before dawn and return to their city home when most of them were in bed. They'd all been latchkey kids. She'd vowed her own child would never, ever experience the same level of what she considered neglect.

"You're a wonderful mother, Toni." He gave her hands one final quick squeeze before he released them. Her fingers immediately itched to smooth his cowlick, put that hanging lock of silver hair in its place. "I'm learning a lot from you."

Tears welled and she blinked as fast as she could without looking like a love-struck puppy. "Thanks."

He gave her a quick nod, and with regret she watched the tender moment dissolve as he stood.

"Let's get the focus back on Sierra. She's going to be a teenager in six months. She's still our sweet baby girl, always will be. But as you've hinted at, conflict's coming. I'm hoping that being here allows me to be a more dependable parent, more present for Sierra. Which should, in theory, lessen the tremendous burden you've been shouldering. But I need your help to make it happen. You have to let me in, Toni."

She blinked, at a loss for a coherent response. Not if she was going to keep a semblance of composure. They'd shared so little time together this last decade, but in the few months he'd been back, Brandon had somehow figured out the secret code to unlock her heart.

You've never changed the combination to your heart.

Brandon didn't seem to notice her inner turmoil as he walked to the sink. The faucet turned on, water slinging against her stainless sink, the squirt of the dish soap unmistakable. Washing his mug behind her back gave her the reprieve she needed from his direct attention. When she spoke, her voice scraped against her throat.

"This is the first time you've acknowledged that I've been doing the heavy lifting." That anyone had, really. Her siblings were supportive and adored Sierra, no question, but they had their own lives to worry about, and they certainly each had pressure-cooker jobs.

He grasped her shoulder as he stood behind her, and it didn't surprise her this time. Instead, her neck, collarbone, shoulders all released the tension of their conversation.

"It won't be the last." His quiet words struck a chord of intimacy she wasn't willing to examine. Not with him standing so close, when all she had to do was stand, turn in to him—

No.

She did stand but kept her back to him until she cleared the island and walked to the back door.

"This was a lot more than I expected for a 'coffee talk.'" She made air quotes and tried to grin, desperately needing to break the intensity between them.

"This was good. We need to do it regularly. Let's figure out which days and times work for both of us. In the meantime, text and call whenever. I'll do the same."

"Sounds good." *Please leave before I do something stupid.*

"Friends?" He held out a hand. The same hand that had comforted her, twice, in the last five minutes. Her body tensed, though, as if he'd wielded a knife. Except the taut coil in her stomach wasn't from fear or impending danger.

Get him out of here.

"Friends." She allowed her hand to be swallowed by his, expecting—hoping for?—a quick, short-lived gesture.

And shocked both of them when she reached her other hand up to his nape and pulled his face down to hers.

"Toni?" His query was even, and his neutral expression hadn't changed, but she saw his pupils dilate, heard his sharp inhale. Most telling? He didn't take a step backward.

She closed the distance between them.

Their lips met in chaste surprise, probably the most platonic contact they'd ever shared with their mouths. Until the tension that had been ratcheting deep inside her took over, insisting upon release.

Brandon's hands were on her face, holding her close as his tongue slid between her lips and began a deep, caressing exploration of her mouth. She groaned, on tiptoe, leaning into him, trying to remember that she was the initiator here, but logical thought had never been a part of their physical relationship.

Their bodies might be thirteen years older than they'd been when they last made love, but muscle memory didn't fail her as she wrapped one leg over his and brought her pelvis snug up against his. His hard length confirmed that Brandon wanted her, too.

A distant rumble began and she absentmindedly identified it as thunder, but then remembered that thunderstorms weren't usual in the Pacific Northwest, that rain wasn't predicted for the near future.

The rumble turned into a groan, then his lips left hers. She cried out in protest at the sudden loss of heat. Brandon's explosive expletive threw cold reality on her desire, dousing her lust. She opened her eyes.

"That was unexpected." His gaze burned into hers, his breathing as off-kilter as hers.

"I don't know what made me…" she began. But she did know.

"I do. Know what made you do that." He let his arms drop to his sides, stepped away, opened the back door. Daylight spilled in and the rustle of leaves she'd been meaning to sweep since November reached her ears. "The same thing that had my tongue halfway down your throat." He ran his fingers through his hair, looked outside through the storm door window. "We've never had a problem in bed, have we?"

She shook her head. "No. It was the healthy communication part that troubled us."

He looked at her again, his mouth curled in a rueful

grin. "Right. Well, we're going to have plenty of time to work on our communication skills now." He opened the storm door and stepped onto the back porch. "Talk soon."

He left as quickly as he'd shown up, jumping from the top step to the ground just as Sierra did, and made his way next door. Only when he disappeared into his house via his back sun porch—such an oxymoron in the cloudy Pacific Northwest, she thought—did she go back inside.

Her lips still hadn't recovered from the kiss, and neither had she. Self-recrimination was pointless. She'd had an occasional date here and there, but in the end had always preferred to spend any free time by herself or with one of her siblings. It'd be so easy to tell herself that she'd kissed Brandon because she was sex-starved.

But the days of lying to herself about anything were long gone. Her last remaining lie about Brandon—that he didn't get the security requirements of raising a daughter—had been shattered by this conversation.

Her worry over Sierra's safety wasn't something she thought she'd ever completely let go of. How could she? She was a mother, whether or not her career involved the worst threats to society. She wasn't willing to yet admit that their time alone together today had eased a bit of her anxiety, either.

Or a lot of it?

But there was no mincing hormones when it came to Brandon. Her attraction to him wasn't one-sided. Unlike Brandon, Toni wasn't able to shake this off, though. The last thing she wanted was to confuse Sierra that her parents were any more than that—her parents. Not a couple, not lovers.

Still, she was going to watch for the school bus this

afternoon, even though Sierra wasn't going to be on it. Just in case that same pickup drove by. Brandon didn't have to know she might be engaging in a bit of obsession, and Sierra wouldn't as she'd be in orchestra practice.

Brandon's support and all, she was still in the security business and took the tiniest threat against her daughter to heart. A heart she'd kept isolated until what she had to admit had been one of the hottest kisses of her life.

Chapter 8

Toby Clayton believed he was nothing if not a master of disguise. He'd learned how to evade his enemies while still in diapers. From the mountain lions and bears in the family's rural backyard, to his older brother, Fred, what he'd learned as a kid continued to pay huge dividends as far as he was concerned. And thanks to the crooks Daddy's business drew in, and the multiple law enforcement agencies that had trailed him through the years, Toby also knew how to hide. How to disappear in plain sight and get what he wanted, however he wanted it.

It didn't hurt that he possessed multiple identity kits, all including fake passports. He'd entered the US two weeks ago under just such an ID, and his clean-shaven face combined with a red wig meant he looked nothing like the real Toby. Today he looked and felt more himself, allowing his heavy beard to grow back along with his gray hair, which he dyed black. He still had his vanity, especially after living in Argentina for the past several years. While money bought him whatever women he wanted, he liked to believe his good looks would have attracted them if he'd been penniless. He never thought he'd miss the place Daddy had sent him to, but as he'd

become reacquainted with his native country, he realized that it wasn't how he remembered it.

The family estate in eastern Washington had been
trashed by the feds when they took in Daddy and that
bitch Veronica. Mack Logging and Manufacturing was a
shell of what it had been, with only the logging part still
in operation, managed by a skeleton crew of longtime
employees who'd never dealt with the shadow business
Daddy had cultivated over the years. The shadow business was the moneymaker, the earnings of which Toby
managed from overseas.

He pounded the steering wheel. Washington State just
didn't feel like home anymore. But he knew his way
around well enough to accomplish what he'd come back
to do. It was up to Toby to get justice for the Clayton
family name.

"And take care of myself for once," he muttered to
himself in the empty cab.

Today he wore what he'd worn for twenty-odd years
working as both a logger and as his father's right-hand
man in shaping the Clayton network. He laughed, thinking about how the cops called it a "crime syndicate."

Syndicate, my ass.

As if they were all running around like bandits in the
backwoods of Washington State. In truth, he'd managed
more accounts and interests for his family name than
most hotshot corporate suits ever did in a lifetime.

In his twenties he'd loved working for Mack Logging and Manufacturing as a logger and do-whatever-
Daddy-needs guy, and he still wasn't a big fan of where
Daddy had shoved him away to, Buenos Aires. He'd
learned passable Spanish in middle school, but the local

Argentinian dialect was often spoken too quickly and was too difficult for him to follow. He'd been able to hold a conversation with the migrant workers who came up to Washington every year during the bigger logging seasons, but trying to talk to a stuffed shirt at a Buenos Aires bank was another matter. Fortunately, most of their accounts were actually kept in Belize. His Argentina residence was a way to keep US law enforcement guessing—and to let them think the Claytons weren't so smart, since Argentina wasn't known to have the most secure banking system. That had been his idea, the first action he'd taken to show Daddy he wasn't the black sheep that first Fred, then Veronica, had painted him as.

He'd dreamed of coming back to Washington and working in the mountains again, of the cedar scent he'd missed so much on the grimy streets of Buenos Aires where he was forced to hang out. No fancy, upscale tourist areas for him. The whole point of being overseas was to keep a low profile.

Careful what you wish for. That was Daddy's favorite saying when they were kids. Things had happened so quickly these last months, and he still didn't have a handle on all that had gone down at company headquarters last fall. Hadn't wanted to know any details, in fact. All he wanted was control of the money.

But when Fred, his older brother, had sent a message to him from his jail cell, Toby knew enough to lock up their numbered accounts as best he could and get on the next plane to Seattle. Via Hawaii, to throw LE off his trail. Not that they were on it. He grunted. Yeah, he'd outsmarted countless uniforms.

This morning he'd dressed as a logger in a flannel

shirt, industrial overalls, a ski cap and a down vest. He kept a warmer jacket in the truck's cab for when the winds picked up—they always did in the PNW, at least in the mountains where he'd grown up. He wasn't too sure about Seattle and this particular suburb. Nor did he care.

All he cared about was revenge. Eye for an eye, but in this case, one Cascade Confidential CEO for the three Claytons Cascade Confidential had helped send to jail. Not that he gave a hoot about Veronica, but she bore the family name.

Putting on the lumberjack clothing and driving his brother's pickup had been easy as pie, natural, almost comforting. But it was a reminder of when he'd still been working for Daddy in person, seeing his old man and brother each and every day. Before he'd been almost nabbed by the police for taking care of some Clayton family business. Sure, it had involved the elimination of a group of particularly stupid rival syndicate goons. Nothing he wasn't used to. But he'd been spotted by a waitress in the local diner just minutes before the jerks had disappeared off a nearby street.

He'd messed up and hadn't taken care of the witness— he'd seen how she'd looked at him the next time he'd come in and known he should whack her. But he hadn't, and she'd blabbed to the police. Daddy's PD informant had told Cal Clayton to make Toby disappear.

Toby had had less than a half hour to get the hell out of Dodge and on a plane to South America that dark day five years ago.

He smirked to himself. He'd been sent away for doing Daddy's dirty business, and now he was back to take care of the dirtiest part of upholding the Clayton reputation.

As smart and fancy as the Cascade Confidential security firm's website appeared, Toby thought they were flat-out stupid. He'd been able to track down each of the siblings who ran the regional offices, from Portland to Seattle and Coeur d'Alene. He was after their head honcho, CEO Antonia O'Malley.

Antonia was the sister of the woman who'd helped the feds bring down the Clayton dynasty. It was too much trouble to go after Willow O'Malley, though. She lived in Coeur d'Alene, and she'd worked alongside some FBI loser during the Mack takedown. They were both too much trouble to try to get to, much less punish, from what Daddy said.

Better to go for the weak link, someone who might not have the same street smarts as Willow. Antonia O'Malley fit the ticket perfectly, as it appeared all she did was office work. She didn't appear in any online searches like her siblings who'd served as cops or military did. In fact, she was going to be too easy. He'd make it more of a challenge for himself by having fun with her before he killed her. But first, he had to nab her.

He chuckled to himself. This was like playing hide-and-seek in the woods out back when he and Fred had been kids. He'd outwait Fred, only to pounce on his back and knock him down in one quick action. He'd almost always beaten Fred, much to his older brother's frustration.

He shook his head. That was a long time ago, when they'd been brothers in all ways. Not like today, when the only bond Toby felt toward Fred was blood. Simple luck of the genetic draw. Still, blood was blood, and the Clayton blood had been threatened. *Unacceptable.*

This stakeout was so damn boring. Could the cul-de-sac be any quieter? The scent of motor oil that permeated the truck cab stirred memories of long days with a chain saw in his hand, full days of supervising major cuts up and down the eastern mountains of Washington State. He'd felt as if he could do anything back then, be whomever he dreamed of. And he'd always dreamed of being a logger just like Daddy.

Until his dream of running the Clayton business was shattered for the sake of his freedom. He'd planned to come back home as soon as Daddy had things under control again, as soon as Cal Clayton was the kingpin of the PNW when it came to all things human trafficking and illicit drug dealing. Daddy's last words to him at SeaTac had been "You'll be home for Christmas, Toby, just hang tight." He ended up coming home for the holidays, all right—five years later. He'd arrived home last month to a shattered legacy, thanks to the feds.

No, not the feds. Cascade Confidential was the real enemy that had taken his family down.

He hated having to rely on information from Fred and Veronica, but he'd do what he had to. All he needed was to get the money back in his hands, under his sole control. Fred couldn't be trusted and Veronica was nothing more than a gold digger who'd used sex to lure Daddy into matrimony.

Daddy probably wouldn't live to see the benefit of what Toby was doing for their family; chances were he'd die in prison. Fred, too, though he might get a lighter sentence or at least get kept in a loony ward instead of a state or federal pen.

Fred was something else. He should have been a movie star, the way he could act. He'd even fooled Toby for the first several minutes of their reunion last month, when Toby had finally been able to get into the locked-down criminal psychiatric ward where Fred was kept. Until Fred's scary grin had turned into a curled lip and he'd quietly sung the first refrain of "Blue Suede Shoes." Elvis had been their momma's favorite, and Fred had used every ounce of his comedic and musical abilities to keep her smiling at the end of her life. Especially those last months in hospice care.

It had almost been the end of the Claytons right then and there. Daddy had gone on a months-long bender, leaving Fred and Toby alone in their house as teens. The logging company had suffered but managed, thanks to several longtime employees who prayed and hoped Cal would come back to himself and find a way through his grief. Cal Clayton had come back home, but with that bitch Veronica, only a few years older than him, on his arm.

He'd left his pristine Mustang in the garage at the logging warehouse back at home and traded it out for his brother's clean but battered pickup. Driving west through a mountain snowfall had made the truck look more like what Toby was posing as, a wannabe lumberjack, cruising city neighborhoods for extra cash.

Everett was so different from the urban setting he'd lived in since he got sent to Argentina. There were trees here, same as back home in eastern Washington. Not as dense, mind you, but enough to cause a problem when the ground got soaked for a few days, followed by the raging gales that hit the PNW every other year or so. And once one tall pine fell, more were to follow. Trees were like dominoes. Daddy had taught him that, too.

His phone buzzed in his overalls' front zipper pocket as he sat in the cab of the pickup truck, watching. Taking notes. Knowing that the information he gathered would be Cascade Confidential's demise, sooner than later. It was an unknown number, but the area code was Washington State and he was hoping for a call from Fred.

"Toby Tree Services, how can I help you?" He'd thought it was smart to use his real first name. Less chance of messing up. His current passport and ID docs all said he was Willard T. McAdams. If pressed he'd claim the T stood for Toby.

"Call from Frederick Clayton, Washington State Psychiatric Corrections Unit."

"I'll accept." He waited while the operator put the call through. A brief blast of a horrendous cover of "Stairway to Heaven" later, he heard Fred's voice.

"Toby? You there?"

"I'm here."

"Where is here? You sound far away."

Toby looked around at the light poles in the friendly Everett neighborhood he'd parked in. At the way the homes lined up so nicely up and down the street, except where the lots arced in a perfect half circle. About ten houses down, where his target remained.

"Far away from home, yeah." He'd never liked big cities, Seattle and its surroundings included. "I'm keeping busy." He knew better than to mention what he was up to, not on a monitored line. But Fred knew what Toby had planned. They'd spoken about it on his single visit to his brother that the officials had allowed.

Now that he'd returned to the truck, he had eyes on the house. He couldn't make out Antonia or the man who'd been sitting with her in her kitchen moments earlier. The strange dude had showed up about an hour after a yellow school bus had driven away. He'd seen several kids waiting at the top of the cul-de-sac and figured they were from homes nearby. "Today has been productive, brother."

"Careful." Fred's growled reminder to reveal nothing about their plan lit his fuse. Fred had always been in charge and still thought he was. Toby fought against throwing his phone into the truck's windshield, the hell with the consequences of either a broken phone or cracked glass.

Play it cool.

"I'm not some dumb kid anymore, brother," he grumbled. "Listen, Fred, I want you to know that I'm here for you, man. Whatever you need."

Silence.

"Fred?"

"That's mighty kind of you. What's best for the family is all I've ever wanted."

"You know I'll always do everything in my power to keep us together. To keep you safe."

"Don't forget to clean my blue suedes for me," Fred said, as if asking Toby to bring him a milkshake or fancy smokes on the next allowed visit. But it was code from way back. "Blue suedes" meant their family, what they stood for. Sticking together. "Clean" meant to do whatever it took, whatever Daddy told them to.

"You know how tough the stains on suede can be, but not to worry, buddy. I have some special cleaner in mind this time."

"Sounds good. Listen, do me a solid and tell Pops

I'm thinking about him." Fred wasn't allowed to communicate with Cal Clayton. Neither Fred nor Cal could communicate with Veronica, either. Toby thought it was overkill, himself.

"Will do." He waited until he was certain the call was disconnected before he allowed himself the belly laugh he'd been holding back. Yeah, sure. Let Fred and Daddy think he was taking care of them. Veronica, too. Salvaging the family name was all he was doing for them. Getting the cold cash in his hands was his real reason for risking jail time. It was high time he put himself first.

None of them had ever done a damn thing for him.

Chapter 9

"I take it you and Willow went over her recent summary of the cold case during your call this morning?" Aubrey's voice was all business as Toni sat across from her in the crowded café. It was one of their favorites, family owned and midway between Everett and the Seattle CC office.

"Yes, and I take it that you actually read the reports she sent. I didn't, and she was none too happy with me about it."

Aubrey snorted. "It's my job to keep up with details, since I work with Denice on the CC archives."

"I know, but I could have at least read over the first page. I forget about her military background, that she's really great at giving us bullet points to keep us in the loop. She's only worked for us the last what, six months?"

"But it feels like she's always been here." Aubrey finished Toni's thought. "I feel as though we've regained the sisterhood." They both laughed. As the three eldest siblings, the sisters had always had one another's backs. "I'm really glad you agreed to meet me today. I miss you in the office."

"Me, too. Brandon's getting Sierra after school, so if I get caught up in some unexpected traffic I don't have to worry about it." She did want to be back in time to see the school bus pull up and make sure that there weren't any unknown vehicles casing their neighborhood. Brandon was probably right; their neighborhood was safe, and Sierra was in no imminent danger. But she couldn't shake her concern.

"Something's bothering you, though. What is it? If you don't want to share, that's okay, too." Aubrey sat back and held her mug of the house special between her hands. Toni was doing the same with her latte. It was cold and blustery, a typical PNW January day.

"You're still the peacemaker, you know that?" Toni jested. Aubrey was in the middle of her and Willow, and the brothers were seven and nine years younger than Willow. The three sisters had effectively been their own family unit before Jake and Kevin showed up.

"I like to think of myself as more of an empath. 'Peacemaker' sounds too much like what Brandon does for a living. Or did."

"He's still doing it, the diplomacy, but on a contract basis."

"And how is it going, seeing so much of him?"

Toni swallowed. "I actually don't see him as much as you'd think. We both work full-time, inside our homes, and when one of us has Sierra, the other can work longer hours. He's not what's bothering me, by the way." Well, Brandon and his nearness hadn't been bothering her until that darn kiss a couple of hours ago. "I'm worried about Sierra, is all. Her safety."

"Because of what Willow said about the Claytons coming after their perceived enemies, or the dust that Willow's stirring up with the missing girls cold case?"

"The cold case. I'm not concerned about Toby Clayton. If he's smart, he's not going to try to come back into the country any time soon." She put her cup down, looked out the front window of the small shop, at the passersby who either wore a hat, their hoods up or had their hair whipped around by the wind. "And I can't even honestly say I'm worried about a threat from the cold case. Not at Sierra. She's an unknown on the CC website."

"What about a threat to you?" Aubrey's eyes were steady. An attorney who'd turned from trial law to become the CC operations manager, she also served as the legal adviser for their company. Her logical mind and calm demeanor proved invaluable when CC had to deal with clients whose emotions were getting in the way of sound judgment.

"I'm not unaware of my surroundings. I take all the necessary precautions."

"Do you think that maybe it's time to actually share the burden of worrying about your kid with her other parent?"

"That's a sucker punch. Where is this coming from?"

"You've always been so keen on the fact that you and Brandon are coparents. And I have to say, you're both amazing. Look at Sierra. The kid is brilliant, well-adjusted and has a bright future."

"Yeah, until the drugs, sex and online bullying show up in her life."

"It all shows up in every kid's life, and you know it. She has you and Brandon. The three of you will get through her teen years. I have faith in you."

Spoken like the single, childless aunt that Aubrey was. Toni appreciated her honesty but was reluctant to lean into the idea that she could simply let go of her worries over Sierra's safety.

"Um, thanks?" She eyed Aubrey. Her sister wasn't done, judging by the way she looked down at her half-full mug, her perfectly manicured nails a bright red contrast against the marine-blue pottery glaze.

"It's not a compliment but a fact. I call it like I see it. And don't do your 'you're not a mother' roll of the eyes with me."

"I didn't roll my eyes!"

"I'm talking figuratively and you know it."

"Maybe." She sighed. "I don't see where you're going, though, when you say I need to share my burden." She didn't believe worry was something one could share, like a hot fudge sundae or a vacation.

"Lean into Brandon being here, Toni. For the first time since you had Sierra, you have someone you can count on 24-7. Sure, you had Mom and Dad before he came back, and you've always had me or even the brothers. But we're not Sierra's parents. We'll never have the worries you do, or be able to discipline Sierra like we would our own kid. But you and Brandon, this is what you're good at. Sharing the parenting role, which includes the worries. That's what I mean by *share*."

"Gotcha." She really didn't, but she also wasn't in the mood to get into it with Aubrey. Toni would lose any argument with her sister. Debating, like fieldwork, wasn't her forte.

Aubrey shook her head but offered a wide grin. "You don't get my point, and that's okay. I hate seeing you wound up all the time, sis."

"Well, unless you have a machine that can transport

me to when Sierra's a healthy, safe and contributing adult member of society, you're going to have to live with me like this." She smiled, hoping Aubrey would lighten up. She'd had enough grilling about her relationship with Brandon from Willow.

"I love you no matter how you are, sis. But allow me this last observation."

"Okay."

"It seems to me that Brandon has really gone out of his way to make your life more manageable as far as raising Sierra goes. So there's a good reason to back off of the worry wagon. Have you ever considered that worrying is a form of control?"

Aubrey paused, as if expecting Toni to object. But she couldn't, because no one more than Aubrey knew the stress Toni had been under as a single working parent. She had Brandon's emotional and financial support with their daughter, but that wasn't a big help when she had long hours of work ahead of her and Sierra needed to be picked up at school and fed and all the myriad tasks she did as a mom still needed doing. Aubrey had seen her break down on occasion, letting tears of frustration roll down her cheeks on her worst days when the overwhelm became too much. And of course she was a control freak. She was the eldest O'Malley. It was in her genetic code.

"I can't argue with the fact that I'm a control freak, Aubrey. I guess it could be one way I try to control the uncontrollable. But I don't think it'll ever be enough to stop me from worrying about my kid. Look how much you worry about Maple and Syrup." Aubrey doted on her two Persian Himalayan cats.

"Do not bring those two into this. Did I tell you that

Syrup ate all of Maple's kibble again this morning? He's going to weigh thirty pounds if I don't figure out how to stop his gluttonous ways." Aubrey smiled. "Life is short, is what I'm getting at. I want you to be happy, and the only time I ever saw you genuinely full of joy was before you had Sierra, when you and Brandon were together that one summer. You were happy when Sierra was born, of course, but I always sensed you were nursing a broken heart." Before Toni could set Aubrey straight—that she'd been the one to break things off with Brandon—her sister continued. "I don't believe in coincidences, either. That house was still available at the right time for Brandon to take it. He wouldn't have unless he either knew or hoped you might come around."

"Come around?" She tried to play it cool, really she did. But her cheeks betrayed her. Aubrey didn't miss the red patches, either.

"You're blushing, and you're too young for a hot flash."

"Don't be so sure." She grumbled and stood up, Aubrey doing the same. "I do have to get back to the house." No way was she telling Aubrey that it was so she could double-check for any strange vehicles in the neighborhood. Not after this conversation. They gave each other a quick hug before going their separate ways.

Toni was grateful for the twenty-minute ride home. She needed the time to decompress and let go of the thoughts clamoring for her attention.

They were all about Brandon.

He watched Antonia O'Malley's residence through his salt-streaked windshield until the sun went down. It would have been easier to see details if it were clean like the windshield on his Mustang, but the banged-up pickup was more incognito, better for his disguise. So far, he hadn't gained anything significant for his purposes. Antonia had left the house for a while but returned before he had a chance to really case her place. Besides, that neighbor of hers had been in and out of his house several times this afternoon, and not on a regular schedule, from what he'd observed. Once had been when he'd gone for a jog, the other times he'd gone out in his fancy car. He might come back at any time now. Toby would need to wait. He couldn't afford any witnesses. This had to be a clean catch.

His stomach rumbled and he looked at his phone. He'd left the neighborhood exactly twice, both times to take a leak and grab some chow. The sandwiches he'd wolfed down had been a far cry from the heavy-protein meals he'd been subsisting on in Argentina. Daddy and Fred had no clue what he'd been up to down there. They thought he was learning the ropes of managing overseas accounts as an underling for one of the cartels his daddy was affiliated with. But when Veronica took over the business so quickly and hired that jerk assistant Fred had told him about, he knew he'd better have all the Clayton financial ducks in a row. Toby had still called in to Veronica weekly, just as he had with Daddy. But with Veronica he always said he had nothing to report. He'd convinced her that it was the same he'd told Daddy. Unless one of the accounts disappeared, he'd say, "Nothing new to report."

He'd learned a lot from Carlos, the man who'd taught him which Belizean and other overseas banks he could trust to put Mack Logging's "extra" earnings into, and when to move them to other, safer accounts.

Carlos hadn't been watching his every move, though. Toby had a nice purse for himself. But he was going to triple it after he did this last gig.

He stretched. The school bus had come and gone two hours ago, right after Antonia got home. She'd come out before the school bus arrived, and for a few seconds he'd thought she was staring right at him before she went back inside. He figured she was taking a break from work. But she wouldn't have seen more than the glint from his windshield, anyway, unless she was using the same high-powered binoculars he was. And she'd been carrying nothing more than a cup.

The kids got off right in front of her driveway, as in the morning, and while he didn't have a direct line of sight to the bus door, he watched every last one of them go into a different house on the street as the bus pulled away. No one went into Antonia O'Malley's, which wasn't a surprise. He'd found no evidence online that she had a kid—and he was hoping she didn't have a husband or wife, either. If he was lucky, she lived all alone in her big house and taking revenge would be easy. Fun.

He'd changed the truck's license plates—he wasn't an idiot—and placed different magnetic signs over the Mack Logging logo on both side doors. It had been tempting to steal one off a different random tree service's truck, but he figured it was too risky, so he'd used an online printing service to make the fake ones and had them shipped overnight to a PO box. He'd paid for both the magnetic signs and the post office box with the credit card that matched his fake passport. It was too easy to get caught by a security camera at either a gas station or other roadside establishment when the cops came snooping, and he didn't want Mack's logo caught on camera.

Two neighborhood cars drove by. Folks on the way home from work, he figured, judging by the time. So far so good—no one had given him a second glance much less a first one. People were wrapped up in their own lives, and he was confident his door signs kept any suspicion at bay.

By the time Antonia O'Malley got close enough to see his door signs were temporary, it'd be too late for her. She'd be right where he wanted her.

Helpless.

Toby grinned in the dark cab. It didn't feel so cold or damp anymore. He could taste the success of the solid plan he'd come up with

He yawned. It was late, and the fresh air plus staying alert all day had done him in. Time to drive away, regroup, go back over his checklist. When he made the O'Malleys pay for what they'd done to his family, he wanted to enjoy every second of it and not have any worry that he'd forgotten something.

Rope, check. Duct tape, check. Rifle, check, pistol—

His mental list screeched to a halt as a familiar vehicle drove by, its taillights sleek and sophisticated, indicating a luxury brand. He knew that car, as it had passed uncomfortably close to his truck earlier.

The car belonged to the house next to Antonia's. An hour ago he'd watched the owner's garage door open, the car reverse down the driveway and drive past him, out of the neighborhood. Figured the man worked from home since he hadn't come out earlier in the day except to jog, and his other jaunts matched up to errands, not going into an office. So many people worked from home now, didn't know what it meant to earn a buck the hard way. His gut ached as the embers of resentment he'd carried since he could remember ignited, wrestling with his acid reflux until his stomach felt like a tangle of barbed wire. He might hate his daddy and Fred, but he still respected how Cal had instilled a solid work ethic into them. Kids nowadays could use some old-fashioned belt buckle discipline, if you asked him.

Time to get a move on.

He sat up so fast he bonked his head on the door frame. "Ow."

He watched the car as he rubbed his temple. Toby was pretty certain the driver hadn't noticed him earlier, and probably hadn't just now either, with it being so dark. Still, he'd better wait a few more minutes, until the car pulled into the garage and the door lowered behind it. But it stopped in the middle of the driveway, its taillights bright, and then turned off as the driver must have put the car in Park.

"C'mon, c'mon." The jerk could read his texts once he was inside.

Toby needed to piss, bad. He went ahead and started the engine so he'd be ready to go. His bladder's urgency increased with each jump of his leg, needing release. Lowering his driver's side door window, he breathed in the cold night air. Anything to distract him from the much-needed bathroom break. The gas station with the outdoor john was a few blocks over, on the main drag that wound around the water and eventually led to I-5, and it was the quickest way to relief.

Come on, dude.

Toby wished he was nearer the woods—it wasn't sociably acceptable to piss on the side of the road in America. Definitely not in populated areas like here.

His hand froze on the gearshift as he watched a most unexpected scene unfold on the neighbor's driveway. A slim figure got out of the passenger seat, grinned at the driver and waved. Because he'd opened his window, and because the light breeze was blowing in the right direction, a single phrase reached his ears.

"I'll tell Mom. See you later, Dad!" The figure, a girl he guessed couldn't be older than nine or ten, turned on her heel and made a beeline…for Antonia O'Malley's home.

Toby grabbed his phone and with shaking fingers keyed in metadata—he'd learned what that was in Buenos Aires—that quickly showed him what he needed to know. The house next door to Antonia's had last been sold this past summer. Six months ago. It had closed two months later. A quick search using the county, the address and "owner" yielded that the owner was Brandon Anderson. So he and Antonia had different last names.

But his daughter had gone to Antonia's. Was it possible that Antonia O'Malley had a daughter? He hadn't counted on this surprise when he'd spotted O'Malley on various social media sites, mostly business-related. At least she was smart enough to keep her kid off social media, like a good mother would.

A good mother, though, would be very upset if anything happened to her kid. More than if something happened to herself, in fact.

"Well, what do you know."

Chapter 10

On Thursday, Toni stared at the notification on her phone. It was from an app she didn't recognize. A very popular dating app, in fact. Toni had never used a dating app, and definitely not this one. Maybe the notification was spam.

She opened the message anyway, intending to delete it after she found the source or gave Willow whatever information she needed to track down how the app got onto her phone in the first place.

Hi. I'm new to the Seattle area, in a suburb up north. I like international travel and all things security-related.

Toni blinked. What the heck? Who was this?

Her thumb hovered over the read-more icon, and she bit her lower lip. She was the CEO of a top-tier private security firm, for heaven's sake. What was she doing?

"Getting to the bottom of this is what I'm doing," she muttered, and let her thumb touch the screen. "Just try me." She'd recently reviewed the security procedures they led new clients through and this was a perfect way to practice how not to handle anonymous messages or notifications.

The app was not only on her phone, but it appeared she had a full profile. Including the photo of her in her sport bikini from when she'd paddle boarded with Sierra last summer. Worse, her alias was "Undercover Mom."

"Ugh."

Her phone lit up with a call from Brandon. He always texted first. Unless something urgent was going on with Sierra. Internal alarm bells rang as she fought back the unwelcome panic.

"Is everything okay? Did the school call you?"

"It's fine. I'm not calling about Sierra. It's all good, honest. You okay?"

"Yeah." She gulped in a huge breath. "You usually text first."

"I do, and I'm sorry. This isn't about Sierra, per se. Not directly, that is." He sounded…cautious. While she waited for him to go on, she looked at the dating app, and at the profile of the person who'd sent her the message.

Another beach shot, but this one in Thailand, where Sierra and Brandon had met his family for vacation two summers ago. She recognized the photo of Brandon as one half of the one he took with Sierra.

Sierra.

"You still there, Toni?"

"I am."

"Do you happen to have a profile on the dating app—"

"Never Too Old?" she interrupted, figuring out where this was headed.

He let out a sigh, but she couldn't tell if it was relief or exasperation. "Yes. That's the app. I've never even heard of this one." Did that mean he used other dating apps?

Don't ask a question you don't want the answer to.

"Let me guess. You have a message from me? Or rather, 'Undercover Mom'?" She went back to her messages, and sure enough, there was a note in her sent file. To "Nomad Looking for Security."

"So you're telling me you're not 'Undercover Mom'?" His voice deepened with humor.

She read aloud what she now realized had to have been Sierra's handiwork. "'Let's get together for fun and more.' Jeez. She went to all the trouble to do this but then writes a weak message. Tell me, does that sound like something I'd say to you?"

"I don't know." She envisioned him shrugging, the way that made her crazy when she wanted him to be serious and he refused to. "It's a long time since we— since we…" At his falter, her lips immediately burned with the memory of how recent their last kiss had been.

"Since we've dated. Been a couple." She finished it for him, ignoring the surprise kiss.

Silence.

She opened her mouth to speak—

"We did a heck of a lot more than date, Toni." The reminder that they'd been more than boyfriend-girlfriend, more than lovers, shouldn't have sent the zaps of regret and guilt through her heart, but it did.

"We were a lot younger then. And we didn't know what we were doing." They hadn't known Sierra would be conceived, that they'd agree to raise her while they lived separate lives.

"I disagree, as we clearly knew enough about what we were doing to produce a child, but let's table that for another time. What are we going to do about our daughter breaking into our phones, downloading the app onto them and setting up profiles posing as each of us?" Brandon had always been good at getting straight to the point. Keeping his emotions out of a discussion. "I didn't realize she had my passkey memorized."

"You gave it to her?" She couldn't keep the incredulity out of her voice.

"Not for her to use it nefariously. She asked to see if my connectivity was better than hers…" He grew quiet for a moment, and then she heard his low chuckle. Blood immediately pooled between her legs, pulsing up to her nipples. Brandon's laughter had always been an instant turn-on. "I've been had, haven't I?" He laughed again.

"Well, I do have to say it's pretty ingenious. She had to have been planning this for a while." Toni meant it. She already thought her daughter was beyond smart, but this was another level of intelligence she herself hadn't had at the same age.

"Probably not any sooner than when we each bought our new phones," Brandon reflected. They'd gone to the phone store together, all three of them, as it was time for Sierra to have her own phone and Brandon needed a new one. Toni still hadn't figured out how to use all the new functions and relied on Sierra's help whenever she got stuck.

"You're right. I changed my passcode then—"

"As did I, and we both insisted she give us her passcode with the explicit understanding that she would never lock us out of her phone."

"But we failed to insist she had to stay off *our* phones. I ask her to fix things on mine quite often, actually." Admiration for her daughter's intelligence and tech prowess warred with her disappointment at Sierra's wrongful behavior.

"I suggest we make sure we have her passcode, that she hasn't changed it." Brandon's tone had grown somber. He was in protective-dad mode. Which for some weird reason made her hormones buzz all the louder.

You're losing it. Turned on by tough love as much as Brandon's whiskey-deep voice.

"I agree. We need to confront her together." She hadn't checked on Sierra's passcode, as Sierra had never given her reason to not trust her with her own phone. "And now we'll have to make her leave her phone out of her bedroom, no matter whose house she's at. She had to have done this either at night or on the school bus." Students were allowed to have phones for emergencies only, and the school rule was for their phones to be locked in their lockers during the day.

Brandon's sad sigh vibrated over her earbuds, eliciting a flood of empathy for him.

"Brandon, it's okay. This isn't your, or my, fault. It just is. Sierra's a kid, and she's supposed to do things out of character like this. I don't like it, either, that she betrayed us, went behind our backs."

"Funny, you sound like me when I told you to stop carrying all this worry on your shoulders."

"I suppose I do." Toni had no argument.

"Listen, Toni, what's bugging me is something far more serious. I'm not so concerned about her breaking into our phones, but why she did it." Brandon addressed what she'd been internally avoiding. "I think this is about her heart, not her mental acuity. She's never indicated that she wants us to be more than her parents, but she's definitely been giving it a lot of thought." Brandon's concern struck a raw nerve, and she blinked back tears. Thank goodness they were on the phone.

"You're right, I'm afraid. We've normalized our co-parenting until now. She didn't know anything different, to be fair. And we never lived next door to one another. Add in that she's at the age where she's becoming aware of a lot more, relationship-wise. She's not a little kid who accepts whatever we tell her."

"We need to sit down with her, together, and work it out. It might get uncomfortable, but we'll get through it." Brandon sounded like his diplomat self again.

"But we need a game plan before we do." Toni wasn't going to budge on this. "We have to present a united front." She did not want to contradict one another in front of Sierra.

"Our game plan is the same as it's always been— get the answers we need, answer her questions and do what's in her best interest." Brandon clearly didn't want to spend more time working it out, which was fine with her. They were on the phone, not in the same room, and yet the tingles of awareness his presence caused were just as potent. She didn't want to be tempted into another kiss, or more.

"Okay." She drew comfort in how well they'd hashed this out. "How about we talk to her on our family game night tomorrow?" It was her turn to host the weekly dinner that they'd decided to have shortly after Brandon moved in.

"Great. See you then." He disconnected before she could reply.

Before she'd say something she might regret, like *maybe Sierra's picking up on something between us.*

"You two don't get it. I'm really good at figuring things out, like Aunt Willow and Uncle Kevin. Why can't you see that instead of punishing me for making my own dating app?" Sierra sat at the dining room table in Toni's house, arms crossed across her chest.

"Stop deflecting, Sierra." Brandon hoped his pride at how good of an argument she was putting up was hidden from his daughter. He made quick eye contact with Toni, who raised her brow. Nodding—he interpreted her body language as *see? I told you she's a handful*—he pressed on. "Why do you think we wouldn't believe you're smart enough to create an app?"

She rolled her eyes, and Brandon was surprised Toni didn't call her out on it. This must be the part about being available and listening that Toni had mentioned when he'd first returned. To not take all her actions personally.

"Dad, Mom, you're missing the whole point. You keep treating me like I'm in elementary school, like I'm six or seven."

"Give us some specific examples." Toni's request was blunt.

"You keep telling me to practice my oboe, pay attention to reading and French." She expelled a very angsty, very dramatic sigh. "But I'm more interested in programming, creating websites, hacking—"

"Hold it." Toni stopped her and looked at Brandon. "Let's catch your dad up. I take it you never told your dad about your career aspirations?"

Brandon swallowed a laugh. He'd no doubt Sierra took

herself very seriously, but really, she had "career aspirations" at age twelve? Whatever happened to "what do you want to be when you grow up?"

"Dad. I want to be like my aunts and uncles and work for the family business. I'd be so good at it. I've always scored tops in all my classes, but especially anything to do with computers."

"Okay, well, that's great to know so young—er, so early—what you want to do with your life. A good focal point. Your mom and I will support you, of course. But know that whatever your, er, career aspirations are, you will succeed by being a fully rounded individual. That means a broad range of all the educational basics. Sure, you might not play oboe if you end up doing PI work. But having the musical training expands your brain in ways no other study can."

Sierra stared at him for a full second before she looked away. "Which means you agree with Mom," she grumbled.

He looked to Toni, who met his gaze…and smiled. They were such a great team when they put their minds to it. Warmth began under his rib cage and began to spread—

Nope. Not going there.

"Let's get back to the focus of our discussion, dear daughter." He tried to inflect some humor into the heavy vibes radiating from Sierra's small frame. "Your mother and I want to make it clear that we're always going to be here for you. We're a family, whether we all live under one roof or not." He coughed at a sudden tickle in his throat.

Having trouble swallowing your own BS?

"Yes, we're not going anywhere," Toni smoothly continued. "We—your dad and I—don't need to be a romantic couple for that, Sierra. You can count on us no matter what."

"You two still aren't getting it." Sierra sat up straight. "I know you're both here for me, that you both love me." Her eyes, the same shade as Toni's, sparked with passion, with belief. "But you have to admit, you're both living boring lives. You work and you focus on me. I was only trying to make you see that."

"Really, Sierra?" Toni's words cut through the lousy alibi.

Brandon looked from his daughter to his—to Toni. The two most important females in his life faced off in a mother-daughter glare. Until Sierra sat back. "Okay, I was sticking my nose into your business."

"And?" Toni was locked on.

"I'm sorry. I won't do it again."

"Okay, then." Toni sat back, too, and Brandon's lungs expanded. He didn't think he'd ever participated in a tougher negotiation his entire diplomatic career. The stakes were much higher to him now. This was about family. About love.

A love he was never going to be able to share with Toni.

Are you going to give up that easily?

"Mom, it's your turn." Sierra didn't look up from the cards she'd pulled as she prompted Toni. Toni had to admit that her heart wasn't in this game, but after their family discussion, she and Brandon had wanted to lighten the atmosphere. They'd agreed to a very complicated board game that was Sierra's favorite. It involved fantasy world building, and all the rules made Toni's eyes water.

"I think your mom has had enough for tonight, baby girl. Plus, it's getting late." Brandon's voice rumbled playfully over the dining room table, and Toni couldn't have stopped her responding laughter if she'd wanted to.

"Hey, I'm improving at this game. I'm holding my own tonight, am I not?" She sat straighter and rolled the die. A three. "Argh!"

Sierra and Brandon cheered. The low roll meant she'd never catch up to their places on the board. "Well, I was holding my own. I'm out. Tell you what. You two duke it out for the winner and I'll get dessert."

"Yeah, Mom, you go get the ice cream." Sierra grinned. *Phew.* Her girl was back, and harmony was restored, if only for tonight.

Toni kissed the top of Sierra's head as she walked out of the room and went into the kitchen. The stove light was the only illumination and she left it for a minute while she pulled three tubs of ice cream from the bottom-drawer freezer and then three deep bowls from the cupboard. It was scary how quickly she'd grown used to the three of them being together. They'd had their talk with Sierra about their very unromantic relationship, that she shouldn't put expectations on anyone else's relationships, especially her parents'. It wasn't going to be more.

But what if it was?

She paused at the sink, looking out through the window. Thoughts of being more than a coparent with Brandon occupied more space in her head than ever. So she turned her focus to what always soothed her—nature. A full moon hung over the tips of the cedar trees that surrounded this part of their neighborhood. The line of woods separated them from the more industrial parts of the city, revealing the shadow of the mountains past the trees without the manmade lines of the storage and boating facilities. The hush of night was palpable as the drone of Brandon's baritone and Sierra's comparable chirping settled over her like a mantel, providing a musical score any filmmaker would envy.

She lifted her arm for the light switch to the right of the window as a flash of light in her backyard drew her up.

What the heck?

Instead of flicking on the kitchen light, announcing her presence to whatever was in her yard, she left the ice cream bowls on the counter and scurried to the back door. As she reached for the flashlight she heard Sierra giggle, Brandon's jovial reply. Should she—

No. She'd never needed a man to chase away a raccoon or a fox from her yard. She sure didn't need to call Brandon to help with a random rambunctious teen who'd been drinking beer in the woods behind her property.

The motion sensor on the back porch light hadn't activated, so she turned it off from the inside. She stepped onto the back porch in complete darkness save for the moonlight. Carefully closing the door behind her, she allowed her eyes to adjust to the inky black and forced herself to breathe more deeply. She'd been more emotional than usual, ever since Brandon had validated her parenting skills. And maybe since that handshake, since the jolt of awareness had reminded her that she was human.

Handshake? You mean the passionate kiss.

She ignored her inner monologue and got back to tiptoeing into her backyard. Creeping around her own property wasn't something she regularly did. In fact, the last time she'd been out here was when a pair of raccoons—

Crunch.

She froze. That didn't sound like a raccoon. It sounded more like a footstep of the two-legged variety. The sound hadn't come from the edge of her yard, either. It was closer. Her ears strained to catch it again. Her heart pounded so loudly in her ears, her breath scraping like sandpaper over plywood, would she be able to hear it again?

Crunch, crunch...

Definitely footsteps. Followed by rapid pounding. Someone was getting away. And they'd been trespassing.

Not in my yard, buddy.

She clambered down the three steps and ran to the side of the house, to the fenced-in side yard she shared with Brandon's property. A dark figure was briefly illuminated by the front-yard lantern. It was only a split second but it was enough for her to realize it was indeed a person, that they were bigger than her and that they were pushing through the gate that opened to the front lawn. She made it to the gate and saw them again, running toward the street.

"Hey!" she yelled as she pursued the interloper. "Get back here! What do you think—" She gasped for air. Her muscles needed the oxygen from her breath more than she needed to chastise the jerk who'd been lurking outside her home.

By the time she neared the sidewalk, the runner had disappeared. She stopped. There was no way to determine if they'd turned right or left at the cross street, and even if she could, she'd never catch up to them.

"Toni?" Brandon's shout came from close by and she turned back to see he was two strides from her, a distance he covered in a blink. He placed his hands on her shoulders, the firm grip shooting warm reassurance through to her toes. She had to fight against leaning into him, letting him figure out whom the trespasser had been. But she didn't try to shrug his hands away, either.

"Let me—" she puffed. "Catch my. Breath." Not for the first time, she wished she were as interested in working out as her siblings, that she would have been fast enough to take down any bad guy who came her way. "I'm not a runner."

"It's okay, Toni." Brandon's voice reassured her. He waited for her to settle, and he must have felt her breathing slow, because he dropped his hands to his sides.

"I got up to use the bathroom while you were getting the ice cream, and I heard you yell. What were you chasing?"

"Who. It was a person. A guy—I think it was a guy—was in my yard. Next to the house. In between our houses, and they ran out through the front gate."

"Was it a kid coming back in from the woods? I saw a few trot between our houses last weekend, late. I didn't mention it because you'd already told me to expect it." He sounded puzzled as to why she was so unsettled. And he was right—she had warned him about the teen foot traffic. In lieu of a nearby coffee spot or empty parent's home, the woods and their convenient location to the neighborhood made it a favored party locale. "Party" encompassing everything from gaming to booze to weed and psychedelics.

"I don't think so… I don't know." Her mind raced. "I have a motion-detector light on the back door that should have lit up if they'd come through the yard, so you're probably right."

"Hang on. Something spooked you. The first time you saw them was on the side of the house?" Brandon turned and strode toward the gate, still open. She jogged alongside.

"It was the side yard, where I heard his steps." The ball of fear in her belly eased with Brandon next to her, with seeing his determination to get to the bottom of whatever had just happened.

"It was probably a kid and your shout scared them off. But let's make sure." Brandon switched his phone flashlight on, and she did the same.

They swept the ground with their beams as they stepped onto the lawn, noting the large footprints in the dew-soaked grass. They walked through the gate together. Something bright caught the light and she stopped.

"Looks like they dropped something." Brandon stepped forward, knelt and reached to pick up the object.

"Wait! Don't touch it." She stepped closer, knelt next to him. And gasped. A long, serrated blade lay against the house. "Why would a teenager be running with an exposed hunting knife?" She looked around, tried to come up with a reasonable explanation.

"Why do teens do any—" Brandon began.

"Wait." Fear welled again, threatening to morph into panic. "Brandon, it's under Sierra's window!"

"What's under my window?" Sierra stood at the far corner of the house, peering around from the backyard. She was backlit by what Toni assumed was the porch light, so she must have turned it on.

"I told you to stay inside, Sierra." Brandon's tone had an edge Toni had never noticed before. Protective, in a primal way.

"*Dad.* I'm just checking—"

"Inside, now." Brandon wasn't budging. His stern tone with their daughter comforted Toni as much as if he'd put his arm around her.

We do want the same thing.

"Listen to your father, Sierra." Toni backed him up.

"I'm not a kid, you know," she huffed, but disappeared, the back door slamming behind her, emphasizing her opinion.

"That's a first." Brandon's low tone hinted at humor. What he found funny in a situation like this was beyond Toni.

"What's that?"

"We worked together as a team without talking about it first."

"We've always been a good parenting team," she replied.

"From an eagle's-eye view, yes, of course. But we've never been in the same place at the same time to draw a hard boundary for her safety. We must be doing the right thing, because she's forgotten common courtesy."

"You're right. It's our job as her parents to tick her off." Toni's mouth lifted at the corners despite her worry over Sierra's security.

"Yes."

She sensed Brandon's gaze on her but didn't try to meet it. Not because it was too dark, but because after Sierra's safety, protecting her own heart topped Toni's list of priorities.

They stood in silence, and she wondered if he was trying to put into words the same thing she was. There was something inexplicable happening between them. First the kiss, and now actually being in sync with how to handle Sierra's behavior. Was it the intensity of the last few minutes, or something more?

What do you want it to be?

She forced out a sigh and raised her phone to call the Cascade Confidential forensics expert, her brother Kevin. She looked at Brandon as she waited for the call to connect.

"I'm calling my brother—he worked forensics with Seattle PD before joining CC. You're probably right—this is nothing more than rowdy teenaged behavior. But I need to make sure."

"Great. Glad we have someone to rely on. I don't think we have any reason to call the cops, do you?"

"Let's see what Kevin says." She had to remember who she was, whom she worked for. Cascade Confidential. There was still a Clayton at large, and Willow was deep diving into a cold case that could have wide-reaching implications for the O'Malleys. But she had questions.

Who had been in her backyard, and why?

Chapter 11

Saturday morning she and Kevin rehashed what she'd told him on the phone last night. He'd suggested she call the local PD and give them the knife. An officer had responded and taken a report within the hour. She'd had a sleepless night.

Talking to her brother face-to-face via the computer screen was more soothing than their short conversation last night had been.

"It could be absolutely nothing, Kevin, but I want your take on it."

"I think Brandon's right—it was probably a rando who'd gotten high in the woods and was taking a shortcut back to the neighborhood. You spooked him, so he took off." At thirty, her younger brother was a forensics expert and had served five years on the Seattle PD. She relied on him to fill in where her lack of experience couldn't. Especially when it came to evidence, weapons and police procedure.

"And an open knife dropped out of his pocket? It wasn't in a sheath, Kevin. I think he, or she, was holding it in their hand."

"Kids do stupid things, Toni."

"I know." Maybe Kevin, and Brandon, were right. "Maybe I am overreacting."

"Hold up." His palm filled her screen for a second before he lowered it. "You have a PhD in criminal psychology. Is there something, some detail, you haven't mentioned, that's troubling you?"

"No, nothing I haven't already told you. I guess it's clear I've made a mountain out of nothing. I'm not the forensics expert you are, or the surveillance expert Jake is."

"And you're not a lawyer like Aubrey, and you didn't serve in the Marines like Willow. Poor old Toni, never great at sports, stuck with being the most intelligent and efficient among us O'Malley siblings." Kevin's teasing tone took the sting out of what in her estimation was sadly true.

"I know my weaknesses, brother."

He paused, and she watched his gaze go past the computer camera to somewhere in the far reaches of their Seattle office. Acute longing struck her. Toni missed going into headquarters on a daily basis, missed being able to walk over to her brother's desk instead of needing to set up a secure video call. But she didn't miss the apartment she and Sierra had lived in, the pace of life in an urban setting. This part of Washington State, near Everett, was so much better for both of them. She continued to go into the office at least once per week, but it didn't feel as if it was enough.

You could go in more often, with Brandon here.

She'd fought reliance on Brandon. But now that they'd had several heart-to-hearts, the armored protection she'd firmly nailed around her heart was unlocking. And perhaps not surprisingly, her trust in him was growing. As long as they kept their relationship platonic, that was. She knew she couldn't handle getting romantically involved with Brandon ever again and keep any semblance of calm in her life. Not with Sierra here to watch from the sidelines. Sierra's heart would be broken when it didn't work out.

Because it would never work out for Toni and Brandon. They'd had their chance, and he'd made a clear decision to put his career first and she'd put her family first. A solid relationship required more than a shared child.

"Earth to Toni. You're beating yourself up again, sis, and there's no reason for it. Has it ever occurred to you that your weaknesses are indeed your strengths?"

She rolled her eyes. "I don't need a pep talk, Kevin." No way was she going to correct him and risk bringing up what she'd really been thinking about. Her nerves were still frazzled from last night's backyard drama.

"Hear me out, Toni." Kevin's demand made her blink. *Oh boy.* Her little brother was about to launch into one of his beloved-to-him affirmation talks. He'd made a TED talk once, and while it garnered decent viewing stats, they weren't enough to convince a New York publisher to buy the motivational book he'd written while still a cop.

When he'd decided to leave the PD and join the family team, Toni was silently grateful, as Cascade Confidential needed Kevin's forensics experience—and his team-building skills. She was adept at management but didn't have the patience—or, frankly, the time—to bolster employees' spirits.

"I'm listening, bro." In the bright sunlight at her dining room table, with Sierra safely at school—Toni had driven her this morning, forgoing the bus—last night's almost-altercation with the unknown trespasser seemed much less of a threat. Forgettable, even.

Save for that blasted deadly blade. Shudders ran down her spine and radiated through her rib cage, forcing her to shake out her hands.

"You okay, Toni?" Dang it, he'd seen her shiver. She hated when any of her siblings saw her vulnerability. Toni was their official-unofficial boss. Yes, she was the supervisor, no question, but in her estimation each of the siblings supposedly under her responsibility was actually much better trained and more experienced than she. Still, she was the oldest of the bunch and had been more like a mother to her brothers, twelve and fourteen years her junior.

"I'm fine."

"Fine my butt. Listen, sis, relax. It's all good. As I was saying…" Kevin launched into, yep, another pep talk. Which she was so ready to simply nod along to, to appease him. Anything so that he'd keep talking and eventually get to his point.

"…stalking a high-end security firm like Cascade Confidential is completely normal—to be expected, in fact. It's a sign of our success."

"Wait, stop." She leaned over her laptop. "What did you just say?" Had she heard him correctly? "There's nothing 'normal' about being stalked, not when said stalker left a weapon under my daughter's—your niece's—bedroom window." And who had said anything about being stalked? Weren't they talking about a random unknown just moments earlier? A flush of heat rose up her neck to her cheeks.

He sighed. "What I said is that CC is getting more

and more recognition in the public eye. Our profile is no longer under the radar, so to speak."

"We always have had a higher profile, though. Mom had the mayor's and the governor's ears by the time she retired. For years before that, in fact."

"Yes, but that was by word of mouth, at least in the first twenty years or so of the company. The last ten years social media has played into it. It's impossible to stay covert when everyone carries a camera on their phone."

"I do hear you on the social media part." Toni had had to educate herself on social media and keep up with all the new platforms—it was part of being a responsible parent. "But we don't advertise on social media. All we have is our website, and that has remained as bare-bones as possible while still attracting clients." CC didn't have any social media profiles, either. Clients found them via an online search that yielded their site, or through word of mouth. Most often when one of their classic, embossed business cards passed from one happy customer to a prospective client. Most often their referrals came from attorneys whose clients had called on local law enforcement one too many times because of a security threat, breach or worse.

"Of course we don't pay for promotion. That's not my point." Kevin's impatience tickled her funny bone. He often mistook her obstinance for ignorance, but she let it go. Another factor in their generational gap. "But whenever we've helped secure a location, whether it's for a concert or a global conference, our agents are out there, wearing our logo apparel, leaving cards and contact information. That's promotion, plain and simple."

"And your point, beyond what you've already mentioned?" Toni didn't want Kevin to think she didn't appreciate his insight, but they both had work to do.

"One video taken by a fan can turn into a viral post. While most of the camera phones are aimed at the teen idol or sport star CC is protecting, there is a small percentage of users who will always zero in on the most minute details in a video clip. Especially if one of our agents has to subdue an unruly concert goer. Physical confrontations make great social media content. A viewer interested in security, or breaking through it, can zero in on our agent, see our logo and look us up."

"And find out that we're tops at what we do. Gotcha."

"Not everyone likes the job we do, Toni. And if we're keeping a stalker from getting to their target, which we do very well, I might add, they could decide to come after us. Put yourself in the position of being an über fan of your favorite musician." Kevin's forensic and profiling background was evident. "You've spent years tracking your idol, finding every tidbit on the internet about their lives, spent all your extra cash on concert tickets. You travel to venues around the country, maybe the world, to be close to them. You're finally in a place where you can actually touch them—front-row seats, mosh pit, VIP meet and greet, whatever. And you get a little too touchy-feely. So a CC agent holds you back. So now you're angry, outraged. Your focus of obsession transfers to CC and how we prevented you from being with the true object of your obsession."

"Obviously you're talking worst-case scenario, since it hasn't happened yet, right?" Annoyance tightened her shoulder muscles. Kevin's insights were way more than she'd asked for. Really, all Toni wanted was to know the gates were secure between her house and Brandon's, to get a few motion detectors in place, upgrade her minimal security system. "I really hope I'm overreacting. To be honest, if the knife hadn't been under Sierra's bedroom window, I would have let it all go as the rando teen you described. My inner mama bear was spooked, is all."

"Maybe. But use this as an opportunity to up your physical security game, Toni. Better to be overprepared and never need the solid system you've put in place."

"If it wasn't for that knife…"

"I'm glad you called it in. If the local cops come up with a connection, though, you may never hear about it, even with CC's LE ties and back-door handshakes. If you trust my police background, then trust me when I say I think it'd be a good idea for you and Sierra to stay at Brandon's, at least for a few nights. Brandon's not on anyone's radar and if—it's a big if—this is really a stalker who's after CC, they most likely are coming after you. They probably wouldn't know you have a daughter, since you've been so good about keeping Sierra away from anything CC-related. For the same reason, they wouldn't know Brandon is her father or related to you in any way."

"Thank goodness Sierra knows to keep her social media locked down, and I limit her to a single video account." The O'Malleys were nothing if not personal security–aware online.

"Really?" Kevin's doubt was palpable. "You believe her?"

"Of course I do." She knew her daughter. "You gave her the personal security talk last year, remember?"

"I do. But that was a year ago, Toni. Didn't you tell me you just bought her a phone? It's only a matter of time before she breaks whatever rules you've set. It's what teens do."

"Tell me about it." She refrained from telling him about Sierra's faux–dating app creation, though. She wasn't in the mood to explain to Kevin the complicated web that was her relationship with Brandon. "I know she's growing up, Kevin, believe me. I deal with her mercurial moods on the regular."

"Sounds familiar." Kevin grinned and made a face that usually had her giggling. Today his attempt at calming her had the opposite effect.

"Give me a break. You were still in diapers when I was Sierra's age."

"Yeah, I guess you're right," he conceded.

"It's just that we're close, you know? It's been her and I for so long. At least, it was before Brandon moved in next door." Since Brandon had come back, Sierra and she hadn't had as many mother-daughter opportunities. Toni was grateful for this, as she'd often felt stretched to the breaking point between Sierra's care and her job at CC. But she couldn't fairly blame Brandon's assumption of the more day-to-day responsibilities with Sierra for throwing a blanket over the connection she'd once had with her daughter.

"Hey, Toni, I was just kidding. Whether Sierra's doing more online than you know has nothing to do with your parenting skills."

"But what about Brandon's skills? We're different in how we interact with Sierra, that's for sure." The words escaped before she engaged her filter, and regret made her stomach twist. "Sorry, that was rude, and wrong of me. Brandon's a good dad." She meant it.

"Whoa, I thought everything was going great since Brandon moved back. I know he took you by surprise at the housewarming last summer, but you all behaved so much like a regular family at Christmas, all of us took bets on when you're going to make it official. Has he been making life hard for you, though?"

"Are you kidding me? Who's 'we'? And what do you mean by 'official'?" She didn't have to ask, though. The O'Malley siblings loved to joke and insert themselves into each other's lives. Usually within reason, though. Thinking she and Brandon were anything but coparents was unreasonable.

Is it, though? If they'd seen that embrace in the kitchen...

"We were watching how you and Brandon..."

"Never mind," she interrupted. "Don't try to explain, Kevin. There's nothing for us to get 'official' about. Brandon and I are coparenting Sierra, period. As far as that goes, our arrangement is actually working out much better than I ever expected when he showed up at Mom and Dad's last fall."

"Good to know. That was a crazy day, wasn't it?" He grinned and let out a long whistle. "Let me ask you this, then. We all know Brandon's a good guy, a great dad. But do you think he's good about the physical security of his home?"

"Of course! I wouldn't ever have allowed Sierra to make all the visits she did to him if I didn't." His question stoked her fear, though. "Why would you even ask?"

"I'm just being a good brother, sis. Brandon is a diplomat. He's had plenty of cybersecurity training as part of his previous job, but does he follow the same protocol now that he's retired? Do you know for certain that his computers and phone are locked down tight with strong passcodes? What about his Wi-Fi?"

"I'm sure—" She groaned. "It never occurred to me to ask." This triggered her regret for not vetting Mack Logging and Manufacturing and the Clayton crime family before she'd assigned Willow to that contract.

"It's fine, Toni. This isn't a repeat of last year, which we've agreed was not all on you. Why would you worry about Brandon's house? I wouldn't have thought of it, either."

"Liar." Her monosyllabic response got a laugh out of him.

"Tell you what. I'll come over tonight after work and check out both your place and Brandon's. Make sure both systems are in working order. I'll take a minute to review Brandon's cyber setup, too. Can you clear it with him for me?"

"Of course. But don't feel pressure to make it tonight. Like I said, I'm sure I'm just being an overprotective mama bear."

"No one hopes that more than me. But I'd rather sit down with all three of you and go over your security routine when it's a nonevent."

"Got it." Relief relaxed her tense muscles. She needed to learn to ask for help from her family more often.

That includes Brandon.

Just great. Now she was thinking of Brandon as family, and not solely as Sierra's father. Other than a threat—real or imagined—to her daughter's health and well-being, she couldn't think of a greater risk to her peace of mind.

Or her heart.

* * *

"I've got the goods on who we talked about. And her kid." Toby watched Veronica's eyes widen at his pronouncement. Yeah, he had a great idea and the means to accomplish it. The large mail order of duct tape, zip ties, hypodermic syringes and fentanyl were neatly stored in the spare wheel well of the pickup. All he needed was time and an opportunity. The O'Malley kid was his. Or maybe the kid's name was her father's, Anderson. He'd found that in the public records of homeownership. It didn't matter what she was called, he was going to take her, drug her—

"Don't even think about it." Veronica's scratchy voice intruded on his happy thoughts. Her gaze was more clear, steady through the prison visitor glass. He noticed she had lipstick on, too. As if she didn't realize she was in the joint and he was the one who was free to do as he pleased. The bitch would always find a way to take care of herself.

"You can't go after a child. We want a warning sent to CC, nothing more. The oldest adult sibling is your target. Take care of her and they'll get the message well enough. So will any of their uniformed friends."

Toby clenched his jaw and curled his fingers around the phone handle to the point of pain. He longed to throw the smelly device against the window, to never hear Veronica's smug tone again. But he needed to get one last thing from her, and she knew it.

The passwords and account numbers for the remaining Clayton dynasty funds that had escaped law enforcement to date. Toby's overseas funds had been locked down tight, probably by law enforcement. He'd gotten a tip when he tried to inquire as to the amounts via his burner phone. The transaction had taken much longer than usual and he'd hung up. He knew he'd been had.

Now he needed cold hard cash that only Veronica had the keys to. She'd hidden the account numbers and passcodes, as well as phones dedicated to two-factor authentication, somewhere far away from the home safe. The basement safe was where they'd kept the majority of their money information, as well as a hefty amount of cash. The feds had taken all of it, claiming it had been used in international crimes. But they didn't have the book of important fund information, according to Fred. Only Veronica knew where that was.

He sucked in a breath. "You forget that I don't work for you. I work for my father." Fury swirled in tandem with desperation in his belly. He'd screwed up. He should have never mentioned to Veronica that Antonia O'Malley had a kid. She'd figured out his intention without him voicing it, which infuriated him even more.

"You've been gone a long time, Toby. There's a reason Cal sent you to Argentina. Far from anything you could royally screw up. Until Cal is feeling better, I'm the Clayton family boss. You work for me, Toby. Whether you like it or not isn't my problem. You want the money numbers, you do what I tell you to."

He fought the urge to pound his fists against the window, call her every name in the book. But it wouldn't help him get what he wanted from her.

Once he did, he'd get Daddy and get the hell out of Dodge.

But first, the kid.

Chapter 12

"Come on in, Kevin." Brandon opened his front door wide and held his hand out. Kevin's grasp was firm, warm. Toni had let Brandon know he'd be stopping by, and why. "Toni left to pick up Sierra from orchestra practice—they had an extra one this weekend. They should be here in the next twenty minutes."

"Sounds good. Thanks for agreeing to this on such short notice." Kevin walked in.

"Of course." He shut the door behind them. "Do you want something to drink? A beer, or stronger?" He knew Kevin enjoyed scotch. "I don't have anything very fancy, but there's a single malt in the cupboard."

"I'll take a rain check, but count on me cashing it in soon." Kevin's smile faded. His eyes were similar to Toni's, but that's where their family likeness ended. "I'm here to check out your house for any security issues."

"So I heard. Such as?"

"Easily jimmied locks or windows, loose wiring on your security system, the usual culprits. Is the company you pay for security the one your window stickers say it is?"

Chagrin punched him in the gut. "I didn't subscribe

to the company when I moved in. I don't use the security system because it doesn't work. This house is over one hundred years old and the contacts on the windows and both main doors aren't reliable. I set the system once, when I was doing a walkthrough with my real estate agent, and the alarm went off. I didn't worry about it because the windows aren't going to be opened from the outside unless someone breaks the glass or takes a crowbar to the panes. The front door, as you can see—" he opened it again and pointed at the width "—is solid oak."

Kevin wasn't impressed by the remarkable woodworking in the custom-built home, though, evidenced by his frown.

"So the stickers are for show only." Not a query but grim observation.

Brandon shrugged. "They were there when I moved in last summer and I haven't gotten around to removing them."

"And I suggest you don't. They seem to have worked for you so far." Kevin's tone wasn't patronizing, but it still made Brandon's face heat. He didn't want Toni's brother to think he was a complete Luddite when it came to security.

"It's not as though there's been a spate of crime in the neighborhood, Kevin. I know Toni is upset about the creep from last night, but aside from the hunting knife under Sierra's window, I didn't pick up on anything sinister. There's no reason to think he was going to hurt anyone." Brandon had lived in very sketchy areas of the world where crime was a given simply by going to the market for fresh produce. He'd been pickpocketed, cheated out of fair change from a currency exchange, had his apartments broken into more than once or twice. "Toni researched this neighborhood before she moved in, which is why I was easily swayed to buy the house next to her. Do you really believe the dude last night was more than some kid taking a shortcut home?"

Kevin didn't reply but instead gazed at him with a very familiar expression. Toni's face had worn the same when they'd spoken about her concern for Sierra's safety. The need, in her opinion, to keep Sierra on a tighter leash. It appeared to be a patient expression, but underneath simmered impatience at his inability to keep up.

"You're looking at me like Toni did when I said the same thing. What am I missing here?"

Kevin gave him a lopsided grin. "Sorry—one O'Malley busting your balls is enough. Chances are, yes, it was a local teen meaning no harm. But in our business we don't take anything for granted, and we never assume something was inconsequential until it's proven so. Whether it was a teen or, let's say, worst case, someone preying on either Toni or Sierra, our response needs to be the same. Tighten up house security. Make sure if it happens again we have fair warning. And the ability to review security camera footage is always a plus. Best case, we're adding in security layers you'll never employ. Worst case, you're prepared."

"Sounds like you're going to be here for a while, then." Brandon's stomach growled. "It's my night to have dinner with Sierra. I have chili on the stove. Plan to stay for dinner. I'll get it ready while you check things out. Unless you need me?"

"Naw, I'm good. This won't take as long as you might think. I'll get your entire main floor set up tonight, and I can come back on the weekend to take care of upstairs. Although…" He frowned. "Does Sierra stay overnight here? How many nights a week? Where's her bedroom?"

"Upstairs, across from mine. Depends on the week, and what Sierra wants to do, depending on her schedule. Toni and I have kept it very informal. We want Sierra to feel like she's gained a larger home, not divided between two." Brandon couldn't help the pride that blossomed in his chest. He and Toni made a damn good parenting team. It could be more, but he'd seen her shut down right after their kiss. He wasn't willing to risk ruining the friendship he and Toni were building, not even for what he knew would be mind-blowing sex. Or worse, sex that had heartstrings. And yet, it had felt natural, mandatory, even, to take her in his arms—

"Maybe you'd better put that bottle of scotch on the dinner table, too." Kevin spoke with a joking tone, but the intensity of his gaze—such an O'Malley trait!—made Brandon's internal warning alarm sound. When it came to his family's security, he'd do whatever it took to keep them all safe.

"Mom, Dad just texted that Uncle Kevin is at his place and he's staying for dinner. We're all going to eat together." Sierra spoke from the passenger seat of their car as Toni drove them the fifteen minutes from her middle school to home.

"The three of you will have dinner together, honey. I doubt your father cooked enough for two extras." Toni didn't want to point out that tonight was Sierra's night with her dad, and that meant one-on-one time. On this, she and Brandon had agreed, always, that Sierra needed alone time with each parent as much as she needed time with all three of them. For tonight, Kevin was in the mix, but it still didn't mean Toni was heading over there.

"Dad said you'd say that, and to tell you he has a gargantuan pot of chili on the stove and your presence is requested." Sierra's excitement reflected in her animated inflection, a contrast with the monotone she often adopted with Toni when she was tired or simply being her preteen self.

"Gargantuan, huh?" Toni smiled in spite of the stress that had made her shoulders insanely tense all day. Brandon must want some backup with Kevin. Her brother could certainly spew security information like a firehose when mere mortals like her and Brandon needed a narrower stream of data.

Her stomach rumbled, and she had to admit, Brandon's chili sounded delicious. She'd meant to throw a chicken into the slow cooker before she'd taken her video meeting with Kevin this morning, but she'd been distracted, to say the least. The dozen or so active cases on CC's docket were certainly valid enough reasons for her stress level, but what Kevin had explained to her regarding CC being a criminal target had occupied her thoughts all day. She'd always known it was possible that CC would be targeted by bad players. But she'd considered it a remote chance. And had rarely figured Sierra into the bull's-eye.

"Dad's chili is the best, Mom." At a stop sign, she saw Sierra's thumbs moved furiously over her phone's screen as she spoke. "No offense. You make the best ziti."

"Good to know."

"Please go to Dad's with me, Mom. It's more fun together. You know Uncle Kevin makes you laugh until you pee your pants."

The words were innocent enough, and true. Too true. Not the part about Kevin's ability to crack her up with his dry sense of humor, but the word she'd been trying to ignore since that blasted kiss.

Together.

Toni wasn't blind to how animated and downright content Sierra was when she, Toni and Brandon were in the same room. After they'd confronted her about the dating app, Sierra had stopped trying to get her parents to think of themselves as anything more.

They'd been careful to make sure Sierra understood that while Toni and Brandon were definitely parents who got along well, anything more was no more than a fairy tale. A plot straight out of a kid's movie.

Problem was, Toni realized a tiny vestige of the woman who'd once been madly in love with Brandon still existed. Since their kiss, the line between who she'd been thirteen years ago and the woman she was today had blurred. Significantly.

Damn that kiss. If it hadn't had happened, she wouldn't be wondering if she'd made a mistake all those years ago, if she and Brandon were making the same mistake now, keeping their relationship in the coparents-only zone.

Toni pulled into their driveway, hit the garage door remote opener.

"You're coming in to Dad's, right, Mom?" Sierra spoke as she shrugged back into her backpack. "I'll get my oboe out of the car after dinner."

"Fine. I'll watch you go inside your dad's from here, then I'll be right over after I put your oboe inside." The instrument was worth a small fortune and required protection from the winter temperatures, as well as the humidity.

"Promise?" Sierra opened the passenger door.

"I promise." Toni held back a sigh. Sierra was too much like her, always needing to know the answer to everything.

Sometimes the not knowing was safer.

True to her word, Toni went over to Brandon's in time to take a seat at his ornately carved dining room table, a treasure he'd brought home from his years of exotic travel.

"This looks delicious. Thank you." She said the words perfunctorily, but when Brandon caught her gaze what reflected in his eyes was anything but. Appreciation, interest and…heat. Whether imagined or not, her body immediately reacted to Brandon, and she crossed her legs under the table as if the simple action could counter the need that pulsed between them.

"My pleasure." His tone remained neutral enough.

"We have every kind of topping you like, Mom," Sierra boasted as though she'd cooked the meal. From the festive place settings, complete with Valentine's Day confetti glitter—an undeniable Sierra touch—Toni knew her daughter had set the table.

"Including foil hearts?" She twirled a shiny fuchsia cutout between her fingertips. "Valentine's isn't here yet."

Sierra nodded. "I convinced Dad that you like to celebrate every holiday. But seriously, Mom, look! There's queso, jalapeños and your favorite—sour cream!"

"And corn chips." As she replied, Kevin jogged down the stairwell and gave her a brief nod before turning around the banister and heading for the back of the house.

"How long has he been here?" She directed her query to Brandon as she ladled chili from the large, enameled cast iron pot into each of their bowls.

"He arrived no more than fifteen minutes before you did. Said he'll have my place wired to go before he leaves tonight. The downstairs, anyway."

"Is this still all about last night?" Sierra crushed a huge handful of chips over her steaming chili. "I don't know what you're both so jacked up about. It was one of the high schoolers."

"How do you know about the high schoolers?" Sierra and Brandon asked in unison.

Sierra shrugged. "What's the big deal?"

"The big deal?" Toni couldn't stop the high pitch of her voice. She caught a slight motion from Brandon in her peripheral vision and stopped. He mouthed the words *let me.*

She wanted to yell at him, too, to scream, *See? I told you, this isn't an easy job!* But instead she leaned back in her seat and prepared to watch the show.

"Sierra." One word, spoken firmly by Brandon, conveyed more than Toni's had. At least by Sierra's reaction, it did, because she, too, sat up and back. But she kept her gaze on her bowl, glumly stirring the chili with her spoon.

To his credit, Brandon didn't say another word until Sierra looked up and at her father.

"What?" Said on a prolonged breath, with as much angst as possible. Sierra's expression reflected her belief that her parents absolutely did not understand where she was coming from.

Toni bit back a grin. Was this what she'd put her dad through? She remembered her youngest siblings being irascible at times but didn't recall such melodrama.

"Your mother and I happen to think that your safety is a very big deal, whether you want to believe it or not. And since we're the adults in this scenario, we get to make the decisions about your living space. Having strangers traipse through our backyard is not acceptable. Please answer our question. How did you hear about what high schoolers are doing in the woods behind our neighborhood?"

Tears welled in Sierra's eyes, the same shade as Toni's, as she stuck out her chin in the same stubborn manner Brandon did. While Sierra's obstinate streak could be trying, as it had been last night, Toni had always been grateful for the characteristic that would prove a strength over Sierra's lifetime. It might cause some gray hair along the way, though.

She's really the best of both of us.

"I don't know any more than the other kids do. Sabrina's older brother hangs out with Anna's sister—they're both sophomores—and they like to, you know, smoke back there."

"What are they smoking?" Toni wasn't going to let Brandon question Sierra on his own. They were a team.

Sierra didn't roll her eyes, as Toni had expected. Her countenance had morphed from preteen defiance to conciliatory now that Brandon had made it clear they weren't allowing her to get away with the dramatics.

"Mom, give me—I mean, they're smoking weed."

"The devil's lettuce?" Toni hoped to eke a smile from Sierra, to confirm she still was on her daughter's side, no matter what.

"Mom, *pleeeeeze* don't call it that."

"Do you know where the brother and sister are getting their pot?" Brandon spoke as if they were discussing the weather as he began to dress his chili. He looked casual, completely at ease, and Toni recognized this was his diplomatic training in action.

"I have no idea. But honestly, what is the problem with them smoking marijuana? It's legal in Washington State."

"The problem is that it's legal for age twenty-one and older, and for private, residential use." Toni wasn't going to let this slide. "Even a twenty-one-year-old isn't allowed to legally smoke weed in public, and that includes a park, and definitely my private property, which a section of those woods is."

"Sierra, honey, like we've said before, we're not upset with you, but we all need to be on the same page with what we want for our family's safety. Keeping you healthy and safe is our job." Brandon passed a basket of corn muffins to Toni. "Try them. You know you want to."

"You know I do." Toni took one of the still-warm muffins and reached for the butter. Did he remember they'd been her favorite, or was he just being his usual amiable self?

What do you want from him?

"Folks, what do we have here?" Kevin broke up all conversation, internal musings included, and proceeded to join them in the hearty meal.

For once Toni was relieved to have her brother drone on about all things scientific and digital as he detailed, at length, how the new security system was going to work at both houses. Sierra listened with more interest than Toni knew she would have before Brandon basically laid down the law with her.

Warmth bloomed in her chest, and this time it wasn't from her sexual awareness of Brandon. The cause was just as primal, though. Brandon was the best father she'd ever hope for Sierra to have. Always had been. This forced Toni to take a hard look at a fact she'd always avoided.

Brandon had asked—pleaded, in fact—for her to join him overseas. His reasoning had been that Sierra needed both parents in one place, and that she'd be able to land a job in security with the State Department at the various embassies and consulates he was assigned to. But she'd refused, insisting that her family company needed her.

She'd chosen her family over Brandon. He'd stopped asking her to move when Sierra was around five or six, and the subject had never reappeared.

Regret clambered for a hold in her conscience. Had she made a huge mistake? If she had, why would she ever even consider asking Brandon if they needed to reassess their relationship now?

Sometimes it was best to let things be.

Is it, though?

Chapter 13

The doorbell rang as they were clearing the dinner table, and Brandon went to the door. It was Officer Clemson, who'd done the initial investigation. He stood next to a woman in civilian clothes who introduced herself as Detective Carmela Inez. Brandon motioned for them both to come inside.

"Carmela." Kevin's tone was clipped, and Toni noticed he put his hands on his waist as if he was about to spar with the woman. *Interesting.*

"It's Detective Inez to you. How have you been, Kevin?" She smiled and her tone was lightly teasing, but the glint in her deep brown eyes was unmistakable. She and Kevin clearly had some kind of history.

"I'm good." He didn't elaborate, very un-Kevin.

"We're here to let you know that we think we've identified the trespasser, and it's no one you need to worry about. The incident wasn't directed at your homes or your family." The police officer looked uneasy. "Detective Inez is, ah, working a case that overlapped with your complaint."

"I wouldn't have come out here without conclusive evidence and corroboration from the suspect, but when I saw it involved your family, I knew I could trust you with the information." Carmela spoke to Kevin and then turned to Toni. "I was on Seattle PD with Kevin for several years before I transferred to Everett PD, and Cascade Confidential's reputation is stellar."

"Thank you. I appreciate that." Toni motioned toward Kevin. "I'd like to think we all work as one big team with local law enforcement."

Carmela nodded. "That's music to my ears, believe me."

"Why don't we sit down?" Brandon motioned to the family room, where the Everett officer and detective each took a seat on the leather sofa and Toni took one of the two armchairs opposite. Kevin remained standing, arms crossed, expression bland. Toni made a mental note to dig for the tea between him and Carmela at a better time.

"Sierra, you can do your homework upstairs." Toni hadn't missed Sierra's apparent disinterest in the action, her head bent over her laptop as it was when she did homework. It was all an act, Toni was certain. Sierra had inherited both of her parents' intelligence, and their curiosity. To a fault.

"Okay." She went obligingly, but not before she smiled at her Uncle Kevin, who winked. Toni bit back a smile.

Once Sierra's bedroom door closed with a solid *click*, Toni focused on Carmela. "What have you got?"

"This is absolutely between us. We've had a stakeout two streets over for the last few nights, after reports of possible drug dealing in the neighborhood. It's part of a wider, ongoing case of fentanyl distribution we—Everett PD—are working alongside several other state and federal agencies."

"Any link to the Clayton family out east?" Toni asked. At Carmela's hesitation, she explained. "We cooperated with FBI on that takedown last year."

Carmela nodded. "I remember that from the reports. As a matter of fact, yes, it's highly probable that this crime ring was working with the Claytons before they were apprehended. But that's not why we're here." Carmela leaned forward, her elbows on her thighs. "Without going into too many details, an undercover Everett PD officer was in an unmarked police car at the time of your trespassing incident. A suspect ran by the car and jumped into his vehicle and drove off. This was right after a uniformed cop responded to complaints from the neighborhood on the other side of the woods that your property backs up to. Teens were making a lot of noise in the same woods that we believe your trespasser emerged from. Our officer called the license plate of the car in. It belongs to a fifty-three-year-old man from eastern Washington, in the mountains."

"So you think the trespasser was the drug dealer?"

"We don't know. He doesn't have a criminal record, and while we're assuming he might have been dealing, there was no evidence to back our theory up. The local PD out east has taken over his investigation. We believe the drug dealing has dried up in these neighborhood streets, because word invariably got out that we were on it." Carmela's manner was incredibly professional, although Toni saw the way she seemed to avoid looking at Kevin.

"So the dealer drove from eastern Washington, just to take his supply to his core customers, in the woods here?" Kevin walked over to the empty chair and sat down. "When the police showed up, he picked Toni and Brandon's shared property to run through because it was closest to his parked car?"

"Is there any news about the knife? Did you get prints?" Toni asked.

Carmela held up her hand. "Hang on. One question at a time. Yes, we do believe the dealer would drive out here, because this isn't the only neighborhood he was supplying. Dealers often run drops all night long, wherever they'll get the cash. And yes, we believe our officer flushed him out. It's coincidence that he ran through your property." Carmela paused, waiting for further questions. When none came, she continued.

"The knife was clean. No identifying marks on it. Anyone could have dropped it next to your house at any time, frankly. Unless you have security camera footage you haven't mentioned?" But Carmela already knew the answer. They'd told the responding officer last night as much. Before Kevin had updated their systems, both she and Brandon had nothing in the way of outside security footage.

"I'm sure that knife wasn't there before. But you're right, we can't confirm it wasn't left there at a different time." The side of her house wasn't a place she looked at very often, especially in the winter. Disappointment weighed on her. She'd wanted a definitive answer and there would never be one.

"It was a long night for all of us, Ms. O'Malley." Carmela must have sensed her disappointment. "Look, I made it clear when we arrived that I'm not able to provide you with any more details than needed." Carmela's chin lifted and her eyes narrowed before she let out a sigh. "But we really came here to reassure you. We don't think the trespasser was targeting you or your family in any way. I hope this can give you some peace of mind. We don't see any credible threat to your family, to either of your homes." Curiosity flitted across her features before she resumed her professional demeanor. Toni attributed it to her wondering why two parents of the same child lived next door to one another. Surely she'd seen every familial arrangement conceivable as a cop who'd made it to detective?

"Forgive me if I don't feel reassured about my family's safety." Brandon stood and walked over to the wood-burning stove, where he shoved his hands in his pockets and paced. "I'm not unfamiliar with what drug use can do to a community. But if we know the local kids are getting together to smoke dope, and we know where, why aren't you doing more to prevent it?"

The officer cleared his throat. "Sir, we are on it, but we have limited resources, and they've been diverted to the undercover case. We definitely spooked the kids out of your woods last night. But the truth is the kids are just going to find a new place to gather. The dealers will always find the kids, too." His description of criminal whack-a-mole was sadly too true, Toni knew.

Dismay soured the delicious meal she'd enjoyed as her worry over Sierra and their neighborhood churned acid in her stomach. She swept her gaze over the officer, Carmela and Kevin. When it landed on Brandon, she realized she'd failed him, failed Sierra.

"I swear I scoured the police reports for this neighborhood, going back the last ten years. If I'd known it'd become a cesspool of criminal activity, I would never have bought here." She thought out loud more than aimed her comments at anyone in the room.

"I'm going to stop you right there, Ms. O'Malley." Carmela spoke with authority. "This isn't a bad neighborhood. In fact, it's one of the safest in the Everett area. There haven't been many reports of any crime until the last few months. You had no way of knowing the teens here were going to attract a dealer with ties to big syndicates."

"Maybe not, but the local high schoolers didn't just start meeting in the woods since we moved here. It has to have been going on for a long time." She remembered meeting classmates at the local park when she'd been a teen. She and Aubrey had saved one another's skin more than once. But that was long before weed was laced with fentanyl.

"Probably, but I can't speak to that." Carmela stood. "Before, we were worried about beer, booze, cigarettes. Now, since marijuana strains are more potent, and some of it's laced with fentanyl, we're looking at the need for a much faster response time."

"I know. Thank you for taking the time to come talk to us, Detective. And please, call me Toni." Toni walked over to the front entry and slipped two business cards from her leather tote, which she gave to Carmela and the officer. "Please don't hesitate to contact our agency with any questions you may have, or with any additional information. If we can in any way help you rid our community of this threat, we will."

"Much appreciated. Thank you, Toni. I'm Carmela." Carmela shook her hand and left with the officer. Brandon shut the door and turned to Toni.

"Do you feel safer?"

"Not really, but I probably just need a day or so to calm down. Everything she said made sense." She shrugged. "We've done all that we can for now, right?" Toni looked at Kevin. "Is there any additional layer of security we haven't installed?"

Kevin shook his head. "Not unless you want to build a brick wall around your homes. What you have in place will give you fair warning to call for help if needed, and the alarms that go off will scare away ninety-nine percent of most intruders."

"That's all good, Kevin, but it's the one percent I'm worried about. Isn't that the kind of person who'd come after us?"

"You're asking me to tell you that every crime is preventable, sis. You know I can't do that." Kevin stood with his hands in his pockets, a soft frown forming.

"Is this why you left the force?" She'd never come out and asked him, just accepted he wanted to work at the family business.

"The daily ugliness is real, but no, that's not why I left." He didn't elaborate, and she exchanged a glance with Brandon.

"I'll clear the dishes if you don't need anything more from me." He'd never enjoyed the stickier side of O'Malley sibling dynamics.

When Brandon was out of earshot, she opted to find out more about the smart detective.

"Don't even try to pretend there wasn't more to your relationship than police work."

Kevin's cheeks flushed and he snorted. "I knew it wouldn't take you long to ask."

"I know it's none of my business."

"So why do I think you'll keep pressing me for details?" Kevin tilted his head, and while she appreciated his attempt at humor, she noted the sad lines under his eyes.

"I promise that this time I won't." Toni walked back to the dining room table and picked up the few remaining dirty plates. "I'll finish with this cleanup and then head home, as long as we're all done with the security talk."

"I've done as much as I can for tonight." Kevin wasn't about to turn down the change in subject.

Brandon walked back to the table from the kitchen and held out his hands. "We can talk more in the morning, Toni. Go home." Brandon took the pile of plates from her arms. "I'll finish loading the dishwasher."

"That's my signal to vamoose." Kevin walked to the door and grabbed the leather jacket he'd hung on the antique coat tree. Toni wondered where Brandon had acquired the ornate yet sturdy piece. There was so much she'd missed out on by staying in Seattle and not making good on their Vegas marriage thirteen years ago.

No. You missed nothing except heartache.

They weren't who they once were, and better to find out long-distance and as coparents than to have had her heart broken.

So why did her heart ache at the thought of the road she hadn't taken?

"I'll head out too, then." She needed a break from this domestic scene. That's where her regret had to be coming from. The constant back-and-forth with Brandon, be it chauffeuring Sierra or disciplining her or maintaining their family game night. It was too easy to think her on-paper-only-marriage with Brandon could be more.

The cold air hit her cheeks as she walked across their lawns to her house, but it wasn't enough to shake the sense that she was already in too deep with Brandon. Her heart was definitely at risk.

Chapter 14

On Sunday morning, Toni initiated a video call with Willow. Sierra was still at Brandon's, and since today wasn't a school day, she knew she might not hear from her for a bit. Sierra loved to sleep in on weekends. Toni was grateful she'd have the alone time with Willow. She needed their sisterly connection that had nothing to do with CC or its cases.

"Hey, I was just going to call you. I've found out more on the cold case that I know you'll be very interested in." Willow took a sip from her USMC mug. "How are you doing this morning? You look…geesh, sis, you look like you didn't sleep at all. What's going on? I mean, besides the fright you had with that creeper in your backyard the other night."

"It's…it's everything." She shared about how Kevin had updated both their homes' security and that they'd all spoken frankly with Sierra at dinner about drugs and what they expected of her. "She's growing up so fast, I don't know if I'm really needed anymore. It's hard to tell what she's taking in and what she ignores."

"Wait, you mean if you're needed as her mother? Stop it. Of course you are. We still need Mom and we're what, almost fifty?" They were actually forty-two and thirty-seven, but Toni didn't miss the attempt at humor by her little sis.

"You know what I mean. She talks to her father a heck of a lot more than me—"

"Hold on. I'm going to stop you right there." Willow set down her mug with an audible thud. "You and Brandon are communicating well, right? So what difference does it make if Sierra's talking to her dad more than you? We did the same thing at her age, and as teens. Remember how Dad was always the fun-loving guy when he was around and Mom would want to throttle us when she came home after a long day?"

"Yes, but—"

"No buts, Toni. Let's get to a subject I know you hate addressing."

Toni's stomach sank.

"Why do I know what you're going to say?"

"What is really going on between you and Brandon? Don't give me that 'we're coparenting' stuff. There's more there, something I honestly haven't noticed between you two since when you were dating. This was before you were pregnant with Sierra, I think. Is Brandon dating anyone?"

"How should I know? His private life is none of my business." If she kept telling herself this, it might be true, right?

"You mean his sex life is none of your business. And you'd be the first to tell me that's BS. Everyone Brandon has a relationship with is your business because he's Sierra's father. So answer the question. Does he have someone in his life, romantically or not?"

"Not that I know of." Judging by how he'd kissed her, probably not. But she'd never asked. He'd never asked her if she was still single. Legally, neither one of them was single. A fact she didn't want to reveal to Willow. She barely acknowledged it herself, except when faced with it, like when they'd enrolled Sierra in school.

"Well, I suggest you find out. And if I'm going to bet, he doesn't. So why not explore having a more romantic relationship with the father of your daughter?" Willow's pragmatism had attracted her to the Marine Corps and made her an excellent cyber expert, as well as a cold case investigator. Except when she turned her skills on Toni.

"I'll think about it."

"Wait—what, really?" Willow resembled Sierra when she'd been told she could have dessert for dinner.

"Hang on. Don't expect this to turn out like the movies. It's just that I've heard what you're saying, and yes, there is something I think Brandon and I need to explore. I don't want Sierra disappointed if it doesn't work out, though."

"So she's said something to you, too? Smart kid." Willow grinned.

Just as with Kevin, Toni didn't want to bring up the dating app fiasco with Willow.

"I was interested to see that the suspect in your trespassing lives in the same town as the cold case girls did."

"Are you serious?" The peace of mind Carmela had wished for her evaporated at Willow's pronouncement.

"Yes. The man, or at least the owner of the vehicle the trespasser took off in, has been identified as Brian Lacey, fifty-three, a resident of eastern Washington. Everett and local PD couldn't positively ID him as your trespasser, as you know, without a photo of him on your property or your positive identification of him."

"There was nothing to see, except the back of him, and he kept his hood up," Toni confirmed.

"It turns out he's related to one of the victims' grandfathers in the cold case. But there's no reason to believe he has anything to do with the cold case. Pine Hills doesn't have a lot to offer in the way of jobs. It was decimated by the opioid epidemic. So his being a dealer isn't a surprise to me."

Relief washed away much of the anxiety Toni had been carrying. If Willow was correct, this would mean the trespassing incident had indeed been a one-off and there wasn't still someone out there watching Sierra.

"Go on."

The click of the keyboard was audible and she saw Willow's gaze focus lower than the computer camera as she called up digital information.

"The man they questioned, Lacey, grew up in the same town as the girls. His grandfather, Obadiah Lacey, was long suspected of being involved in the girls' disappearance, but the police never were able to find any evidence to make a case with."

"You don't think Brian Lacey showed up here to warn Cascade Confidential, meaning me, because of your work on the cold case?" Kevin's concerns about CC being a criminal target came to mind.

Willow leaned back from her screen. "I think you're good, sis. It's awfully close for comfort, but from everything I have in front of me, no one is stalking CC, or you. You're safe. Sierra's safe."

Phew. "It's going to take me some time to process this, I'm sure, but this is the best news I've had all year."

They did a quick recap of the subjects they'd attack on Monday morning and wished each other a good weekend.

After ending her call with Willow, Toni texted Brandon.

Just spoke to Willow. Good news about our trespasser. Is Sierra still asleep? Is now a good time to come over to talk?

What kind of coffee do you want?

"This actually has nothing to do with the trespasser. But I do want to say that I'm a bit relieved. It does sound legit when added to the explanation Carmela gave us." Brandon stood in front of her in the kitchen, sipping from his mug. She did the same, her hip leaning on his counter. The thrum of the dishwasher, which he'd admitted he forgot to run last night, was oddly soothing against her hip bone.

"It does, and I'm relieved. To a point. But I'm still grateful Kevin came out and took care of both of our houses."

"Yes, definitely." He looked into his mug, an uncharacteristically shy action. "Look, Toni, I've been doing a lot of thinking lately." This was sooner than she'd expected, but here it was. The opportunity Willow had suggested she take advantage of.

"About the divorce paperwork we never took care of, right? So have I." It was a relief to have it out in the open. "It's definitely the right time to do something about it."

"Yeah, it's definitely time to do something…" As he trailed off, his gaze bounced from her to the black night beyond his kitchen window and back to her again. The light in his eyes was hopeful, yet his stance was wary.

"What is it?" She held her breath. He needed something from her but was worried about her reaction. Was he about to tell her that he'd met someone? That he needed to be legally single, and not just virtually?

"What if Sierra's on to something? What if we did something neither of us ever planned on, Toni?"

"Spit it out, Brandon." She braced for the inevitable.

"What if we tried to see if making our marriage paperwork real—as in, if we could be more than coparents?"

"More?" She stared at him.

"Yes. What if we made our legal ties…real?"

Cold shock pulsed through her veins, followed by a roiling heat that started in her center and radiated outward. Not equitably, either. The warmth pulsed to her most sensitive areas, the places he'd once known intimately.

"I—I don't know what to say."

"You see, this is the problem, Toni. We are so much better—" he reached up and caressed her cheek, allowed his finger to trace her lips "—at communicating in other ways." His hand felt around to her nape, but he needn't have bothered. Toni scooted up onto the counter, wrapped her legs around his waist and tugged until they met pelvis to pelvis, eye to eye. She reached her arms up over his shoulders and pulled him closer, but he didn't close the last inch. He made her wait. He remembered how she'd loved this game they played, raising the mutual sexual want between them until she thought the tension would break them apart. Her breathing hitched and she squirmed against him, as delighted as she was frustrated.

"This is just our relief over Sierra being safe." Her mind clawed for a reasonable explanation for why she wanted to finish this conversation with their bodies and not words.

"Speak for yourself." His expression darkened and he moved in. Used to meeting him halfway, he was too quick, her surprise at his offer slowing her response. But the moment his tongue slicked her lips, she moaned and fully opened to him.

Brandon's fingers raked her hair back, his hands holding her head still as he deepened the kiss. Eager to participate, she met his tongue stroke for stroke and held on to his shoulders as if they were crossing Puget Sound during a storm, being tossed at the whim of the tempest.

Their sexual chemistry wasn't something born on a whim, though. It was alive and real between them. The days, weeks, months of seeing each other and working as a family unit with Sierra had awakened what she'd so carefully buried along with her broken heart.

She'd never stopped caring for Brandon. Maybe he was right—she should stop fighting her desires and enjoy the ride. Sexually and practically.

Is that's what really going on here?

He broke off the kiss, pressed his forehead against hers. "You're doing what you do, Toni. What's racing around that mind of yours?"

How did he know she'd begun to distract herself from the way he aroused her, from the promise of release that her body desperately needed? A release that she'd never experienced as deeply with any other partner?

She waited until her breathing slowed, pressed against his chest. And met his gaze.

"What exactly are you asking me, Brandon?" She knew it was petty of her, that she should be begging on both knees for him to forget the multiple times she'd rejected his pleas to join him overseas. To tell him she'd made a huge mistake. But that wasn't enough to risk heartache again. Especially now that she'd be forced to see him each and every day, at least until Sierra went to college.

"Isn't it obvious?" He took a step backward and her arms dropped to her sides. She slid down from the counter.

"To be clear, you're suggesting that we try…dating?"

"Well, something like that." He braced himself against the counter beside her, ran his fingers through his hair. Which only made her desire for him more painful as she recalled that only moments earlier those same fingers had been pushing her to her breaking point.

"I'm proposing we try to be a real couple. I'm not sure if it's feasible, in light of the time and hurt we've caused one another. But I believe we owe it to Sierra to try. To see if our marriage will work, or not, between us, before we move forward with an annulment."

"No one could know about it. Not until we know it's working between us." She replied so quickly she knew that somewhere in her subconscious—more likely her heart—she'd been mulling this over, too. "I don't want Sierra to get her hopes up and then crush them."

"You two are married?"

Sierra stood in the kitchen, her silent arrival jolting

Toni out of her sexy thoughts, out of the possibility of what-ifs.

"How long have you been eavesdropping, Sierra?" She tried to muster a stern tone with zero success.

"It's not eavesdropping if it's not intentional, Mother." *Oh boy.* Sierra only called her "Mother" when she was being defensive. Or furious.

Toni moved her gaze from their daughter to Brandon. His expression mirrored her thoughts.

What now?

"It's plain and simple, sweetie. Your mom and I did what was best for you." Brandon spoke as they all sat on the living room sofa, Sierra between them. He'd suggested they all move out here, where the wood stove was cranking and it was more relaxed than it had been standing in the kitchen.

"We never annulled our marriage because it was simpler to be legally married, for your sake," Toni added. "I kept my maiden name, but a lot of women do, so your school never questions it on the emergency contact form."

"It made my paperwork with the State Department easier, too. We could have annulled our marriage, probably should have for adult reasons you don't need to be concerned about. But we didn't."

"You mean divorced." Sierra looked at him. "That's what 'annulled' means."

"Well, yes, but—"

"Our marriage could have been annulled right after we, um, got married because it was an impulsive decision we made when we were on a trip to Las Vegas." Toni wasn't holding back. He was both relieved to have her support and wary of Sierra's reaction. "It was before we ever knew we were going to have you."

"Was I conceived in Las Vegas then?" Sierra's query sliced through Brandon's gut. What was happening to his little girl? Did she even know—

Yes, she knows. Catch up, old man.

Toni paused. "Yes. You were conceived in Las Vegas." She met his gaze over Sierra's head, and her eyes reflected not only the incredible chemistry that had always arced between them, but the ties of bringing a new life into the world. Sierra.

"That's cool." Sierra nodded. "Are you going to get divorced now?"

"We—we don't know, Sierra." Brandon turned sideways and knelt in front of their daughter, took her hands. Toni kept her arm around her small shoulders. "Your mom and I are figuring things out. But no matter what the outcome, you need to know that in all honesty it has nothing to do with you, what you do or don't do. This is a very adult concept we're talking about now. Something that's strictly between your mom and me."

"Okay?" Sierra looked at Toni, then back at him. "All I asked was if you guys were married and why you never told me. I don't need to know about all your adult emotional baggage." Her eyes widened. "Oh, I get it. No one else knows you're really married."

Brandon looked to Toni. She mirrored his warring exasperation and pride.

"Sierra, we're so glad you understand how relationships work, and that you're willing to give Dad and me room to explore ours. And no, no one else knows about the legal marriage." Toni's emphasis on *legal* raised a tiny alarm bell in Brandon's mind. Had Sierra's interruption spooked her? Was she still willing to explore their relationship?

"Not even Aunt Willow or Aunt Aubrey?" Sierra looked at Toni, who shook her head.

"No. I never told them. Not because it needed to be a big secret—it doesn't." Toni looked at him and he saw the silent plea.

"Let's not think of it as a secret. It's family knowledge that we don't need to share with all of the O'Malleys for now. Is that clear?" Brandon was proud of how hard he and Toni had worked to be transparent with Sierra on as much as possible, shielding her from the harsher realities of life only as was age-appropriate. Now wasn't the time to start with the old "family secret" dysfunction they'd both agreed they never wanted Sierra to experience.

"Yes, Dad." Sierra didn't roll her eyes, but he sensed she'd had to fight from doing so. She stood. "Please sit. Now it's my turn to talk."

He sat back on the couch, knowing that to ignore an O'Malley woman was never a good idea.

Sierra stood in front of them, her hair still mussed from sleep, wearing her whimsically printed Christmas pj's that matched his and Toni's flannel bottoms—Sierra had asked they all have matching pj's this first Christmas in the same country—and held her hands up as if she were about to conduct a symphony. Which he supposed was how a kid might view their parents, depending upon family dynamics.

"Okay, Mom and Dad. I have an idea. I think you need to have adult time to yourself to figure things out.

My friends' parents go away for date nights and weekends all the time."

"They do?" Toni interjected and drew a frown from Sierra.

"Mom! Let me finish." Sierra sighed dramatically, but at least she didn't roll her eyes. He knew Toni wouldn't let an eye roll go. He bit back a grin.

"Sorry, sorry." Toni leaned back against the sofa cushions.

"You know I love being with my aunts. My uncles, too, but they're *guys*." Sierra's lip curled when she said the last word. "You need to let Aunt Aubrey or Aunt Willow stay here for a weekend once a month. That's what my friends do. Remember when Emma slept over on Halloween? That was because her parents went to this beautiful spa resort place somewhere." Sierra nodded, clearly pleased with her solution to what she considered their family problem. "Valentine's Day is coming and it's my school's three-day weekend, too. You two go away!" She clapped her hands and grinned at them.

"That sounds good, but…" Toni looked at him, and Brandon sensed she was grasping for a way to wiggle out of a commitment.

"Great idea, honey! We'll get right on it." He stood and ruffled Sierra's hair. "How about we get those waffles going?"

Chapter 15

Toby thought of himself as a very patient man. He was a great hunter, having learned at Cal Clayton's knee. But it had been almost a week of using every disguise imaginable, renting different vehicles, driving into the neighborhood at staggered times of day and night. And still, there hadn't been a chance to nab the kid.

Worse, doubt had crept into his master plan. Had Veronica's order tainted his resolve? Or had she been the wiser, seeing how difficult taking a kid could be? Especially a kid whose parents were more than helicopters—they were damned drones, always right next to her, too close to make grabbing her a sure thing.

And taking a risk of getting caught wasn't an option. Toby knew he didn't have the fortitude to make it on the inside. He wasn't mean like Daddy or Fred, and he hadn't had the hardscrabble life Veronica claimed to have suffered as a child. He didn't know poverty and he didn't know true suffering, and he knew it.

"...why do you think Cal sent you away..."

Veronica's snide question triggered memories he'd rather forget. Of Daddy telling him he was weak, that he couldn't stay on task if he was led by the nose. Sure, he could hunt, but much of anything else…

No. He was strong, and this was his chance to prove himself to Daddy. To show him that he was as worthy a son as Fred.

Maybe he did need to change his plan?

"We'll be fine. Promise." Aubrey stood on the front porch with Toni in the still morning. A week had passed since their talk with Sierra, and somehow Brandon had managed to find room for them at a resort spa. It had been a late cancellation and she was sure he was paying through the nose for their getaway—he wouldn't hear of her chipping in.

Snow clouds loomed to the northwest, and Toni knew she and Brandon needed to get on the road ASAP if they were going to get to the spa resort before snowfall. Sierra was in the driveway, in her pajamas, chatting with Brandon.

"I know you and Sierra will be okay—it's me I'm more worried about." She wasn't really feeling her own joke, not when butterflies relentlessly batted against her stomach lining.

"You don't have to tell me what's really going on between you two if that makes you more comfortable. We don't talk a lot about private stuff, and with you working from home more, I feel like it's been years since we did anything together. I want you to know that I am one hundred percent here for whatever is going to make you happy, Toni." Aubrey shifted on her slippered feet. They'd always had a bit more of an adversarial relationship, as they were only two years apart, whereas Willow, being five years her junior, had never competed with Toni, nor Toni with her.

Tears sprang to her eyes and she did several wide-eyed blinks, not wanting to muss her mascara. "Come here." She engulfed her sister in a bear hug, relishing the embrace she received in return. "I would never have made it this far as a single mom if you hadn't been here each step of the way. You know that, right?"

Aubrey leaned back and offered her own tremulous smile. She nodded. "I do. I've got Sierra. She'll be fine, no matter what you and Brandon work out. I think of Sierra as my own, you know."

"I do." Toni hadn't given up on seeing Aubrey find the love of her life and having her own family, even if her sister swore she was a confirmed cat mom. She opened her mouth to say as much, then closed it. Aubrey was here to be with Sierra, not listen to Toni opine over her visions for Aubrey's future.

"I've heard Snoqualmie Falls is beautiful right now." Toni couldn't stop talking. Anything to keep her mind off the next two hours alone in the car with Brandon. And the overnight at the fancy spa resort to follow.

"How much of the outside do you think you'll see?" Aubrey playfully hip-checked her.

"Stop." Toni rolled her eyes, leaned down and grabbed her cross-body bag, slinging the long strap over her head before taking her travel coffee mug in hand. "This is the first of what I'm sure will take many, um, times together. To see if it can work, I mean."

"From the way you two look at each other, I'd say that parents-with-benefits is a minimal perk you can count on." Aubrey grinned.

Toni sighed out a laugh. "Would sex be a nice side dish? Sure. But that's all it is. Passion isn't enough to make a long-term relationship last." Her hands trembled at the reminder of what had kept her awake all last night. Not fear for Sierra's safety, or work issues. It had been her hormones, plain and simple, as Brandon liked to say. She hadn't been able to get images of being naked, skin to skin, with Brandon out of her mind.

"Uh-huh." Aubrey grinned and waggled her brow. "You keep telling yourself that."

"Don't mind if I do." She threw the last over her shoulder as she went down the steps and strode toward Brandon's car, as if her hands weren't trembling, as if her knees didn't feel so wobbly.

Sierra's attention switched from her father to Toni. The sparks of hope and curiosity in her gaze at once warmed Toni's heart and scared her to death. Fear returned, but for Sierra's emotional well-being more than physical. The last thing she wanted was to disappoint whatever "married, normal parents" ideas were swirling in Sierra's mind.

"Let's go before the snow starts." Brandon must have sensed her hesitation as he took her bags from her before she replied and put them behind the passenger seat.

"Yeah, Mom, you need to go. Snow's coming! Aunt Aubrey and I are prepared to be snowed in!" Sierra's focus had shifted. "Stovetop s'mores, hot cocoa, popcorn and pizza, plus we have the video games."

"After you do your oboe practice and the outline for your English essay." Toni smiled. "Come here." They hugged and she relished how tightly Sierra held her, even if only for a second.

"Mom, go. You need a break." Sierra pulled away and motioned at the open passenger door. Brandon was already at the wheel, setting up his GPS navigation on his phone.

"Have fun, honey." She slid into the passenger side and almost moaned as the warm leather seat embraced her backside. Instead she shut the door before she changed her mind.

More than heated seats are going to make you moan this weekend.

Yeah, her mind was definitely not going to focus on anything else for the next couple of days.

"Let's set some ground rules." Brandon drove them out of the neighborhood and shot her a quick glance at a stop sign. Toni looked well enough, but by the way she was picking at her cuticles, he figured she was a ball of nerves. "Feel free to adjust whatever controls you need to in order to be comfortable."

"You've already set my seat on full blaze, thank you." She laughed. "It's definitely winter in the PNW."

"Naw. The Pacific Northwest doesn't do a real winter. Not that often, anyway." He merged onto the highway, noting the oncoming traffic from the Cascade Mountains. It was impossible to miss how many of the vehicles had several inches of snow on their rooftops. "The occasional snow dump doesn't count. It's rarely below freezing here, so any snow melts within a day or two."

"True, but it's all relative. I suppose it feels a lot milder to you here than in the remote mountains of wherever you were last year."

Brandon laughed and the years dropped from his

awareness. It was just him and Toni, on the road, alone. Just like before—

Nope. He couldn't go there. The last thing he wanted, and what he feared most, was ruining this opportunity that he believed was their last chance at a real partnership. Sex was all his body focused on. Quite frankly, it was all he'd been able to think about since…since forever, dammit. But he had to wait until he was sure that Toni was certain. That she wanted this as badly as he did.

"I honestly can't remember exactly where I was a year ago." And it didn't matter to him any longer. Had it ever? He'd had a passion for diplomacy, had enjoyed his career. But his longing to provide a more permanent base for Sierra had been stronger.

To be closer to Toni.

"I know where I was." Toni laughed. "I was in the Seattle office, contract requests for the upcoming summit unending, and worried that Sierra was adjusting to her new school. She did, and all my worry was for naught."

"I'm very grateful for the time you put into finding your house. I wouldn't have been so quick to put a bid on mine if you hadn't, that's for sure."

"I still can't believe you bought a house from overseas. You could have asked me for help. I would have been happy to be your power of attorney here for all the paperwork."

"Would you have, though?" He had to ask, had to know if she still harbored any regrets about him becoming her neighbor.

She laughed. "No, not right away I wouldn't have, you're right about that."

"Ah, I think it worked out, don't you? If I had asked

you last year…" He recalled the quarrels they'd had via email about Sierra's status in school and being bullied, before Toni had moved.

"I owe you an apology, Brandon. I know I treated you like dirt the last year we were in our old house and I was displacing my guilt over Sierra's school bullying onto you."

"Hey, what's a coparent for?" He reached over and squeezed her hand, which had been resting on the console between them. The shock of awareness that physical contact with Toni initiated had never faded. The electricity between them was at once welcome and a warning. *Tread lightly here.*

"Back to our ground rules. I have to say this aloud, Toni. Nothing is going to happen between us this weekend that you don't want to happen. We're just laying the groundwork for the future possibility should we decide to move forward with our relationship."

"Spare me the diplomatic lingo, Brandon. And what if I want a no-strings sex-only relationship?"

His gut tightened and he fought against the full erection that tried to push against his jeans. He cleared his throat.

"As in coparents with benefits?" It was a poor attempt at a jest, he knew. But he was unable to do much else, as he had to concentrate on the road and not his sexual desire for her. Remaining focused on the drive was becoming more difficult with each mile his odometer measured. Her sexy musk—floral and pure Toni—had filled the car the minute she closed the side door, teasing his attraction into full-blown lust.

"More like intimate coparents, I'd guess." Her tone

had dropped into a key that reflected her introspection. "We left a no-strings-attached relationship in the rearview mirror the night we conceived Sierra."

Had they ever? He swallowed, gripped the steering wheel tighter. "That remains the single most incredible night of my life. Right up there with the night Sierra was born."

"I know I didn't express it at the time, but I was so grateful you were there, Brandon." Her sincerity matched the severity of the birth. Toni had developed preeclampsia, and if not for the fast action of the entire labor and delivery team at UW Montlake, he would have lost at least one of them. Possibly both. The memory singed the jubilation he'd been riding since Toni had agreed to go away with him this weekend.

"You were a champ, as was Sierra. Nothing was going to keep her from arriving hale and healthy."

"No." She sipped her coffee, turned in her seat to face him. "I often wonder, if I hadn't had such severe postpartum, would I have made a different decision?"

"About us, you mean?"

"Yes."

"You might have. I might have, too."

"What do you mean, you might have? There wasn't a decision for you. I was the one who refused to meet you even halfway."

"As I see it today, Toni, there was no halfway, not when it came to my career as a diplomat. By its nature, it's not a Stateside occupation. Not permanently. I could have considered other options for my career. Law school, maybe, and then I could have gone into contract negotiations."

Her silence forced him to risk a quick glance at her. She'd turned back forward, and her profile contrasted starkly with the forest backdrop as they approached the foothills of the Cascade Mountains.

"Did you hear me?"

"I did. And do you know, I never, not once, thought of you refusing to make a choice. I really made it all about me, didn't I?" Her bemusement tugged on his heart. Or something similar that lay under his rib cage.

He cleared his throat. "We were a lot younger, both used to our very independent lifestyles, and if I recall correctly, you'd been used to playing the field, as had I been. We were both self-centered, Toni. It wasn't only you."

"But I made it the hardest on us both, and Sierra, by refusing to go overseas with you."

"This isn't going to get us anywhere. We can't change the past, Toni."

"No, we can't."

He reached for her, unable to take his gaze from the heavily trafficked highway. "Take my hand." He held his arm out, palm up.

A hesitation, and then her palm met his, their fingers curled around each other as if they'd never stopped caring for one another. As if they'd been together instead of a world apart for the last thirteen years.

As if they had a chance to begin again.

Chapter 16

Toby hated when things didn't go his way. For the last two weekends, the kid had bounced between the two houses, and he'd gotten glimpses of both her parents, who never seemed to leave the kid alone for one damn minute. Veronica's warning echoed in his mind even if he didn't agree with her. But he wanted that kid.

Except he never had a good enough shot to nab her, and from the schedule he'd carefully kept track of, of all three people, he still didn't have a solid plan of when and where. How, no problem.

But maybe this would be his chance. He kept far enough behind the late-model sedan to not draw Brandon Anderson's attention, but close enough to not lose them on this stretch of highway that would be stop-and-go within the hour. As soon as snowflakes hit his windshield, he'd better shorten his tailing distance. Not that he was concerned about being spotted, to be frank. These two parents didn't know dick about security. From what he'd read online and figured out tailing her, Toni was a book person. Had a fancy degree in forensic psychology. Book smart, but no street smarts like her sister Willow. That was why she worked from home, he figured.

The jackoff father didn't seem any better. He still got a good belly laugh when he remembered how they'd come out onto their front lawn when that lowlife had run out from in between their houses. If he'd had his rifle he could have taken them both out then, but he'd spied the stakeout—did those cops really think no one else picked up on them being there? He knew the cops would be on the way when he saw Antonia lift her phone to her ear. People like the O'Malleys were in tight with the law.

He'd noticed a third person this morning, a woman, and was positive she was another O'Malley. She looked just like Toni, and from the send-off where the kid was still in pajamas, he suspected Sierra was being babysat by the petite woman. He didn't want to mess with a break-in at the house, but if he confirmed that the parents were going somewhere overnight, he'd be able to circle back and get the kid. And who knew, maybe he'd get a chance to grab the aunt, too. If he did, he could forget about the kid and definitely get the account information he needed from Veronica.

Daddy and Fred didn't know how lucky they were that he was on the case. He'd have them all living their best lives on their own private island within a week, because he'd hire a top-notch lawyer to get them paroled. Once he got the passcodes from Veronica, he'd make sure she never heard from any of the Claytons ever again.

"Here we go." Brandon turned off the road at a sign marked with the resort logo.

"Talk about the perfect parent getaway. We're not that far from home, but it feels like we're in Montana." Toni was happy to be anywhere that could give her a break from the recent stresses of her job, of blending her life with Brandon's. She sat up straighter. Was that what she'd really been doing, with all the back-and-forth of how she felt Brandon should be parenting Sierra?

Was this what she'd wanted all along?

"That's why I picked it."

"You found it, how? Online?"

"At first, yes, and then I drove out here a month ago and checked it out."

"A month ago? We didn't decide to do this—"

"Until last week, I know." He expertly pulled up to the front entrance and placed the car in Park. "I was hedging my bets. Old diplomatic tactic."

She laughed. "How successful is it for you, usually? Hedging your bets?"

"I don't know. I'm too risk-averse to ever use it. But you're worth a risk, Toni."

Her stomach leaped to her heart as their gazes met. No longer did the sparks in his eyes ignite a warmth in her center, but instead lit a full flame. She leaned across the armrest—

Tap tap tap.

The valet was at the driver's side and opened the door. The cold rush of air cooled her cheeks, and she busied herself with getting out of the car. Fat snowflakes began to swirl into the overhang, and she shivered, but not from the chill.

Nothing was going to douse the red-hot heat that lived in her lower belly.

Toby grinned as he parked on the far side of the lot that made a semicircle around the imposing stone building that looked more like a hunting lodge than a hotel. But sure enough, it was a hotel. A very exclusive resort, complete with spa.

He wasn't grinning at the spa "treatments" that he didn't even comprehend the need for—one reason he never had women in his life except for sex. They were money grabbers, all of them. No, Toby was happy because in the short span of eight minutes he'd downloaded the hotel's app and hacked into it. He might not be the smartest street criminal in Daddy's mind, but one thing Toby could do was break into computers that didn't have the tops in security.

The app itself was pretty strong on its integrity, but it was Brandon Anderson who was the fool. He used the same password as he did on his home Wi-Fi. Toby had hacked into Brandon's Wi-Fi without a problem, but getting onto his computer had proved more difficult. Too many firewalls. Toni's Wi-Fi had been solidly locked down, which he'd expect from a CC employee, or boss, or whatever she was in reality.

"Well, lookie here." He spoke to himself, sure that no one who saw him would wonder if he was talking to himself or to a real person on the phone. "I'll let you get nice and comfortable on that massage table, Antonia. It'll help the medicine go down smoother." He guffawed and slapped his steering wheel. He was damn funny, if you asked him.

Brandon tipped the valet and carried each of their bags into the lobby. He didn't want to risk a doorman delivering their bags at the wrong moment. If he'd read Toni's glance and body language correctly, this getaway was going to be more than talk, more than coming to an agreement on how to move forward. She wanted him as much as he did her.

He'd already checked them in via the resort's app, and he had a surprise awaiting Toni. He glanced at his smart watch. It was in an hour and a half; they'd made good time. Frustration followed quickly on the heels of his need to be with her. Naked, lost in each other. He wanted this to be special. Sex was something they'd always been good at, and they'd both acknowledged, more or less, that being coparents with benefits wouldn't be a stretch.

He wanted more, and he hoped his read of Toni's desire was accurate, because as he'd said aloud, he was risking it all here.

Including his heart.

"Look, Aunt Aubrey! It's really a blizzard!" Sierra ran to the front entry, where she'd piled every single piece of winter outerwear that she owned. "Oh my gosh, my ski gloves do not even fit anymore." She groaned.

"No frets, love. Here, use mine." Aubrey pulled a pair of well-worn bright neon-pink gloves from a humongous tote bag. Why didn't adults use nicer-looking bags and luggage? Mom had carried around Sierra's old diaper bag, of all things, minus the changing pad, which she'd been using as a computer mat for when she worked in her car when Sierra's orchestra practice ran late.

"Okay, thanks. But what will you use?"

"I happen to have a brand-new pair of mittens I made myself last weekend when I found out there was a chance of snow." Aubrey grinned as she dangled patterned mittens in both hands.

"Are those…cats!" Sierra groaned. Aunt Aubrey was the best, but she really had way too many cats. And plants.

"On one side, yes. But check it out, I did something different on the other side." She flipped the pair to reveal bright green shapes with red pins…no, not pins. Needles. Cactus needles. This time Sierra did groan.

"Aunt Aubrey, remember when we watched that rom-com movie and you said you wouldn't mind meeting the right person? A man who would love you as you are, you know, a cat woman with too many plants?"

"Yes?" Aubrey laughed, but then her eyes narrowed and her smile faltered. "What are you saying, my dear niece?"

"I'm just sayin' that maybe guys don't notice you because you dress like…" Uh-oh. Her face got hot. Really hot. Why did she always open her mouth at the wrong time? Like when she had Mom and Dad doing exactly what she wanted but then she gave herself away by fessing up to a lie?

"Don't mind me, Aunt Aubrey. I don't know what I'm saying. I'm so excited by the snow I don't know what to do!"

"How about let's get bundled up and go enjoy it." Aubrey leaned over and put an arm around Sierra's shoulders. "I think you were sweetly pointing out that dressing the part of a cat lady—not the superhero kind—with weird taste in home decor might be a turn-off?"

Sierra giggled. "Ewww. Aunt Aubrey. Stop. I don't want to think about you doing, you know…"

"Sierra Abigail! What on earth did you think I meant? I was talking about finding a reading companion. Get those salacious thoughts out of your mind right this second!" She tickled Sierra under her chin as if she was still a baby and they both burst out laughing. Sierra hugged her aunt, tight.

"I love you, Aunt Aubrey. You get me."

"We're two peas in a pod, sweetie. Now, c'mon, let's get a move on. We want to be back inside in time to have our rom-com marathon."

"Yay!" Sierra squealed and got back to getting dressed.

Sierra loved snowstorms. They were some of her favorite memories with each of her parents. Of sledding and skiing with Mom at Mount Baker in the Cascade Mountains. Of first learning to ski with Dad at Whistler, when he'd been visiting Vancouver for some kind of international peace conference. She stopped for a sec as she picked out the boots she wanted—her warmest, with the shearling lining. Quite a few of her classmates were vegan and had made comments about leather goods, but Sierra had lived with Dad in countries where all that was an impossibility because of the poor standard of living for the locals. And she liked meat well enough, but also knew from Mom that no one needed to eat as much of it as they thought they did. Sierra was okay with wearing her boots because she'd researched the company and they made sure all the animals used in their products were humanely treated, and the entire animal was consumed, from the warm boots and slippers she loved to the organic lamb stew Dad was the best cook at.

"Nice boots. Ready?" Aubrey stood across from her, and they both started to laugh again. They were bundled up, all right, from head to toe, including the matching rose-and-green balaclavas that Aunt Aubrey had made for them this Christmas. With the knit masks, all that was visible of their features was their eyes, both the same shade of bright blue as Mom's and Grandma's.

"Wait, we need to send Mom a selfie!" She reached for her phone, only to remember she'd left it upstairs in her bedroom when she'd gone up to find her base layers. "I'll be—"

"No, hang on." Aubrey's arm stopped her. "Let's use mine." They took a quick photo and Aubrey sent it off. Before Mom replied, they were out the front door and into a literal snowball.

Sierra breathed in the snow scent and pulled down her balaclava so she could catch the flakes on her tongue. And coughed when a cold mass of wet hit her smack in her face.

"Gotcha!" Aubrey laughed and ran for cover behind the huge rhododendron that looked like a hulking polar bear with a full inch of snow coating.

The snowball fight was on.

Chapter 17

Toni's stomach swirled with the same tingling expectation that she had on Christmas Eve. As a child, she and her siblings had thrilled to the magic of the season, racing down the stairs in their sprawling family home that Aubrey now occupied along with Kevin. Jake had lived there, too, until he took over the Portland office last year.

It wasn't Christmas, and she was a forty-two-year-old adult woman who knew what she wanted out of life. Or had, that was. Before Brandon's unexpected full-time arrival into her world, she'd thought being Sierra's mom and enjoying her career were the be-all and end-all. But lately she'd become more aware of her own needs than ever. For a partner to share life with. To have great sex with, of course, and lots of it. But to her, that meant a relationship she went into with complete abandon. No-strings physical intimacy didn't interest her. It never had.

Was she willing to become not only entangled but totally bound to Brandon again?

"Why so quiet?" He stood next to her in the elevator, where they'd been told to go to the fifth floor, the top of the hotel. Brandon hit the five button and they waited for the doors to close. *Please let us be alone.*

Her silent wish was answered when no one else entered the elevator. The doors quietly swooshed closed. Palpable tension sparked between them. She wouldn't be surprised to see the arcs as her body heat pooled in all her most sensual places.

Unexpected shyness stole over her as her mind warred with her body's response to his nearness, with what they both knew was coming. Yet it had been years since they'd been together, not counting the two kisses in the last two weeks.

In for a kiss...

"I don't know where to start." She licked her lips and looked at him. Pure lust burned in his gaze, and with one smooth action he dropped their luggage and pulled her to him. His mouth met hers in a white heat that forced her body up against his, making him lean against the elevator wall as their tongues met. His hands pulled at her bottom, and she gasped at the juxtaposition of how strongly she pulsed between her legs while her knees went weak, unable to hold her.

Ding.

He pulled back, his arms still clasped around her, and looked at the open door. "Let's go." His clipped tone triggered a rush of memories. Brandon was rarely hurried or impatient. Except when she'd made him so hard he couldn't see straight, as he'd told her so many times when they'd been together.

Never had she been more grateful for modern technology as he opened their door with a single swipe of his phone. Hotel apps were truly miraculous.

"Get in." He held the door for her and she walked into a large room with a panoramic view of the mountains.

The snowfall made it feel as though they were truly inside a winter wonderland.

"Brandon, this is—"

"No talk." His hand was on her shoulder, spinning her around.

"We said we were going to take it slow. We're here to talk, Brandon." She wrapped her arms around his neck as she spoke and wiggled her hips against him. He groaned as she licked his throat. His deep voice sent shivers of delight across her chest, down, down, to the deep pool of need between her legs. She sighed, as if disappointed. "But if you must, we can have sex first."

She pulled his head down until his lips met hers. The need in the elevator remained, increased. Her body and mind screamed for her to hurry, to get the release she craved, but her heart wanted to savor every single bit of their reunion. Union being the ultimate objective.

Nipping his lower lip, she slowly unzipped his parka, moved her hands down his sweater, up under the hem, and stroked his belly. Undid his belt—

"Stop. Otherwise this will be over before we hit the mattress." He gave her a hard kiss, then turned her around to face the large king-size four-poster bed. "Hold on."

"Oh, do you mean like this, Brandon?" She couldn't help but string out the tension as she shoved out of her jacket and reached for one of the posts, posing with her bottom closest to him.

"More like this." He tugged at her waist from behind. "Take your top off." As she lifted her sweater over her head, he pushed her leggings down. She heard his belt buckle hit the floor and she stepped out of her tights, took off her lace bikini panties. Looking over her shoulder to see him, she was stopped by his hot palm between her shoulder blades.

"Stay right where you are, Toni." His voice was the perfect cross between a bark and a caress. She heard soft swishing behind her as he finished undressing. She reached to remove her bra—she'd picked her favorite black lingerie set—but his hand covered hers, pulled her naked bottom up against his erection. The bedpost's carved design pressed into her palms as she held on, wanting this exquisite contact with him to last forever.

He unclasped her bra and she slid it off one hand at a time, only able to keep her balance because he'd wrapped his arm around her waist, rubbing his hard length against her cheeks. Before her bra hit the floor, Brandon used both hands to hold her breasts, kneading them in the way she'd always loved, waiting until she cried out to move his fingers to her nipples and gently, then not so gently, squeeze. Tug.

"Brandon, we've got to…" Her lungs struggled to keep up with her racing pulse, her legs shaking from her need.

"Stay. Right. There." She gripped the post tighter. The quick blast of cold air to her bottom heightened her anticipation.

"Hurry, please," she panted as the condom wrapper crinkled. Then his hot palms seared her hips, and he pulled her up against him again.

"Do you want it here, Toni—" he rasped as he spread her cheeks, placed himself against her "—or on the bed?"

"Here," she breathed out, needing the release now, not wanting to break the physical contact long enough to get on the bed. This was pure magic. Pure Brandon.

Pure us.

Taking her at her word, he pressed into her until she opened fully. When she involuntarily closed tightly around him, tears sprang and ran freely down her cheeks at the exquisite fit.

No one knew her better.

She moved in tandem with him, allowing his hands to guide her hips. The tension she'd thought was at its maximum heightened again and again, until she thought she couldn't keep up, she'd never reach the peak they both needed.

"Hang on, babe." He breathed the words at the same time she felt his arm circle her waist and his fingers touch between her legs. As if no time had lapsed since they'd last made love, he touched her, swirled, pressed.

Toni shattered.

"Brandon!"

He responded with a deep thrust, his own shout, followed by a low groan.

Toni couldn't remember the last time she'd so totally lived in the moment. There was nothing but her, Brandon and…

Love.

"So much for not doing anything we don't want to do." Toni sat on the small sofa that overlooked the gorge, the view mostly obscured as snow was coming down in a sheet of white. She sipped the mug of tea Brandon had made her from the kitchenette and snuggled into the spa robe that had been hanging on the walk-in shower wall. The soft fabric was delicious against her skin, which smelled of the hotel's lemongrass lotion she'd applied after they'd taken a long shower. And made love again, this time on the bed. The pillowcases were still wet from their hair.

Brandon sat down with his own mug of coffee and put his arm around her shoulders. "We've never had a problem with sex. Did you do anything you didn't want to? Did I do anything you'd prefer I hadn't?"

She smiled. "No. And you know it."

"Were you worried about Sierra?"

"Do you mean while we were making love?" She bit her bottom lip. She'd wanted to leave out that word—love—for now. Emotions weren't facts.

But love is an action, a living and breathing commitment.

"Since that's about all we've done—" he looked at his watch "—for the last two hours, yes." They both laughed. She'd forgotten how good it felt to share joy with him.

"No, I didn't think of her once. But now that you mention it—" She leaned over to the coffee table and reached for her phone.

"Hold on. If you call now, she's going to think you don't trust her. And Aubrey is right there with her, honey."

"She is. You're right." Her fingers hovered over the screen. "Tell you what. I'll send a quick text, say we got in safe, no worries. That way it puts it on us."

"Sounds good." His lips, still darker and fuller from all the kissing, curved into the smile she hadn't seen in thirteen years. *This is the life.*

She sent the text, and the sense of being safe and secure, that she was doing what was right for her, returned. She leaned back against him. "Can it always be like this? Awesome sex, no arguing?"

He kissed the top of her head. "Always, no. But most of the time, yes. We're getting ahead of ourselves, though. It's not even dark yet, and you've got someplace to be."

She sat up and twisted to look at him. "I do?"

He looked at her with such reverence she felt her heart squeeze and tears welled. Toni blinked, looked away.

"Hey." His fingers gently guided her chin toward him, wiped a tear that rolled down her cheek. "What's going on?"

"I'm happy, is all." She tried to smile, but it was futile as a sob escaped her. "Don't you remember that I cry whenever things get to be too much?"

"I do, but explain to me how we're too much."

Now her smile was solid, the tears diminishing. "It's—it's everything. There's so much to lose…"

"We're not going to lose anything we decide to keep, Toni. That's the beauty of this. It's our relationship, our family, our show to run."

"I love that." She sat up straighter and rubbed the tears from her cheeks. "Now, what was that surprise you had for me?"

This place might look fancy on the outside, but they could learn a thing or two about security. Toby had thought his goose was cooked when the too-thin spa receptionist had come out of the employee bathroom and given him a double-take. He'd nodded as though he belonged there.

"We've got the sauna running smooth again." He smiled.

"The sauna?" She tilted her head at a comical angle

and he couldn't help but think how easy it'd be to twist it, to hear the snap of her neck.

Easy, boy. Save it for Antonia O'Malley.

"The heating element needed a quick clean, is all." Now he was in true bullshit territory, as he knew nothing about saunas except that he liked to sit in one after a hard workout. And after sex.

"Oh, okay, gotcha." She walked away quickly, as if she knew everything about the spa. Pride was every man's, and apparently woman's, downfall if you asked him.

Before another employee could question his presence, he ducked into the men's locker room, prepared to say he was there to check on a maintenance issue. No one was in there, so he headed to the private bathroom stalls and locked himself in one.

And waited.

"The table is heated, so please let me know if you need it warmer or cooler." The aesthetician worked at the small sink as she spoke. Toni luxuriated atop a massage table, the warmth soothing her back and the featherlight blanket providing the perfect added layer.

"I will, thank you." She breathed in, trying to identify the essential oils used by the spa. "Roses?"

"Yes, and cedar during the winter months. I'm going to put some cleansing oil on you first." The woman massaged the oil into Toni's skin and then wiped her face with a moistened warm facecloth. "And now your first mask. This will be for exfoliation." Her skin tingled as the woman brushed gel onto her skin. "I'll step out for a few minutes while that does its magic. Are you okay? Do you need anything?" Her hand was on Toni's shoulder.

"No, I'm wonderful, thank you."

"Be back soon." The door clicked closed behind the facial provider and Toni took in a deep breath, releasing it as she sank into the most relaxed she'd been in…years?

It wasn't just the sex with Brandon. Or the hope that they might really make a go of it again. She'd finally let go and trusted another adult's judgment with Sierra. Leaving Sierra with Aubrey or any of her family was never difficult, as she totally trusted them. But so soon after the trespassing incident, and Willow's concerns over her cold case heating up, had rattled her.

"It's okay." Brandon's reassurance had worked. She was here, her body was still humming from fantastic sex and she was being treated to a luxurious spa treatment thanks to Brandon's prior planning. This was so thoughtful of him.

The door swooshed back open and closed again. With an audible *click* she hadn't noticed the first time the aesthetician had entered. A waft of an aroma that clashed with the soft surroundings reached her and she opened her eyes.

And looked into the eyes of a man staring at her.

"Scream and you're dead."

Chapter 18

*K*eep him talking.

She didn't know where the thought came from, didn't know what the hell it really meant, but she had nothing else to hold on to. Not when a hulking man wearing a ski mask and overalls that looked like the pockets held everything from knives to handguns stood mere feet away.

And he'd locked the door.

"Who are you? If you want money, I don't have anything here. It's all in the locker room. There, in that robe on the door—take the key from the pocket. Locker 105A." It was her voice, but her body didn't feel attached to it. She'd sat straight up when she realized it wasn't the woman who'd come back into the treatment room, but otherwise she hadn't moved.

This must be fight or flight. Looked like she was going to have to do a bit of both. Slowly, slowly, she began to inch her toes, her feet, her legs—

"Don't move or you're dead." He pulled out a dark handle and clicked the side switch. A blade popped out. Long, glinting with the faux firelight from the LED candles.

Toni gasped and held the blanket more tightly against her chest.

"What do you want?"

He grinned. "I want you, Antonia O'Malley." He touched the tip of the blade with the index finger of his opposite hand. "This is very sharp. You won't feel it, not right away. But if you make one more move that I don't tell you to, I'll bury it into your sternum before you can scream."

She had no doubt he spoke his truth. But her truth, what she was about to fight for, was deeper than the risk of a killer's blade. *Sierra. Brandon.* Their family's future.

"Get off that bed—" He was interrupted by the rattle of the door handle, a quick rap.

"Toni, are you okay?" The aesthetician was on the other side of the locked door.

She opened her mouth to scream, but he leaped to her side, slapping a smelly, sweaty hand over her mouth and pressing the blade against her throat. A whimper escaped her, but his hand muffled it to nothing.

"I told you to shut up. I'm going to move my hand, and you're going to tell her you're fine." His furious whisper against her cheek moved her hair, sent chills of dread down her back.

"Toni, please, open the door." More insistent. Worried.

At her silence, he added pressure to the blade.

What would Willow do?

She gave a tiny nod, and he removed his hand. The knife he kept in place, a sinister reminder of what she risked.

"I'll be ready in a sec." She spoke loudly, unable to muster a shout or yell, not that she would. Not with cold steel against her jugular. "I need to make noise like I'm getting off the bed," she whispered as she tried to see him with her peripheral vision.

"Go ahead." He lowered the knife, only to press the tip into her spine, in the same place Brandon had caressed earlier. She swallowed a desperate cry and she swung her feet over the side of the table. She was dimly aware of being naked save for her panties. It didn't matter. All that mattered was that she survived.

Everything went in slow motion as she kept acting as though she was going to listen to him, and her peripheral vision saw his paw reach into a front pocket. He withdrew a syringe and her mind shifted into chilling clarity. He was going to drug her and then kill the attendant. If he got her out of here, Toni instinctively knew she was dead.

Sierra. Brandon. She had to fight to see them again. Her family—*Aubrey, Willow*—

What would Willow do?

Instead of allowing her feet to hit the floor, she quickly spun on her bottom, leaned back on her elbows and planted her feet into his chest as forcefully as she could, kicking him backward. He fell against the counter, knocking over a row of glass bottles with a crash. The force of her kick shoved her sideways, and she dropped over the edge of table, her head hitting the floor with a sickening thud that send stars across her vision. No, no, no! She couldn't pass out. Not yet.

Hang. On.

"Run! Call nine-one-one!" She screamed as best as her sore throat would allow. She crawled toward the door, reached for the stool to pull herself up. But it had wheels and she had to lean on it, using her legs to get to the door. Nausea threatened but then receded, her adrenaline finally kicking in

"You bitch!" He was back on his feet quickly, too

soon. She looked over her shoulder to see him lunge again for her, but this time she wasn't frozen from fright, couldn't yet take flight, so she had no choice but to fight for her life. She got to her feet, grabbed ahold of the misting contraption that had been shoved aside, lifted it and swung as hard as she could.

And missed. The attacker ducked, then came around the table, forcing her to the back of the room, against the wall, where she screamed again. He was coming for her, but his hands were empty—he'd dropped his weapons.

She seized the opportunity without the threat of a deadly needle or blade to squeeze around to the other side of the table, closest to the door. When he rounded the table, she squatted and grabbed the rolling stool. Lifting it over the table, she let out a painful yell and shoved it at his head.

His head bent back and he lost his balance, falling against the side wall. The stool's wheels spun as the seat fell onto his chest. A grunt escaped him.

It was the break she needed. Toni quickly opened the door and stumbled out into the corridor, where she saw her attendant turn the corner and disappear into the reception area. Toni ran after her, shouting the entire time. But her legs grew heavier with each step, the corridor tilted, and black spots crowded her vision.

No. She couldn't pass out, not yet. She had to keep going.

Before the killer caught her.

That bitch had gotten away, but as far as Toby was concerned, she done him a favor. Oh, he'd get her eventually, no problem. But first? He was going to get her kid.

He figured he had a half hour jump on them, maybe

an hour, especially if he'd banged her up good enough for them to call in EMTs. There was the risk they'd call the cops back in Everett, that the kid would be moved. But he'd take his chances. He'd messed up when he'd called her by name. That had been stupid. But he'd been so sure he had her. Turned out the meek mouse was a rat in disguise.

Excruciating pain stabbed behind her eyes before she opened them. A familiar voice drew her from the depths of the blackness, and she lifted her lids.

"Toni." Brandon's face loomed above hers and she pushed at him, tried to sit up. And promptly vomited into the wastebasket that had been placed next to the sofa she lay on.

"Where is he?" She grabbed the wet washcloth from him and wiped her mouth, her face.

"Take it easy, babe." His hand was on her shoulder. "EMTs are on the way. What happened?"

As her consciousness returned, so did her awareness. She and Brandon weren't alone. They were in the waiting lounge area of the spa, where she'd sipped on ginger tea before…

"A killer. Came in the room when she left." She tried to swallow. "Can I have some water?"

"Here." The receptionist—her head couldn't be as bad as it felt, not if she remembered the woman, right?—handed Brandon a glass of water with a slice of lime. He held it to Toni's lips and she gratefully sipped it, the cold liquid like gold to her weakened body.

"Slow, babe. You want to keep it down."

She took one more slip then impatiently shoved his hand away.

"Where is the killer? The man who attacked me? Where—where's the woman giving me a facial?" Her mind thought *aesthetician* but her tongue still felt too heavy to say it.

"She's okay. They're tending to her." Brandon's gaze looked away briefly.

"You're lying. Help me up, damn it. I have to call Willow. Kevin—"

"Babe, there's nothing they can do for you right now. Not in a snowstorm. Look, this was a random event. The police are coming, too, and they're going to need all the details you can give them."

"We'd like to hear your observations, too, Mrs. Anderson." The uniformed security guard she'd been vaguely aware of sat down on an ottoman across from her, sparing her the pain of having to look up at him. "I'm the head of hotel security. Do you know who hurt you?"

"No. Never saw him before, but even if I had, he wore a ski mask." Her head pounded as she tried to clear her mind. "He had, he had a knife. And a needle. He was going to drug me!" Or was it worse? Was he going to kill her? The memory of his menacing demeanor, the way his eyes were so lifeless, so disconnected from what he was doing…

Brandon's face went white, then fury sparked in his deep brown eyes.

"I'm okay, Brandon. I got away." She briefly told the guard what she remembered. As her head cleared, her mind began to race. She turned to Brandon. "Call Sierra. Make sure she's okay." Her mother's instinct shifted into high gear. "I'm not feeling good about this."

"Of course you're not. You were attacked!"

"And your attendant was seriously injured. This is

someone who has no regard for anyone's welfare." The security guard spoke with an air of authority. Brandon shot him a glare. Before he followed the silent reprimand with what she was certain would be a very undiplomatic response, the sound of pounding footsteps reach them.

"The EMTs are here." The guard nodded in satisfaction. As if he'd handled the entire situation. Vaguely she realized she'd find his demeanor amusing if she hadn't just fought for her life.

"She's shook up, and like I said, it seems she took a really hard knock to her head, but she's okay." Brandon stood outside of the spa reception area as he spoke to Kevin. With the way Toni had pleaded for him to check on Sierra, he'd gone a step further and reached out to Kevin. He figured Kevin's assurances would go further with Toni when it came to security.

"My sister's a tough egg. She'll be okay. But I think you both need to get out of there ASAP." Kevin was right to the point. "I'm just out of a meeting with Willow—"

"Does she think this is linked to the cold case she's working on? As in, is there another stalker out there, or did the suspect the PD thinks was the trespasser hire someone else to keep tabs on Toni?"

"No, Willow doesn't believe this has anything to do with the cold case." Kevin paused, and Brandon's gut roiled with powerlessness. What now? "It's worse, Brandon."

His pulse pounded in his ears and his stomach sank. He watched through the glass doors as an EMT moved a penlight back and forth in front of Toni's eyes. He'd witnessed accidents overseas, had needed the in-depth first aid training he'd been required to take as part of his previous profession. He thought he was immune to blood or another's pain. But not when it came to his loved ones.

She'd never stopped being a part of him.

"Spit it out, Kevin."

"Willow thinks this has to do with the case she worked on with Jay. You know about the Claytons, right?"

"Yes. Toni gave me the big-picture view, and I was there at your parents' with all of you at the housewarming last fall." A family event that had turned deadly when the takedown of one of the sons of the elder Clayton had happened. The same day he'd surprised Toni with his return. It seemed eons ago.

Kevin let out a long sigh. "Long story short, one of the brothers, Toby—the other one, Fred, is in jail, along with the elderly father and stepmother—is suspected to be back in the country. The Claytons ferociously defend their turf and their reputation. And they have a bone to pick with Cascade Confidential since Willow helped bring them down. They wouldn't go after Willow because she's too much of a threat, especially since the Claytons perceive her as part of the entire FBI op that worked against them. They'd aim at a soft target. Brandon, we believe Toby Clayton is the man who attacked Toni. He must have followed you two from home."

"Okay, well, she chased him away. Surely he won't try to come after her again? At least not here?" Keeping Toni safe was all he was thinking about.

"No, but he could decide to go after what matters most to Toni. To both of you."

Brandon saw red at the edges of his vision. "Sierra."

"Yes."

"Say no more. We'll head home as soon as they give

Toni the okay to move. If she can't go, I'm going. Have you already told the local police?"

"That's just it, Brandon. From the weather and traffic reports we're getting in our office, the snow isn't going to let up until at least midnight. It's for all practical purposes a blizzard. It's how these PNW storms go. It may be another twenty-four hours before they open the highway home."

"There are side roads I'll use. I have chains on my tires." He'd put them on halfway up the mountain when they drove in.

"No, don't go anywhere. Stay with Toni. It's too risky in this weather. I'm on my way to your place now. I'll stay with Sierra and Aubrey until you're back, or until we find out that law enforcement has apprehended Toby Clayton, or the man who attacked Toni, if it wasn't him."

"Got it." He'd feel a lot better if he knew the bastard was already in custody. He trusted Kevin and all the O'Malleys. They were who you wanted on your side when the devil came to call. But Sierra was his daughter, his heart.

So is Toni.

He ended the call and immediately texted Sierra. She didn't respond, but she could have left her phone on silent as she and Aubrey watched a movie. He sent a quick text to Aubrey, too. As he reentered the reception room, he wondered about how much he should he tell Toni. She needed rest, and there was nothing they could do right now.

Toni had never been a woman to wait on the go-ahead from someone else, though.

Chapter 19

Toby inched down the slick mountain road, one of many vehicles in a long line of traffic that he'd merged with on the local route that led to the main highway.

"C'mon, c'mon." He looked into his rearview mirror but only saw a line of headlights, which, after about the second vehicle, was obliterated by the heavy snowfall. There wasn't a lot of traffic coming toward him, which made his stomach heavy. His concern was validated when he realized that each car in front of him was being forced into a U-turn and passing him going in the opposite direction.

He had to come up with a quick story, and fast. Next in line to speak to the state trooper, he slowly crawled the truck to a stop and lowered his window.

"Highway's closed. Make a U-turn and try again tomorrow morning. Do you have a safe place to stay?" The trooper motioned with an LED flare.

"Yes, sir, but I'm fully equipped to handle the snow. I'm part of a logging team that's been called out to move the downed trees. I've got my chains on, and my chain saw's oiled in the back." He offered a grin but was careful to keep it casual. Nice and easy. *Act as if you have the right to be there.* Daddy's words ever since he'd gotten caught after his first robbery attempt at age eleven.

"Chains aren't enough, not at the rate this is falling." The trooper wasn't hearing it.

"My tires are jacked up just enough. Trust me, the roads are worse off the highway, and I've made it this far." He patted the outside of the door with a gloved hand. "I've been doing this my whole life."

The trooper's gaze narrowed on the door's logo, and he shifted with impatience. Toby didn't believe in prayer but he hoped the cop was too distracted with the weather to notice that the door logos were magnets. Toby heard the flakes hitting the son of a bitch's parka, saw him look at the line of cars snaking up behind him.

"Whatever. You get stuck, it's on you. I'll say you went of your own volition." The trooper took a step back and waved Toby around the blockade, then returned to his post.

Toby rolled up his window and drove onto the closed section of highway. "Sucker."

He'd never been more grateful for a snowstorm. He figured the curtain of white between him and the trooper was the only thing that had saved him from having to add assaulting an officer to his record.

The good news was that if he'd barely gotten the go-ahead, no way were Antonia O'Malley and her boy toy going to get through.

Sierra O'Malley was primed for the nab.

"This is insane, Brandon. I'm feeling better by the second. I have contacts, CC has a solid network of LE support. I'll call in a favor and get us a truck to drive home. We can come back for your car later. If any two people can drive through this storm, it's us." Toni stared at him with her uninjured eye as she held an ice pack over the other side of her face. "I can't sit here while some madman might go after my daughter. And she's not answering my texts." Worry lines formed between her brows as his internal alarm bells clanged. Sierra and Aubrey hadn't answered him, either.

They're watching a movie.

The EMTs had suggested Toni get a CAT scan when she could, to rule out a concussion. But since she was improving and had a decent lump on her head—indicating the swelling was outside of her skull and not inside—they were fairly certain she'd be fine. There was no way of getting her to a medical facility, though, not in the storm. "It's more risk that it's worth, sir. The snowplows are having a rough go of it, so even if you had a four-wheel-drive truck, it'd be too dangerous to get on the road right now." The young EMT didn't mince words with Brandon or Toni, whose protest was weak enough to convince Brandon that she wasn't, in fact, "fine."

"First, we have no choice here, Toni. Even if we made it down the highway to the main exit, they've shut the highway at least through tonight. Your attacker can't get out, either. And the chances of him being caught are high, with the roadblocks." He walked over to the sofa and sat on the edge, not wanting to shake her. She hadn't said anything but he could tell by how weak her voice was that she was hurting. "Kevin is there, as is Aubrey. Sierra couldn't be in a safer place."

"I never should have agreed to go away." Distress underscored her mental anguish.

Brandon fought against the defensive stance his body

tried to take. He knew this might be a possibility—that she'd blame their trip for putting Sierra at any risk whatsoever. He'd gladly take the blame, but he didn't want to lose what he and Toni had shared earlier, either. A new start.

"You had no way of knowing you'd be assaulted. And I know you're convinced the attack is related to one of your cases, but chances are high that it isn't." He lifted his phone from the coffee table. "Here, let me read you the text chat between me, Kevin and Aubrey."

For the next several minutes, Toni remained still on the sofa as she apparently listened to him read the texts that had flown between them in the short time the EMTS tended to her. He emphasized the part where Willow had reported that Toby Clayton wasn't known for being a smooth criminal, and in fact, appeared to have a history of violent unpredictability. He'd bumbled so many assignments his father had given him that Cal Clayton had finally kicked Toby out of their criminal operations, save for the minimal accounting that he managed from Buenos Aires.

"So you see, we're getting ahead of ourselves, Toni. We can't be one hundred percent certain that this is Toby Clayton's doing. It's still possible that it was a random act of violence by a criminal who preys on women. Spas are like a magnet. To that type of sicko, you were an easy target, laying vulnerable."

A knock on the door interrupted his attempt to soothe her. He recognized the head of hotel security through the peephole and let him in.

"Can I speak to Ms. O'Malley?"

"Of course." Brandon led him into the suite.

"We have security footage we'd like you to take a look at. It's not great, but maybe you can verify that this is the man who attacked you." The guard sat on the edge of the sofa next to Toni and held his tablet up for Toni to see, with Brandon on the arm of the sofa next to Toni.

Toni scrutinized the frames as they played out. A bulky man with a ski mask appeared, running from the spa room where he'd attacked her, Brandon assumed. Toni remained stock still, until the feed was taken over by another camera, on the outside of the hotel. The same man exited the hotel, into the white wall of falling snow. But not before the video captured that he'd removed his mask.

"Oh my goodness." Toni's words formed on a sharp exhale, and her face paled, which Brandon thought impossible as she hadn't been anything but ghostly white since the attack.

"Toby Clayton. That's him." She held the side of her head and grimaced. "The fuzziness from my head wound kept me from figuring it out until now, but the security footage proves it. That's why he seemed familiar—his build and profile look almost exactly like the photos we have on file. The ski mask made it hard to ID him."

"Thank you, Ms. O'Malley." The hotel security manager stood. "I'll inform the police." He let himself out. As soon as the door clicked closed behind him, Toni grabbed Brandon's hand.

"We have to get to Sierra. Now."

"We can't." He spoke through clenched teeth, fighting the same urge to leave now, to track down this bastard. "He's not getting anywhere near Everett until tomorrow morning. We'll be home by then, you can have police guarding our houses. I'm sure the police will arrest him before that." Brandon silently prayed his words were true.

"Damn it! I've cost us too much time. I'm getting

the truck." Toni wasn't listening to his reasoning. She pushed herself up into a full seated position. Her torso swayed and he leaned over her to help ease her back against the cushions.

"Easy, now. You might not have a concussion, but that's an ugly bump, and you were knocked out for bit. Your body needs time to recover."

"Sierra doesn't have time!" A sob escaped her and pierced his heart as though it were a titanium arrow. "Why did we leave with a storm coming, anyway?"

"None of this is your fault, Toni." But he had a sneaking suspicion she thought it was *his* fault. "Let me call Kevin again—"

"No, I'll call my brother. Where's my phone? Have we heard back from Sierra or Aubrey yet?" And there it was. She referred to Kevin possessively, a verbally drawn line.

Toni didn't consider him part of her family.

He was relegated back to being her coparent, period.

"If Kevin was already there, or if your sister would leave her damn phone on, I'd agree. But she's effectively alone in that house right now."

"You just said there's no way Toby Clayton could get there in this snowstorm."

"No. And the PD as well as state troopers have assured you that the highway remains closed."

"Yes. Kevin's in constant contact with them…" She looked at her phone. "You know, it's not like him to fall off the radar like this. He should have been there an hour ago, even considering the extra time needed in this storm." Her hand trembled as he watched her send another text to her brother. "Oh, forget this." She hit the screen with her finger and held the phone to her ear.

Helplessness threatened to overwhelm him. He was an expert in negotiations, not in handling complicated family dynamics, and certainly not in navigating a truck with a snowplow through blizzard conditions. Even if they'd secured a truck and gotten through the roadblock, Toni wasn't up to a drive. Not yet.

He watched her wait for Kevin to answer, then leave a message when he didn't. Her hair was mussed, the blood from the surface wound at her temple crusted into her scalp, her black eye actually a vivid shade of purple and crimson. She was the most beautiful woman he'd ever known. The years had added to her natural beauty, her inner wisdom illuminating her essence. Deep longing tugged at his gut. They'd come so close, so near to becoming a solid family.

"This is ridiculous." She placed her phone in her lap and stared at the fire he'd lit earlier. "This is a joke, right? We're literally stuck in a luxury resort while our daughter is a sitting duck in her own home. I can't even get ahold of the sibling I know can handle this mess best." She shot him an accusing glare. "I knew I should have trusted my gut. We never should have left Sierra. We're leaving now."

"You're right. Let's get out of here." He couldn't fight her, didn't want to fight her. He was beyond worried about Sierra, too.

He wasn't a believer in fate as much as doing the work that was laid in front of you, and taking it day by day, sometimes moment by moment. But it sure seemed fate had it out for him and Toni. Their timing had never been right; they'd never synced to a point where being a couple again might work.

And now the threat to their daughter, no matter how remote, had pried Toni away from him.

She'd never trust him again.

Toby sat and watched the house for a good while after he arrived. He'd messed up at the resort and couldn't afford to screw this up too. He had to snatch the kid before another wrench got thrown into his plan.

The snowstorm made it easier than ever to sit here without worry of being spotted, as the visibility had been so low and it was dark. Absolutely no one was out on the streets, which also helped. But the storm was just about over, and he'd have to make his move. He tried to ignore how the ground reminded him of the winters when he was a boy in the mountains. When life was a lot simpler. When he didn't have the weight of springing Daddy and Fred from prison, of needing Veronica's approval so that he could get those bank account passcodes. At least she appeared to have bought into his lie. She really believed he'd get her out of jail, too. *Stupid bitch.*

He figured it was smartest to make his move after both the babysitter and the kid were in bed, but before the snow completely stopped. Definitely before sunrise. If he was lucky, he'd get inside, grab the kid and take off before the woman ever woke up. He'd studied the floor plan from the real estate app he favored and had memorized every nook and cranny.

Before anyone could say "boo," he'd have justice for his family—and a nice rainy-day fund thanks to Veronica. She'd have no choice but to give him the information once he completed this side job. He had the goods on her and would spill it to the local cops they'd had working for Clayton industries ever since Daddy had turned them decades ago. The Clayton cop friends would make a lot of Daddy and Fred's evidence disappear and leave it all pointing at Veronica. No amount of money would get her out of her cell, even if he agreed to help her. *Never.* He allowed himself a quick laugh, watched the cloud of his breath form between him and the windshield. He'd had to turn the engine off to keep his profile as low as possible.

He looked at his phone. It had been over an hour since the last of the lights had gone off. He'd bet the porch and garage lights had motion detectors, but at this hour it didn't matter if it lit up the whole neighborhood. He'd be in and out and on his way to eastern Washington within the next ten minutes. He sat up fully and reached to turn on his engine when two headlights appeared in his side-view mirror. He quickly hunched back down, grateful he hadn't depressed the brakes yet. Whoever this was would have seen the red and white rear lights and his goose would have been cooked.

A Jeep drove past, but his side window was too frosted over for him to make out the driver. As he watched, it pulled into the dad's driveway and he cursed. Who was this and what were they doing showing up now? Oh, he knew what was going on. They'd come back early, to protect the kid. Somehow they'd gotten a vehicle that would get them through the snow. The father's sedan wouldn't cut it, that's for sure.

A single person got out from the driver's side, no doubt the father, and he waited for Antonia to follow on the right. But as the kid's father remained outside, no one else got out of the car. Toby watched as he opened his passenger door and pulled out some kind of duffel bag. So no one else was with him.

Figures. He'd left Antonia pretty banged up. Instead of walking into his house, though, the father walked through the several inches of snow that carpeted the front lawn and began to make his way to the girl's house.

"Hell's bells." The O'Malleys and Cascade Confidential were on his last nerve. He quickly grabbed the entire bag of hypodermics he'd brought, and the vial of propofol. Thank goodness for the Clayton family's hidey-holes, as Daddy called them. There were several scattered about the Mack Logging and Manufacturing compound, the family estate, and in the woods on state game lands for backup. He'd been dismayed to find all but one of the Mack hidey-holes cleared out, probably by the feds after Veronica and her boy-toy assistant, that idiot Derek, had gotten themselves taken in. Stupid jerks, both of them. Red-hot anger blurred his vision and he stilled, consumed by the urge to ruminate on the wrongs committed against his family. Against him. But he had to catch up with the girl's father before he got inside the house.

Kevin slung his duffel over his shoulder and trudged through the snow to the side gate. He wanted to do a complete walk around before going into Toni's place, to make sure there was no evidence of a trespasser. All three of his older sisters were wound pretty tight, but he put Toni at the top of the doom and gloomers. He figured it was because she was the only one of the five of them who was a parent, and he knew from his own circle of friends that once they became parents, the worry was nonstop.

He didn't expect to find anything—no one had been

able to get out in this storm. He'd passed a pickup truck on the way into the cul-de-sac, but was covered in snow. It had been sitting there a long time.

There were all kinds of snow indents across both Toni's and Brandon's front lawns. A snowman—er, snowwoman—sported what looked like a bikini—the snow had frozen atop the three triangle patches—on the front lawn. But the tracks of Sierra and Aubrey playing in the storm had been covered by at least another inch of snow since they'd gone in for the night.

He opened the gate, pushed against the heavy snow piled up on the other side. His breath puffed out in large clouds and he noted that the stars were coming out from behind the last of the storm's clouds. The wind had whipped the storm away as quickly as it had materialized.

Pounding footsteps sounded behind him. *Too close.* As he dropped his bag and turned, a hit to the side of his throat, just above his shoulder, had him reflexively reach up to grab his attacker's hand. But his arm, his hand, hung limply at his side. Was that the sting, the pinprick, of a needle on his neck?

"Your kid is mine, loser." A deep-throated growl. Was it Toby...Clayton? *Must...warn...Toni...*

Darkness swirled and he felt himself falling, falling... and then the darkness was total.

Sierra watched the snowstorm videos on her social media app with delight. Aunt Aubrey had tucked her in—she hadn't the heart to tell her aunt that she didn't need to be tucked in anymore—over an hour ago. They'd had a long day outside and then come back in to enjoy the amazing dinner Aunt Aubrey heated up. It had been

Sierra's favorite takeout from the grocery store. Mom didn't usually do takeout because they were on a budget and she said that processed food wasn't healthy for either of them, especially a growing girl.

She missed Mom.

As if summoned by magic, her phone lit up with an incoming video call. She pressed accept.

"Mom!" she whispered loudly, as she didn't want to waken Aunt Aubrey.

"Hey, honey bunny." Her mother's face seemed…

"Mom, what happened to you? Did you guys go skiing or something?" Her mother looked like she'd been in a fistfight. "Your eye looks positively sick!" Sierra breathed out in awe as she took in Toni's black eye. "Are you in a car?"

"We were walking on the scenic view paths and I took a bit of a tumble, is all. I'm fine. Your dad and I, uh, borrowed a truck to come home a bit earlier so I can rest. I figured you'd still be awake." Mom grinned, but one side of her mouth didn't curve up as far as the other.

"Mom, you don't look so hot. And I am still awake. Aunt Aubrey and I played outside for, like, hours, then we had dinner and watched *Sleepless in Seattle*. She brought over Grandma's caramel corn."

"Oh my goodness, did she have that left over from Christmas?" Mom sounded like herself, at least.

Sierra shrugged. "Don't know. It did taste a little stale, now that you mention it."

"So you're under your covers, eh?" Mom's lips lifted in the smile that let Sierra know Mom was really missing her.

"Yeah. I don't want to wake Aunt Aubrey up. I think I wore her out."

Mom laughed. "You probably did. She's used to a quieter life."

"She needs to meet someone, Mom. She loves her cats, but I think she'd be happier with a partner."

"Life's about being happy as ourselves first, honey. If we choose to be with someone, it's just that. A choice. Don't ever think you need a partner to be whole." Mom's image wobbled. Probably the storm interference. She'd read about how weather affected cellular connectivity.

"Where's Dad?"

"Driving, of course." Mom flipped the phone so Sierra could see Dad's profile, but in the dark it was kind of blurry.

"Hi, Sierra. Listen to your mom. We'll be home soon."

"Did you two have fun? Before you fell, I mean?" She knew each of her parents enjoyed the outdoors and especially snow but had never seen them doing so together. The image of all three of them making a snowman made her smile. "Are you and Dad, you know…"

"Yes, sweetie pie, we've had…fun." Mom's face looked so serious! "No matter what, your dad and I will always be the best of friends, trust me. Like we told you, our relationship is our concern, not for you to worry about. All we care about is how you're doing."

"I'm doing fine, Mom. Is there something else going on besides your fall? Anything I should know?" She recalled Aunt Aubrey leaving the living room to take a call earlier. She'd been on the phone a long time in the kitchen, out of Sierra's earshot.

"No, nothing comes to mind." Her mom was keeping something from her, Sierra was sure of it. But getting Mom to spill the tea was never easy, and she was getting really sleepy. They'd be home by the time she woke up in the morning…

"Tell me something, though, Sierra, did Uncle Kevin make it to the house?"

"Uncle Kevin?" This shocked her out of her drowsy place and she sat up. She shook her head, puzzled. "No, he wasn't supposed to come over, was he?"

Mom's face, the half she could see because she had that ice pack on it again, scrunched up. "He's—he's going to stop in for a bit."

"What's going on, Mom?" Sierra knew Uncle Kevin wouldn't just *stop in*. He was too busy. And probably out with his friends this late on a weekend night. "Dad?"

"I'm still here." Dad's profile reappeared and she immediately relaxed at his smile. "We're having Kevin do some follow-up on the systems he installed. Nothing to get alarmed about. We just thought he'd be there by now."

"Well, it's been a crazy blizzard outside!" She told them all about the fun she'd had with Aunt Aubrey. Every now and then she heard Mom laugh or say something quiet in the background. When Dad looked at the phone for a second, she gave him the "shhh" sign with her index finger over her lips and mouthed, *Is Mom okay?*

But she wasn't sure if he saw her since his focus went right back to driving.

"Like your mom said, walking around the paths to get to the viewing spots for Snoqualmie Falls was treacherous. We're lucky that all she did was trip. No broken bones, though. Just a noggin-boggin.'" Sierra giggled at his use of the childhood term for a bonk to the head.

"What time was Uncle Kevin supposed to come over?" She looked at her phone clock. "It's already almost three in the morning."

"I'll check on that and get back to you. But you need to go to sleep, honey. Did Aunt Aubrey activate the alarm?"

"Yes, I helped her." She rolled her eyes. "She really doesn't like anything modern, does she?" Her parents had called her, she assumed, because Aunt Aubrey notoriously turned her phone off at night. It was a point of conflict between Mom and Aunt Aubrey since their business was security and Mom said that Cascade Confidential never slept. Aunt Aubrey said that was great but she needed her solid nine hours a night.

"Okay, good. Now, get to sleep and—" Dad's image blurred, and when the camera focused again it was on Mom's face. "Get to bed, Sierra. Stop scrolling."

"Okay, Mom. Love you."

"We love you too, honey." They disconnected. No way was she going back to sleep now. She shoved off her covers and got out of bed. It was colder than ever tonight and she looked for her fluffy pink robe. After she put it on, she tiptoed to her window and moved the Venetian blind aside to peer out. The snowfall had lessened, but the wind was howling, making the light snow hit the glass like pellets. It didn't look like a snow globe anymore but like the video clips of desolate landscapes that her earth sciences teacher had them study during their meteorology lessons.

She quickly texted Uncle Kevin.

Heard you're coming over. I'm the only one awake here. LMK when you're here and I'll open the front door.

Adding a heart emoji, she thought about how much Uncle Kevin liked sweets, just like her. Which reminded her of the caramel popcorn that she'd not eaten a whole lot of. Her stomach rumbled. Mom's order to get to sleep echoed in a far corner of her mind, but the image of the bowl of fruit on their counter—Mom had restocked before she'd left with Dad—lured her out of her bedroom, down the hall and into the kitchen.

The bananas were still a few days from ripening, which was actually how she preferred them. She used a steak knife to get the peel going and perched on a kitchen stool while she munched on the slightly bitter fruit. Sierra enjoyed the cozy feeling the darkened kitchen, lit only by the stovetop light, gave her. Nestling down into her fuzzy robe, she almost didn't see the shadow cross the side window. Fear pricked, but then she remembered Uncle Kevin was on his way. He'd probably checked out Dad's house first.

Eager to surprise him at the door—he still hadn't answered her text, so she assumed he either hadn't read it or hoped she'd be asleep by the time he showed up—she quickly opened the security app on her phone. With a few deft taps she disarmed the front door and slid off the stool. She'd wait up for him, no problem. She could play her favorite phone app game until he showed up. Padding into the living room, she headed for the front door. Sure enough, Uncle Kevin's silhouette moved across the wide picture window as he headed for the door. Perfect timing!

Sierra jogged the remaining steps and turned the dead bolt, opening the door wide.

"Surprise!" she shouted into the howling wind.

But the surprise was on her, because the man standing in front of her was definitely not Uncle Kevin.

Chapter 20

Sierra immediately shoved the door closed, but the not-Uncle-Kevin bad guy shoved against her, hard. She fell to the floor on her butt and let out the loudest scream of her life.

"Shut up!" A large, gloved hand smacked her across the face, sending stars through her vision. Sheer rage exploded from her, but she was powerless to use it until she caught her breath. Crawling on her belly away from him proved futile as he grabbed her ankles and yanked her backward.

"Aunt Aubrey!" she yelled, but with her stomach on the floor and her lungs gasping for air it sounded more like a whimper.

"You relax, kid." He had her on her feet but held her from behind in a chokehold with her toes barely touching the floor. She'd lost both slippers and tried to kick his shins in vain. He had his hand clamped over her mouth, and she gagged at the acrid odors of petroleum and cigarette smoke.

Don't let them get you in a vehicle.

The lifesaving tool from the several videos and classes she'd had about safety from strangers became her focus as she tried to keep him from taking her out of the house and then carrying her across the front lawn to a truck. When he tossed her into the back seat of the F-250's cab—she'd studied trucks and cars, as she'd noticed Uncle Kevin and Aunt Willow seemed to know all the different makes and models—he locked the door before she could reopen it. He seemed to be fiddling with something outside, and she watched as he removed his gloves and pulled a hypodermic needle from his jacket pocket.

Sierra didn't know of a tool that would work when getting drugged by a kidnapper.

"You didn't realize I have as many connections as a diplomat, did you?" She spoke from the passenger seat while reclining, the ice pack on her temple.

"Let's say I appreciate what you and CC do more than ever." The number of vehicles on the roads had increased as they first wound their way out of the mountains on I-90 and then onto the 405, avoiding both the more scenic, rural routes and going directly into downtown Seattle. The city had been cleared of snow, but so had Everett's main streets and they were minutes from home.

Brandon couldn't believe their luck, that the weather pattern had shifted farther north and allowed them to take the main highway out of Snoqualmie Pass. There was no way the scenic route they'd taken at their leisure earlier today would be close to plowed.

Things had moved quickly once the weather reports came in. Toni had called in a favor with the state troopers, and as a result he was driving the personal vehicle of a trooper who'd broken an important case thanks to

CC. He'd told them he'd drive Brandon's sedan to them for the swap out within the next couple of days. As much as Brandon was used to smaller, compact models thanks to his years in crowded urban areas of developing nations, he had to admit that the practicality of the Toyota Tacoma pickup was doing what his car couldn't, not in the aftermath of a snowstorm. As it stood, they were due to pull into the driveway in ten minutes, as long as he didn't wipe out on a turn. As he got closer it was obvious the residential streets hadn't been plowed. The storm had come so quickly there'd been little time to get salt on the roads, so he opted for a safe and steady speed, fighting the urge to floor it.

"Any word from Kev or Aubrey?" Her sleepy voice that his body usually responded to in the exact opposite manner of what he needed to be in this moment—unruffled, focused, strong—broke into his thoughts.

"No, not yet." They'd both texted and left voicemails on her siblings' phones before they left the hotel. It seemed a lifetime ago that they'd driven up to the mountains and had come so close to finding a way to make their paper marriage real. The sex had—

"It's not a surprise that Aubrey turned off her phone for bed, that's so typical of her. But Kevin's never out of touch. He always gets back to me, too." Toni remained professional in tone. As if they'd never had yesterday afternoon and the early evening together.

"You talked to him less than a couple of hours ago and he was almost there. It's still dark, and they're all probably sacked out. We called Kevin in off the slopes, remember."

"I did." Concern edged her voice as she again left Brandon out of the equation.

He ignored the emotional gut punch. His original small doubt about Sierra's well-being had grown into a bona fide concern with each passing mile.

"Sierra's phone is still at the house, which means she is." Toni held the phone over her face with one hand as she studied the Find app, which both she and Brandon used to keep track of Sierra. "That's something, at least. Remember when you told me that making her carry an AirTag was a bit much?"

"I do." He paused. "I was wrong. And before we get back home, we need to talk—"

"About nothing except Sierra's safety. For the record, there's an AirTag at the bottom of her backpack, but that hasn't moved all weekend."

Yeah, she was still furious with him over taking her away from their daughter.

His peripheral vision registered her fingers tapping. "According to the house security app, the alarm's still off. I don't like that one bit."

"Sierra had to turn it off to let Kevin in, remember?" Increasing worry for Sierra overrode his dismay at losing Toni again. This time for good. Guilt scrubbed at his thoughts about himself and Toni. There was no thinking about making things better with Toni until they both knew their daughter was safe and sound.

He knew deep down that it was too late, anyway. He and Toni weren't going to make it as a couple. There'd be time enough to grieve the loss later. First, he had a daughter to take care of.

"I had a hard bonk to my head, but it didn't scramble my memory, Brandon."

"We're just about there." He ignored the sick feeling in his gut over Sierra. It'd taken twice as long as before the storm, but they'd made it.

Toni remained silent, reinforcing what he already knew: Their romantic connection was permanently severed, and it was entirely his fault. He'd pushed her too quickly, forced this trip too soon.

Losing Toni was something he'd have to live with the rest of his life. But there was no life if anything happened to their daughter.

Sierra lay across the back seat of the truck's cab where he'd thrown her. Without hesitation she scrambled for the far side door, but his mean hands grabbed her ankles and yanked, hard.

"Don't bother. Sit still or I'll kill you now." His voice was as ugly as he was. She stilled while the cold air rushed over her from the open door where he stood. As she met the stare of her would-be kidnapper, she shook her head.

"You won't get away with this."

He ignored her as she watched him. He was patting down his jacket. Looking for something. Whatever he was hoping to find in his pockets, it must have been important, because he stopped looking at her. He stared at the hypodermic needle, still in his hand.

He was going to drug her!

Lucky for her, the horrible man was also a stupid man. She knew he was way stronger than her. He'd definitely beat her as far as muscles were concerned. So she had to use her brains. *Call 911.* Her phone was still in her robe pocket, but he'd drug her before the cops could get here. While he kept looking in his pockets, she spied kneepads half stuck into the passenger seat pocket, the kind she knew workmen used. She'd seen them on the roofers this past fall when Dad had his roof installed. Inch by inch she reached her arm over, shaking with the fear that he'd look back at her at any second. He was still focused on the needle. He swore, threw the needle on the ground and started shoving his hands in other pockets. She didn't wait for him to find another one.

Her fingers curled around one of the kneepad straps, and she didn't hesitate. She grabbed it and shoved the thick pad between her neck and pajama top as fast as she could. He looked at her again and she thought she'd been caught. But he said nothing, and she wrapped the collar of her fuzzy robe high around her throat and made a fake shiver, as if she was cold.

He grabbed her by her hair. She screamed as he lifted her from the bench seat, she saw his other hand coming toward her—with the needle. He pressed the hypodermic against her neck and stared at her with the meanest eyes she'd ever seen. But she never felt a telltale prick. The needle had gone into the pad! But she had to pretend it had gotten her.

"Oh no, what did you…" Sierra acted woozy as she figured he expected her to, and, still holding her robe closed, fell back on the seat, on her side. Only then did she allow her arm to drape over the side of the bench seat, as if she were truly unconscious. It was scary because he could do whatever he wanted to her right now, the way she was lying. But he didn't.

He closed the passenger door with a soft *thud*. Sierra prayed that he'd not used child locks on the doors as he walked back around to the driver's door. The wind had died down and the snow had all but stopped, so she was able to hear the crunch of snow under his boots. *One, two, three...*

Sierra lifted up onto her elbows and peeked from between the driver's headrest and seat back. The bad man was at the front middle part of the truck's hood. It seemed to take him forever to make it to the driver's door, but she was ready.

She flipped around, opened the back door—it was unlocked!—and shoved with all her might. The door was heavy but she got it open wide enough to squeeze out. She bolted up the slight incline of their front lawn to the porch.

"Get back here!" The bad man's shout was too close. Fear made her body feel as though the cold air was rushing through her very being, and her hands and feet were numb. She slipped on an icy patch at the base of the porch steps but kept her balance, running straight inside the still-open door and shoving it closed behind her with all her might, securing the dead bolt.

Without stopping, she reached inside her robe pocket for her phone to first arm the security system, call 911, then alert the company via the app that they had an intruder.

Her fingertips didn't find anything in her pockets except old tissues and an empty cocoa powder packet. Her phone had dropped out of her pocket!

"Sierra, honey, what on earth were you doing outside

at this hour?" Aunt Aubrey stood in her pajamas at the threshold of the living room. "Get back to bed, honey."

She opened her mouth to shout, to warn Aunt Aubrey that they were under attack. Instead, they both stared at one another as the door handle clicked from the outside, followed by heavy pounding.

"You can make this easy or hard. Your choice, girlie." The door wasn't thick enough to muffle the sinister intent in the deep-voiced threats.

"Come on, now!" Aubrey reached for her hand and they ran to the back of the house, to the kitchen. "Get down!"

They lay on their stomachs on the kitchen floor, between the pantry and the island. If he came around to the back, he wouldn't be able to see them through the window over the sink, as long as they stayed flat.

"We have to arm the alarm," Sierra whispered. "I can get up—"

"No!" Aunt Aubrey had her phone out, and they both leaned in to listen. Sierra heard a woman's voice.

"Nine-one-one, what is your emergency?"

Aubrey gave whispered details about their situation and location. She set the phone down and Sierra saw it was still connected, on speaker. The dispatcher kept asking Aubrey to stay on the line and to tell her where the intruder was.

Sierra spoke up. "He tried to kidnap me!"

"Ma'am, is there a child with you?"

"Yes, it's my niece."

"Stay on the line—"

The rest was drowned out by the shattering of the kitchen door.

Chapter 21

"Quick, Aunt Aubrey!" Sierra tugged on her aunt's arm, and it made her drop her phone. She reached for it, but another crack rent the air—the man was almost inside. Aubrey left the phone and turned to Sierra.

"I know how to get out of here!" Sierra whispered.

"The garage." Aunt Aubrey understood. "But stay down. Let's go! Quick, quick!"

They belly crawled to the far end of the kitchen, into the small entry that had the washer and dryer. Once out of sight of the thug, they stood up and Aunt Aubrey opened the garage door. "C'mon."

They stepped into the cold, pitch-black garage. The concrete floor hurt Sierra's bare feet so badly. She hopped from one foot to another, shivering for real this time.

"Don't turn on the lights. I'm locking the door behind us." Aunt Aubrey spoke so quietly Sierra could barely hear. Sierra knew Aunt Aubrey had grabbed the basket that hung on the wall above the shelves where their outdoor stuff was.

"We can get away in Mom's car!" Relief gave her hope.

"I don't have the keys—they're in the house. We can't

go back in." Aunt Aubrey's words brought the despair rushing back into Sierra's awareness, but she clung to what she'd seen on a show she and Dad watched not too long ago, where a kid like her was being stalked by a killer.

"I've got it! Let's open the garage door, and run over to my father's. I know how to get into his house without my phone."

"No! Do not open the garage door—he'll hear us." Aunt Aubrey took over. "Let me go first, Sierra. We can't run in between the houses, straight for the front yard, either. He'll see us if he's in your room, or the living room. We'll go around to the other side of your dad's house, and then into the garage. You know the code to open it, right?"

"Yes."

The grave tone was one she'd never heard from Aunt Aubrey before. She followed her aunt, not waiting to hear the man's footsteps inside the house. He'd made it clear he was coming inside. Sierra figured they had two minutes before he'd have searched the house and come up empty. Then he'd come outside.

Running across the grass behind their houses wasn't so easy with the snow coming up to their knees, but they made it clear around to the other side of Dad's house. As they leaned against the wall, Aunt Aubrey peered around it before she nodded at Sierra to keep following her.

"I'll open the garage door!" She ran ahead of Aunt Aubrey, to the keypad mounted next to the door. She flipped the lid and entered the code, triggering the opener's motor to start. The door lifted slowly, and Sierra looked at her house. Lights were on in the front windows, and she saw a large figure moving behind the sheer curtains. He was going to open the front door at any moment.

"Quick, get under there!" Aunt Aubrey must have seen him too. Aubrey shoved Sierra so hard and toward the door that Sierra hit her head on the edge. The door stopped and began to lower. Sierra had just gotten her feet inside Dad's garage and run over to where she knew the main switch for the door was, next to the kitchen entry. She pounded on it and the door opened again. She saw Aunt Aubrey's feet, her knees, and then Aunt Aubrey scooted inside.

Pounding feet sounded on the driveway as she hit the button to lower the door with shaking fingers. She caught sight of the tips of the man's boots right as the door closed with a loud *bang* behind Aunt Aubrey.

Sierra knew it was only minutes until he'd be inside Dad's house. Would the police get here in time?

Toni wanted to allow herself to relax if only the tiniest bit as they approached home. Her anger at herself for trusting Brandon's judgment over leaving Sierra still simmered, but that was the least of her worries. A madman was on the loose and her daughter was his target. She knew it with every fiber of her being. Her child was in jeopardy.

Normally the knowledge of Kevin being there would be a consolation, but a sense of apprehension had settled in her gut and kept building ever since Sierra had disconnected.

At least Kevin texted when he pulled into the driveway earlier.

Her logic was little relief from the anxiety racking her nerves. Toni's body was as taut as if she'd downed three cups of coffee.

"We're probably going to wake them all up." She spoke her prayer aloud as they approached the last turn into their cul-de-sac. *Please let them all be safely asleep!*

"Yeah." His tone was heavy. Brandon felt it, too. She wasn't the only one who'd realized their romantic rendezvous had not only been a mistake, but misguided. Sexual chemistry was one thing; trusting her entire future to one man, when she still had a daughter to raise, was a no-go. Brandon was Sierra's father, so if she didn't trust him, what man would she ever trust?

No one.

She sat up straighter and put her gloves back on, intending to get out of the car the moment they pulled into the driveway. Looking at her hands, she missed their first glance at the houses. Brandon's sharp intake of air forced her attention on him.

He was staring straight ahead, slowing the four-wheel-drive vehicle to a crawl. She swung her gaze in the same direction, to the windshield and beyond. A tsunami of fear froze her in place.

"No!" The strangled cry sounded foreign to her, yet she knew it was from the very center of her soul.

Three Everett PD cruisers and an ambulance were blocking the view of Toni's house. The back of the EMS vehicle was wide-open, and her stomach plunged when she saw a stretcher being shoved inside—with Kevin on it. His eyes were closed and his face appeared blue in the harsh light coming from inside the ambulance.

Toni opened her passenger door and her boots slapped

onto the pavement before Brandon had come to a complete stop. She heard him swear, the slam of his door, his rapid footsteps as he came after her. He was at her side and they were jogging toward Kevin. To his credit he didn't tell her to take it easy or slow down. They both sought one answer.

Was Sierra safe?

"Make a noise and I'll kill you both." The bad man glowered at them from the hallway. He had forced them both into the small half bathroom off Dad's kitchen. They couldn't be seen from the outside in this windowless part of the house.

His voice was awful and Sierra knew that butcher knife that he held in his left hand was one he'd taken from Dad's kitchen. He held a handgun in his right hand. It looked like a Glock to her. She'd looked at a weapons book with Uncle Kevin not too long ago, eager to learn all she could about law enforcement and the tools they used. He waved the gun in front of her face and she saw enough of it to confirm it was a Glock, a Glock 17, actually, which meant it had up to eighteen rounds if the bad guy had a round in the chamber.

"Eyes on me, girlie!" He snarled the command at her.

Refusing to look directly at his eyes, she focused on a huge pimple on the bridge of his nose. This way her brain could figure out a way to survive this bad man's attempt to kidnap her and hurt Aunt Aubrey.

"Whatever you think you want, this isn't the way to do it." Aunt Aubrey's voice was low and quiet, but deadly. Sierra had never seen this side of her aunt. They'd made it into her father's house and had hidden in the kitchen pantry as the man had broken in quicker than either of them expected.

"You have no idea what I want. First, you're going to tell me where your mother is." He jabbed the knife at Sierra, as though he was going to poke her in the eye with it. This dude really didn't know what he was doing. He'd messed up with the hypodermic, but he wasn't going to shoot her, or he'd have done it already. He loomed over her, reminding her that he was definitely stronger than either of them.

But not faster and not smarter. If they hadn't had to hide in the pantry so fast, he might never have found them before help arrived. Aunt Aubrey and she had agreed to go to the attic and pull up the ladder door with its long string behind them. But they never made it.

"I, I, I'm s-s-s-so s-s-s-cared!" She let out a wail she hoped he'd fall for. "Please, mister, don't hurt us. I don't know where my mother is. She doesn't talk to me." She sensed Aunt Aubrey's questioning glance but didn't risk looking at her. "I have to pee!" She crossed her legs.

"Stop crying! And you're going to have to hold it. You'll do more than pi—"

"You need to talk to me. Please stop upsetting her." Aubrey stood up from where he'd made them both sit in the bathroom off the kitchen, the one room that didn't have windows. "She has to use the restroom. Give us that much privacy."

"Ooooh, I'm going to wet my pants!" Sierra grasped her crotch and saw the man's expression change from menacing to confused. He didn't like her crying, and she didn't know why, but she had the feeling he was uncomfortable with being with two women. He wore lumberjack kind of clothes, like her classmate's dad who ran a

Christmas tree farm. Her friend's father was smart, not slow like this guy. Neither she nor Aunt Aubrey could fight him one-on-one so much, but they sure could fool him. She already had, with the hypodermic.

"Unless you want to smell urine all day, I suggest you let her use the restroom." Aunt Aubrey gave zero sign of being afraid. Sierra wanted to be just like her.

"You go." He waved the knife at Sierra. "You—" he pointed the gun at Aubrey "—come out into the hallway with me. Don't think I'm stupid enough to leave you two alone. One false move and you're dead."

"No—" Sierra opened her mouth to wail, but Aunt Aubrey's hand clasped her behind her upper arm, hard.

"That's enough. Listen to the man." Sierra looked at Aunt Aubrey's big eyes, shocked to be spoken to so harshly. But when as she stared, Aunt Aubrey's eye that was out of sight of the bad guy winked.

She got it. Aunt Aubrey was playing it tough, and Sierra needed to follow along. "Please don't spank me, Auntie."

"Then get in there." Aunt Aubrey's approval sparked in her eyes and made Sierra feel better. They were going to get away from this bad man!

"Get out here, now! Or lose your chance." The bad man pointed at Aubrey. She exited the bathroom but looked over her shoulder at Sierra.

"You listen good, honey, and do what the man tells you. Hurry up, now." With her back briefly to the bad man, Aunt Aubrey mouthed one word to Sierra.

Attic.

"Kevin!" Toni went to leap up into the emergency services vehicle but was stopped by a strange woman.

"Toni, you have to give them room to work." She blinked and realized the woman was Carmela Inez, the detective who'd investigated the trespasser from the woods.

"What's going on? Where's my daughter?"

"She's with your sister." Carmela's expression was as flat and unemotional as stone, and it wasn't from the cold. "They're being held hostage by a man we believe is Toby Clayton."

Toni's knees threatened to buckle and she swayed, but she remained standing, allowing herself time to absorb the shock of what Carmela said. "No, that's— How did he—"

"Then what's with all the cops around my house?" Brandon interrupted, and she felt the weight of his arm around her waist.

"I'm good." She shrugged off his attempt to comfort her and took two steps to the van, reaching out her hand to the open door, needing the support she never wanted from Brandon ever again.

"Hostages? He's got them?" Toni gripped the door's edge as a fury greater than any she'd ever felt before exploded in her midsection and made her entire body shake. She would get whoever took Sierra and rip them—

"They're in your house, Mr. Anderson." Carmela spoke as if they had all night. "It appears the intruder entered through the back kitchen door of Toni's house. From the footprints across your backyards, your daughter and your sister got away from him for a short time before he broke into Mr. Anderson's home. We don't have a status on any of them right now, but we're hopeful."

"Hopeful isn't good enough." Brandon spat the words.

"I'm going to get my daughter." Toni pushed away from the van and turned toward Brandon's house. Sierra was in there.

"No, you're not. Toby Clayton is unpredictable. The hostage negotiator is en route, and SWAT is on the way, too."

A single tear ran down Toni's cheek. If sobbing would have helped Sierra, she'd have cried for the rest of her life. Instead a steely resolve rose inside her more quickly than the fury had.

"What can we do? Does she have her phone?" But she already knew the answer. Sierra hadn't texted or called since Kevin had arrived. "What happened to my brother?"

Carmela's skin turned ashen. "We're not sure. We found him in the yard between your two houses, just on the other side of the gate." She pointed at the front gate, now wide-open. Toni saw the deep grooves the gurney must have made. "He was unconscious when we arrived. There's indication that he was drugged, but I can't confirm that. We have to let the hospital figure it out."

"Is he alive?" Toni's breath caught and she looked at the EMTs as they worked over Kevin, inserting an IV, wrapping him in blankets. Warm air pumped out of the back of the vehicle.

"He's got a solid pulse, but he's on the brink of hypothermia." The lead EMT spoke up, answering Toni's question before she turned to face Carmela. "We need to move him now. There's a medevac inbound, and it'll land here, in the cul-de-sac."

"No!" Carmela didn't hesitate. "I don't need anything else spooking the assailant. Can you transport him to the community park two blocks away and have him lifted from there?"

"Yes, ma'am."

Toni, Brandon and Carmela stepped away from the ambulance and Toni refocused her attention on Brandon's home. It looked completely dark, as if no one was there. Her baby was in there with a madman. She sensed Brandon next to her, spared him a glance.

"Our girl's in there." Her voice cracked.

Brandon's profile was an immovable fortress as he stared at his home, the only indication he'd heard her a slight nod.

"It's not Aubrey or Sierra who Toby Clayton wants. It's me." She looked around, noticed that Carmela was in deep conversation on her phone. Probably directing SWAT in. The presence of top professionals didn't do anything to allay Toni's sheer terror, though.

What were the chances they'd arrive in time to save Sierra? Aubrey?

"We have to let the pros do their job, Toni." Brandon said what she suspected he'd uttered more than once during his former career. But instead of sounding authoritative, full of wisdom, Brandon's voice was empty.

So were his words, she feared.

Sierra heard Aunt Aubrey talking to the man but couldn't make out all the words through the door. Her aunt's voice sounded very calm, almost soothing. The man's replies sounded like grunts.

She figured she should wait it out, because if she said she was done and went back out there, the man might try to stab either one of the them.

"Get her out of there." The man's voice was loud and clear.

"Give me space to let her out." Aunt Aubrey wasn't backing down.

Sierra opened the door a crack and realized Aunt Aubrey was at the door and the man was on the other side, by the inner garage door. Aunt Aubrey's hand motioned behind her back for Sierra to run. They'd planned this out.

"I have to wipe myself! I need privacy!" She spoke into the bathroom, hoping he'd fall for it.

"Hurry up, honey." The hidden instruction under Aunt Aubrey's words wasn't lost on her. She quickly, quietly inched out of the bathroom and tiptoed with her back flat against the wall, her presence blocked by the bathroom door that opened outward, until she turned the corner and ran as fast as she could up the stairs, down the upstairs hallway, toward Dad's room.

She heard shouting, a scuffle and something—someone—hitting a wall as she ran, but she didn't stop until she was in Dad's closet, where she clicked on the light to find the string that hung down from the ceiling. She tugged with all her might, causing the ladder to unfold with several loud creaks and a thump when it hit the carpeted floor. Scurrying up the rungs, she got to the top and tugged at the ladder—it wouldn't lift!

"Please, please," she sobbed, this time for real. Aunt Aubrey had been clear that she had to pull the ladder up to lock herself safely in the attic. But the contraption was meant to be pushed up from the bottom. Frantic, she bounced her gaze around Dad's closet, looking for an answer.

The shelf that ran along the one wall of the closet was halfway between the ceiling and the floor. She climbed back down a few steps and then onto the closet shelf, knocking Dad's folded sweatpants down. Leaning over, she tugged at the ladder from the side. It wasn't the best angle, but she got the ladder to budge, and then it began to slide back up. She reached back up to crawl into the attic opening when she heard footsteps pounding up the stairs. They didn't sound like Aunt Aubrey's steps—her aunt would be quieter, stealthy. Sierra's heart sounded in her ears as panic rushed her. She didn't have much time.

The bad man was coming for her.

Chapter 22

Brandon's heart raced in his chest as he ducked below the dining room window, out of sight of the man he assumed was Toby Clayton.

Had Toby seen him? His hands shook as he waited, planted against the side of the house, trying to not make a single sound.

Brandon hadn't seen much inside the house, but luckily he'd observed what he needed to. Sierra had run past and around the corner to where the stairs were, too quickly for him to get her attention. Toby would have been too close, anyway. He couldn't risk Toby shooting Sierra, or both of them. It looked like Toby had already taken out Aubrey, as he spied her long hair, the same shade as Toni's, spilling onto the floor between the kitchen and dining room. He prayed she was still alive.

The police would notice he'd disappeared. Or Toni would, and she'd tell them he was gone. Sierra needed him.

He ran around to the back of the house, tearing off his parka as he went. He climbed onto the recycling bin, which put him chest-level with the low-hanging eave that covered the side of the house. He hoisted himself up and over the ledge in a very clumsy but effective movement, his stomach against the hard, sloped surface of the roof, icy and cold under his hands. He slowly put his knees, then his feet under him and stood. He kept a hand on the wall of the attic as he began to make his way to the back of the house. To the attic windows he'd left unlocked when he and Sierra had been lying the floor last weekend. The double-paned window would allow him quick access into the house, and hopefully he'd reach Sierra before Clayton found her.

The snow made the roof tiles slippery, and it was impossible for him to stay as quiet as he wished, as he had to stomp down with each step to crack the ice layer. The frigid coating on the roof provided enough reflection from the moonlight to illuminate his path so he wasn't doing this totally blind.

He knew his daughter, and if she was smart, which she was, she'd have done her best to hide from the kidnapper. She'd oohed and aahed over the attic when he'd shown it to her and pleaded for him to let her use it as her bedroom. He'd relished the time with his daughter as they worked side by side and had promised her that it could be her room once he had it fully modernized. The cozy niche space could be her place to escape to as a teenager.

In typical Craftsman style it had its own stairwell, but he'd needed the wall space on the bedroom floor to place a humongous hand-carved armoire he'd carted back from Asia. The armoire fit the space perfectly but blocked the attic door, so he'd installed a pull-down ladder from the attic in his main bedroom's closet. Sierra knew how to access the attic, but she wouldn't be able to pull up the ladder once she got up there. And Clayton would no doubt look in the closet as a likely hiding place.

Clayton.

Rage rose and his hands clenched into fists, his vision darkening.

Get to Sierra.

"We can't just stand here." Toni turned to ask Carmela how they were so sure Sierra was still in the house. Maybe she'd somehow escaped and was shivering in the back woods?

But Carmela had walked away, into the middle of the cul-de-sac, still speaking into her phone. SWAT remained nowhere in sight. She turned back to talk to Brandon, but he was gone. Had he taken advantage of the very distracted Carmela and run into his house? She stared at his front door, stymied.

"Don't even think about it." Officer Clemson stood next to her. She'd been so lost since she and Brandon had pulled into the cul-de-sac that she'd never noticed he was also on scene, and she hadn't heard him walk up. "There's nothing you can do right now."

"What is anyone doing right now? Because it looks to me like no one is making a move to save my daughter!" As she vented, she caught movement on the roof of the house.

Brandon.

"You have to let us do our job, Ms. O'Malley." Clemson hadn't noticed the man on the roof, and she knew she had to make sure it stayed that way. "Right now we have every reason to believe your daughter is alive in there. The kidnapper is desperate. He'd planned to get away with your daughter, but from the marks in the snow around the open back passenger door of his truck, she outsmarted him and escaped. Then she and her aunt got away from him again. If he'd wanted to kill your daughter, he would have. She's no use to him dead."

"Sierra…" She couldn't voice the words, much less allow her thoughts to go there. What was Brandon doing on the roof? She didn't want to draw attention to him by glancing over at the house again. Brandon was doing what she wished she'd done, sooner.

Although, who was she kidding? As much adrenaline as her mama bear instincts were pumping through her bloodstream, it wouldn't be enough. She was still hurting from her own escape from Toby Clayton. Even at her full strength she didn't have the self-defense tools that her other siblings possessed. Sure, she'd taken all the mandatory CC trainings with weapons and defensive driving. But she wasn't a natural field agent by any means. No, that was best left to Willow, Kevin and Jake. They were born agents. Aubrey wasn't hardcore as the other three, but she was certainly more athletic than Toni ever hoped to be. Aubrey would do whatever it took to save Sierra, she knew.

When it came to O'Malley genetics, Toni had been born in the shallow end of the brawn pool. She'd had to learn to appreciate her mental abilities. Her advanced degree seemed pointless in this moment, though.

You're Sierra's mother. This was her superpower, and her daughter needed her.

Her gaze flicked to Officer Clemson, confirmed that he was looking at his phone and not paying attention to her. The nearest officers stood several yards behind them. Only then did she chance a better glimpse at the rooftop.

Brandon had disappeared. Her stomach plunged and her hands began to shake. Had he fallen off the roof?

A second quick glance confirmed that no one was paying attention to her. It was all the go-ahead she needed. Before she changed her mind, Toni made a beeline across the lawn, not stopping until she was well hidden behind the mature fir trees that grew on the side of the house.

Sierra needed both of her parents.

Brandon's foot nearest the edge slipped and his stomach plummeted as he waved his hands, expecting to fall through the morning air and onto the icy ground below. Miraculously his foot stopped sliding a hair from the edge and he regained his balance. His breath formed white clouds in front of him, and he was coated in sweat underneath his ski sweater. His body was pumping adrenaline and he had to channel it in the right direction if he was going to save Sierra.

He'd never appreciated more the Navy SEALs and other US special forces he'd had the occasional interaction with while overseas. It was rare, but every now and then one of the elite military units would participate in an international exercise with whatever nation he was assigned to. They'd made feats like scaling a wall and climbing onto a roof look as easy as if they were superheroes with special powers.

Which he definitely wasn't.

Every grain of his primal instinct told him to stop and get the hell off the roof and warred with his desire to see Clayton dead.

He had to focus, to treat Clayton like the despots he'd dealt with in the diplomatic world. *Keep going, no matter what.* Because his heart was running the show here. He had to get Sierra out of the house alive.

They'd worked out fire escape plans within a day or

two of his move-in. Sierra had actually been the one to bring it up. He'd already made sure she knew how to easily get in and out of the house via the front, back and garage doors. They'd gone over how to lock and unlock her bedroom window, in case she couldn't escape via the hallway and down the stairs.

And they'd explored the attic together, carefully picking out the sturdiest beams she'd need to step on to get to the same windows he was heading toward. Except now, the floor under the window was in place. Not stained or permanently in place, but it would give him enough support when he entered.

On all fours, he turned the back corner and crawled up the steep gable, leaning his back against the wall right next to the back attic window. He hadn't considered the attic windows at the front of the house because the flooring underneath them wasn't finished. At this point, it was a good thing he'd headed for the back of the house. He knew that SWAT would spot him and make him stop. Or worse, mistake him for the bad guy and shoot without question.

There was a half foot between the bottom of the window and the roof. Not big enough for him to lie flat without Toby seeing him from inside. He'd have to kneel and risk it from the side. All he had available for a handhold was the gutter—the window frames lay flush with the back attic wall. He knew if he relied on grabbing the gutters while opening the windows, it would be a certain fall. He wore hiking boots with excellent traction. Despite his acrophobia, he had decent balance and he'd made it this far.

He had to go for it. He'd get Sierra out of the attic and to safety before Clayton found her.

It felt like hours that she'd been up here. Where were Aunt Aubrey and the bad man?

She hunkered down lower in her robe and thought about sticking her feet under the layers of exposed insulation on the unfinished half of the attic floor that she'd watched Daddy install a few weeks ago. He'd been updating the "tired Craftsman," as he referred to it, since he'd moved in last fall, but the attic was only half-done. Dad seemed to know an awful lot about energy costs and savings, and he said the old house that she loved so much for all its nooks and crannies had great bones but lots of clogged arteries. Dad had a friend who was a home inspector who'd come over and told him where all the problems were and how to fix them.

The roof had been a big source of heat dissipating in the winter, for sure, because of the humongous attic. Dad said that maybe they'd turn it into her own room someday. She'd carefully walked among the long beams that held up the structure, careful to stay on the support beams and not risk falling through the ceiling into one of the upstairs rooms, as Dad had warned could happen.

She would make this the coolest room ever. Mom would fuss, because she'd made it clear that her house was really Sierra's home. But the more time Sierra spent over here with Dad, the more she loved this house. Mom had picked out a fine enough house, but something about Dad's house appealed to her. Maybe it was all the nooks and tight spots that she imagined putting a window seat in, or one of those old-fashioned privacy screens. Or how she kept finding cool trinkets left behind by the old neighbor who lived here for so long. Last week, Sierra had found a hand-powered cake mixer. Not like the big modern electric one Mom used, but smaller, with two beaters and a hand crank. It worked great for eggs and was a little harder to use with pancake batter, but manageable.

A grin escaped her serious pondering as she remembered that they'd discovered an old box full of love letters the last time she'd been up here with Dad. The tin had been stashed under one of the attic vents. She strained to see where there might be a sliver of light pouring in, but it was pitch-black. She waited for her eyes to totally adjust and then saw where the moonlight had come through the worn roof when Dad first moved in. They'd found the holes in the roof when Dad assessed the attic. Dad had decided to get the new roof installed right then and there. Because of the cost, he told her they'd take it slow when it came to fixing up the attic. So far Dad had worked up here every other weekend or so. Just last weekend she'd helped him lay hardwood planks across the beams, starting under the far windows. Half of what would eventually be a solid floor was in place. She enjoyed fitting the boards together with their tongue-and-groove structure. Dad had taught her the right way to firmly but gently hammer the pieces together with the rubber mallet.

Would she and Dad ever get the attic finished?

Sierra wiped away the tears that dripped down her face. How long had she been sitting here, doing nothing? She had stuff to do. Get out of the attic, away from the house, and save Aunt Aubrey.

Before the bad man found her.

* * *

Toby stared at the motionless body on the floor in front of him. He hadn't meant to knock the kid's aunt unconscious with the punch to her face.

What if she's dead?

"Stop it." He slapped his head. He wasn't going to get caught like Fred had. Whether she was dead or knocked out didn't matter. Either made things easier for him.

All he needed was that kid. She'd disappeared, but he never heard a door open, so she was still in the house.

He crept into the living room and went to the window, careful to stay to the side, out of sight of anyone out there. He took a peek through the slit in a sheer fabric drape. His gut instantly clenched at the sight of so many people, mostly uniformed cops, in front of the house. This wasn't Pine Hills, where the Claytons had kept cops on their payroll. If he got taken in, he'd never get out. He had to have the kid to barter with.

Cold sweat broke out on his forehead, under his pits. He needed his bargaining chip. Time to get that smart-ass kid in hand. He turned and strode to the stairs. He caught a glimpse of movement through the side dining room window but he didn't have time to check it out. The clock was ticking until SWAT arrived, giving him seconds to finish this off. He pounded up the stairs, not worrying about making noise anymore. They knew he was here.

Get the kid.

Chapter 23

"Ms. O'Malley!" Officer Clemson's fierce whisper made her look down. "Come down from the roof now." Officer Clemson stood on the ground below, motioning for her to get off the roof. She'd gotten up here in the nick of time. Thirty seconds later and he would have stopped her.

"I'm not coming down without my daughter." The roof was too steep to risk talking to him. Toni leaned back against the side attic wall, which put Officer Clemson out of her sight.

"Ms. O'Malley!" She ignored him. Time was her enemy, and Sierra's. If Officer Clemson was going to come up here, he would have already. And he knew better than she did to keep it quiet.

Focus, focus.

She'd found where Brandon's footprints had ended and she'd looked up in time to see his boots disappear over the edge of the roof. She'd climbed up as he had, using the trash bin as a step stool. A torn pair of leggings and one fingernail later—it had torn off when she'd grasped the rough edge of the roof, which was miraculously free of ice, unlike the rest of the roof—she'd gotten up here without slipping.

Her breath came in gasps as Clemson kept asking her to come back down. She forced herself to take deeper breaths, to ignore him and calm down. Panic would save no one. So far she'd heard zero noises from inside the house. Screaming or gunshots were the last things she wanted to hear, but the silence wasn't reassuring, either.

Toni's phone vibrated in her pocket, and she pulled it out. The screen lit up with Willow's smiling face.

She pressed her phone to her ear. A warm sensation ran down the back of her hand. It was blood from her broken fingernail.

"Toni, talk to me!" Willow's demand reflected her Marine Corps training. "Where are you?"

"She's still in there, sis." Toni's teeth chattered as she whispered, her parka no match for her shock at Sierra being held by a kidnapper, the snow under her bottom soaking through to her skin. "I'm on the roof. I followed Brandon. He—we got away from the cops and climbed up here. Officer Clemson is keeping an eye on me, but he's not coming up here. He's waiting for SWAT."

"Why are you on the roof, Toni?" Willow's voice was the steadying force Toni needed, a life preserver in the midst of chaos. Her resolved returned.

"I think Brandon's expecting her to head for the attic. They've been working together on remodeling it." A sob escaped her at the image of Brandon and Sierra together, without the threat facing them now.

"Okay, stay calm. You've got this, Toni. Where's Aubrey?"

"They're both in there with Toby." She spat his name. "I'm going to kill hi—"

"Stop. You're going to get Sierra first. Are you sure you need to be up there? Hang on." She paused. "Okay, I show that SWAT is almost on scene." Willow was using the CC police scanner app, no doubt.

"I haven't seen them yet, but the place is crawling with LE. I got up here right before they could stop me. I think I heard them yell at Brandon, too, on the other side of the house."

"Stay right where you are for now, Toni. Is there any word on Kevin?"

"No, nothing. Detective Inez said the EMTs called in a medevac. He looked awful, Wil—" Her attention was caught by the sound of tires on the road, and she leaned out far enough to see through a stretch of tall cedars. A SWAT vehicle pulled up into the cul-de-sac, along with two more cruisers. The ground below her was empty. Officer Clemson had given up on her. "SWAT is here."

"Okay, that's good news, right?" Willow was in full-on sister mode. "You should go. Get off the roof. They might need you to help with the negotiator."

"I—I can't. I have to save Sierra." She heard Willow's sharp intake of breath, imagined her shocked expression, followed by anger at Toni's stupidity. But Willow hadn't had a child yet. She didn't get what it was like—

"Jeez, sis. Okay. Where is Brandon now?"

"I'm not sure. I saw him climb up here a few minutes ago. I don't have time for twenty questions. I need your help."

"You got it. Do you have a weapon with you?"

"My phone?" She blinked against the stinging tears.

Willow was right, and so was Officer Clemson. She had no business being up here.

"Listen to me, Toni. Above all else, do not enter that house, or a room where you know Toby is, without a weapon. In fact, if you want to stay on the roof, make yourself useful if you can, as a point person between Brandon and SWAT. Can you tell them from there?"

"No. Can you?" She didn't want any other distractions once she hung up.

More muffled talking. "Jay's on it." Another pause. "Listen, he's told Detective Inez where you are. Do not move from there."

Toni ignored Willow's order. "Is there anything you can think of about Toby Clayton that the negotiator—" her voice cracked at the implication of Sierra's life being negotiable "—or Brandon can use? Does he have a soft spot for anything?"

Silence. Had their connection broken?

"Willow?" She strained to hear a reply as she watched the SWAT team debark from the back of the truck. Their appearance in state-of-the-art protective gear reminded her of a science fiction movie. Except this wasn't fiction. It was very real and Sierra's life hung in the balance.

My baby girl!

A sob escaped her and she held the phone away to disconnect, assuming the call had been dropped.

"Toni!" Willow's shout reached her and she placed the phone numbly against her ear.

"Go ahead."

"Toby has been in and out of trouble, mostly in, with local LE since he was fourteen. I can't bring up the juvenile records, but his last offense was for assault in the local diner. He left the country shortly thereafter. He's remained on the Clayton payroll, according to Jay." Willow's voice was muffled, and she realized she was asking Jay for more information.

"Listen to me, Toni. The police know you're there, and they're none too happy. Text Brandon that Toby has always been the black sheep, unable to do Cal Clayton's bidding without getting caught. Unlike Fred, who was never arrested until last fall, when he was caught stalking me." Toni recalled the shocked expression on Fred's face when the Montana state troopers and FBI apprehended him on her parents' property. He'd never expected to be brought down, ever.

"Will do. I'll text it." She prayed Brandon would receive her message, that he'd look at the text. He wore a smart watch, so even if he'd dropped his phone he should get the message. "And Willow? Thank Jay for giving up the info. I know he didn't have to." Nor should he have, in truth.

"Jay's part of our family too, Toni."

"Yes." She disconnected and immediately tapped out a text to Brandon. She swore, as her fingers were numb and her injured fingertip was still bleeding.

Toby Clayton has always sought his father's approval. Black sheep of family. I'm on the roof outside of the attic BTW. LMK what you want me to do.

Now she had to wait. Would Brandon be able to use this information? Where was he?

She had to know if he was in the attic, or if Sierra was there, alone and afraid. Getting back up on her feet seemed risky. Even with SWAT knowing she was up here, it wasn't worth risking being mistaken for Toby. Her only choice was to belly crawl.

The weight of her entire body against the roof, even in the slick parka, gave her more traction than her two feet had. Once she was at the back corner of the outside attic wall, she grasped the corner with her hand nearest to the house and used her other hand and both feet to propel her around, until she was on her stomach and perpendicular to the far back wall, just under the window.

She wasn't alone.

Her gaze locked on Brandon, mere feet away.

What the hell? he mouthed.

Before she could answer, a series of three gunshots sounded inside the house.

Bam! Bam! Bam!

Sierra jumped and clasped both hands over her mouth. Her knee hit the corner of a spindle-legged sewing machine table and she was glad she'd covered her mouth to keep from screaming, because she couldn't help the whimper she made when the sharp edge of the table cut into her knee. Crouching down, she looked around the attic. She had to find a hiding place, but where?

"I know you're up there." Another gunshot. "Come down now or you're dead." The man pounded on the attic ladder hatch. She'd pulled in the cord that she and Dad used to pull the stepladder down, so the man was going to have to go get a ladder from the garage if he wanted to get to her. Unless…would he fire through the floor?

The windows beckoned. Could she climb out and get away?

Not without a ladder. The roof under the windows

on either end of the attic covered the kitchen and front porches. She'd have to jump off the roof and into either shrubs in the back or the hard ground out front. There was a big pine tree, though, next to the house. Would it support her weight? Could she even reach past the snow-covered pine needles to its trunk?

Another shot fired. If the weapon was the Glock, like she thought, its magazine held ten to seventeen rounds. It was impossible to tell by the brief glimpse she'd had of the gun, especially with that jerk's big hand around the grip. Hopefully the bad guy only had about eleven rounds left. If she was lucky, even fewer.

Pop pop pop pop pop.

Eight rounds left, max. Maybe seven.

One round was too many, she knew, but if he was so careless as to blow his rounds trying to scare her, she'd bet he still didn't want to kill her. None of the rounds had come through the attic from what she observed. Dad's walls were probably a mess, though.

She'd seen that hypodermic needle, and its contents had soaked the kneepad she'd used to protect her throat. He meant to drug her and use her to barter. That's what the kidnappers did in the crime books Mom didn't realize she had on her ereader, and in the books she took surreptitiously from Granddad's library. She wasn't stupid—she hid whatever adult fiction she was reading inside the big Harry Potter books that Pappy kept, too.

Why he would think she was worth going to all this trouble for she hadn't figured out yet. As soon as this was all over, she planned to find out. Or ask Aunt Willow what was going on. She'd overheard Mom and Willow on so many different video calls it was insane. Mom was in the habit of using her laptop speakers instead of earbuds, which meant Sierra had overheard lots of good tea relating to the security business. Mom always assumed she was upstairs in her room or streaming a show on her tablet. She kept her headset on but turned off to give the impression she wasn't eavesdropping.

If she'd fooled Mom, who was the smartest person she knew, she knew she could outsmart this jerk.

First, she had to get out of the house without him knowing.

"What the hell are you doing up here?" The last person he'd expected to have to deal with in this moment was the one person besides Sierra who meant the most to him.

"If you don't go in there, I will." Toni glared at him. They were both hiding out under the attic window, and several more shots had been fired. They'd heard Toby's shouts, too.

"You need to get off this roof." He spoke through clenched teeth. Toni was in his way. "Sierra needs at least one of us left." Brandon's heart was in his throat as he spat the whispered words. The chance that his baby girl would lose one, much less both of them in one tragic day made the red-tinged vision return.

"You need to listen to me. I have information about Clayton that will allow you to negotiate."

"This isn't a diplomatic situation!" Brandon's jaw ached from clenching, and if it weren't for the fact that their daughter's life was at stake he'd be yelling. "I'm going in to get Sierra out of there, before Clayton climbs into the attic." He moved from his stomach onto his knees, off to the side of the window.

"Shut up and listen! You need to know who you're dealing with." Toni had never spoken so sharply to him, even in the midst of their worst arguments, and the steel in her eyes as she looked at him brooked no argument. "Toby Clayton is unpredictable and violent." She quickly whispered a bulleted list of facts about the loser, never missing a beat. "We both go inside. I'll focus on getting Sierra out of the house, or at least in a different room, and you work on talking the bastard off the ledge. You're the negotiator between us."

He opened his mouth to persuade her to go back to where she'd climbed up, but with SWAT, it would put her in more danger than she was in now. Everyone in or on the property would be treated as a suspect, including them.

More gunfire erupted from inside, and he had to make his move.

"Stay here. I'm going in." He leaned to look through the window.

"Brandon. Wait."

Chapter 24

Something she couldn't identify, had only had a premonition of once before, had forced her last two words out.

"Brandon. Wait."

He stared at her as if looking at a stranger. Suddenly she wasn't on Brandon's rooftop in Washington State, but in front of her parents' home in Seattle. The home she'd been brought to as a baby, and the one she'd come back to after finding out she was going to have a baby. Brandon's baby.

Their child.

He'd stared at her that summer evening, the sun's long pink and peach rays lighting up the sky behind him, making him appear like an avenging angel instead of the man she'd fallen for. Hard and quick. Too fast. Always needing to know she was in control, Toni hadn't considered her emotions when she'd told him that she wouldn't follow him around the globe to the assignment he'd worked for since high school Model United Nations.

"Not even for our child, Toni? Whoever they are, they're going to need both parents."

"We'll be there for them." Tears welled and she

squared her shoulders, nodded. "I'll make sure they visit you, wherever you are, and you'll come to see them here."

"That's not what I meant by *both* of us."

"It's what it has to be, Brandon. You have your dreams," she'd gulped, "and I have my commitment to my family." She'd been too scared to admit what was so clearly the truth for her.

Toni had been scared to death of committing to anyone besides her family. She'd never been given a choice with her family—the commitment to the business, to Cascade Confidential and all it entailed, had been something she'd accepted since she'd run around her mother's legs under her executive desk as she spoke to her agents on the landline telephone.

"What am I waiting for?" Brandon's clipped demand snapped her back to the present. To the decision she'd made today, and would have thirteen years ago, if she'd known what she knew now.

Except that their daughter, the very being who'd kept them in contact for all these years, the girl conceived during, yes, the hottest sex of her life but also at the height of her love affair with Brandon, needed them.

She faced him with the same resolve she'd mustered in front of her parents, but this time her shoulders were shuddering from the cold and her fear for her child. And with one additional trait she'd never given herself credit for. Courage.

"Go get our girl, Brandon."

Their gazes locked, and she saw all the unexpressed longing she'd ever had for him reflected back at her in his eyes. Along with the commitment they'd both never shirked.

Sierra.

"Wait here. I will hand her to you through these windows. You take care of her from here."

She nodded. "I will." It was the most solemn vow she'd ever made. The still-drunk wedding vows in Vegas that were the birth of their marriage on paper only weren't even a dim equivalent.

As she watched, Brandon's focus turned to the attic windows. To Sierra. Toni's heart threatened to break open. The chances of her ever seeing him alive again—

A loud creak sounded from inside the attic. But it wasn't from inside. It was one of the attic windows. The windowpane closest to Brandon was rising.

Toni sucked in a breath and said a silent prayer, hoping against hope that a gun barrel wouldn't appear. She and Brandon were defenseless.

The moment Brandon saw Sierra's face in the window he wanted to whoop at the top of his lungs. His relief was quickly edged out by grim reality.

"Where's the shooter, honey?"

"Boy, am I glad to see you guys! We have to hurry, the bad guy is shooting downstairs." Sierra spoke through the window she'd raised halfway.

"Sierra, come out here." Brandon reached for her.

"I can't get this window up any higher." She grunted as she pushed up against it.

"I've got it." He shoved at the pane, and it inched up. "Dammit."

"Let me help." Toni knelt next to him. "Sierra, get your fingers out of the way."

"Hurry!" Sierra's squeal punctured through Brandon's

crisis-management demeanor and his hands slipped, the combination of sweat, freezing temperatures and the blasted antique window mechanism a terrible storm of doom.

"I've got you now, girlie," Toby's voice boomed, too close.

Sierra screamed.

"Oof!" Toni grunted as she shoved the window another two inches up, which was just enough for Sierra's head to fit through.

"Hurry." Brandon held her shoulders until they had her legs and then her feet out, and Sierra collapsed into Toni's arms. Toni didn't take any time to comfort their daughter as she immediately scrambled sideways, toward the corner of the house, out of view of the attic window.

Out of danger.

Sierra disappeared first, then Toni moved to follow. But she stopped at the edge of the wall and turned back, looked at him.

Footsteps pounded—up the attic ladder, he assumed.

"Brandon, come on!" Toni's cry was a plea he couldn't honor. He had to stay here until both his girls were out of sight, out of the path of the crazy man.

He shook his head and motioned with his hand for Toni to keep going. Toni and he shared a glance he knew would be forever seared in his heart. It conveyed all he never could say to her, would never say to her now.

"Take care of her." They were his last words before a gunshot rent the air.

"Mom, did you see the way the SWAT officers got both of us out of the way so quickly?" Sierra sat next to her on the gurney, wrapped in a blanket. They'd been hustled to the same vehicle Kevin had lain in only hours earlier.

"I did, baby girl." She tried to stay calm, but since seeing the love of her life assassinated right in front of her minutes ago, she hadn't been able to think of anything but. Brandon had given his life for Sierra. For both of them.

The most intense grief attacked her conscience as her heart lamented what she knew would be the biggest regret of her life. Not going with Brandon overseas thirteen years ago was still a huge mistake on her part, but she'd been given a second chance to make it right with Brandon. For Sierra.

For us.

There was no more *us.* Toby Clayton's last shot had fired and she'd seen Brandon's head whip to the side, seen the spatter of blood right before the SWAT officer had yanked her back—

"Toni?" Carmela Inez stood at the door of the ambulance. "Sierra. How are you both doing?"

"We're great!" Sierra responded with the innocence Toni dreaded shattering. How was she going to tell her?

"Toni?" She sat nearest the door, and turned her body to face Carmela so that Sierra wouldn't see her expression.

"Where—where is he?"

Carmela tilted her head as if unsure how to answer. "Toby Clayton has been apprehended. Our sniper caught him in the shoulder, which was enough to flatten him."

"The bad man is still…alive?" Sierra's voice wavered, and Toni quickly turned and hugged her.

"He'll never hurt anyone again, Sierra." Carmela was adamant, and Sierra relaxed against Toni's side.

"And—and…Brandon?" The last came out on a whisper. A keening sob swelled and she turned her head away from Sierra, needing to protect her from the harsh reality until she could tell her what happened.

"Toni." Carmela's hand was on her shoulder, her gaze full of compassion. "He's fine. Brandon's okay," she confirmed. "He took a graze to his head, is all."

"A graze? I saw Toby Clayton shoot him." Toni wanted to believe Carmela so badly, but what she'd seen wasn't something Brandon could survive. Or was it? She'd been pulled back by the SWAT team before she saw Brandon fall…

"You were involved in a very fast, very lethal takedown. It takes time to process it all. But trust me, Brandon's absolutely okay." Carmela spoke with authority.

"Mom, is Toby Clayton the bad man? Because he couldn't have shot Dad. He used up all his bullets."

Both Toni and Carmela turned to Sierra, who'd stood up to face both of them. Toni's breathing was shallow again, trying to comprehend everything her mind was trying to digest.

"Yes, Toby Clayton is the monster who tried to hurt you. How do you know so much about his handgun, exactly?" Toni asked.

"Because I saw it, Mom. He had a Glock and the magazine held seventeen rounds. They can hold eleven, or seventeen, or even more, but eleven is pretty common in the USA. After he'd shot off thirteen, I knew he had the seventeen-round magazine. He had a total of eighteen, tops, if he had one in the chamber. I heard him fire all eighteen before he came into the attic."

"Impressive, Sierra." Carmela thought it was fine that her daughter knew about firearms? It reminded her of her younger brothers.

Kevin.

"Tell me exactly how you know so much about weapons, Sierra?" But Toni already knew.

"Uncle Kevin helps me understand law enforcement topics, is all." Sierra looked at Carmela, then at Toni. "Where is Uncle Kevin?"

Toni turned to Carmela for the answer, tabling her reflexive ire at her sibling for the sake of his well-being.

"Your Uncle Kevin is in the hospital, and he's going to be just fine. He was injected with a sedative that, according to his doctor, has just about worn off."

"That's what the bad guy—the Toby man—was going to give me a shot of!" Sierra grinned. "I fooled him, though."

"You did, and we're going to need you to tell me all this again, for an official statement. When you're up to it." Carmela nodded at them both. "I'll let the EMTs finish up here."

"I want to be with my family!" A loud shout from a figure being wheeled across the cul-de-sac on a different gurney. EMTs blocked her direct view as they guided him over the still icy road toward the ambulance.

Disbelief warred with memory as Toni stood and shed the shiny silver blanket.

"Dad!" Sierra jumped out of the ambulance and bolted for him. Her reaction proved she'd escaped unscathed, at least physically, from the nightmare she'd endured.

Toni followed Sierra, but more slowly, afraid to believe in this vision of Brandon, which was more like a dream. A very good dream.

"Brandon?"

He turned his head, and the eyes she'd thought she'd never see again were alight with joy. When his gaze locked with hers, though, the joy disappeared. Replaced with a quiet knowing.

"Thanks for saving her, Toni." He continued to hold Sierra to his chest, and for once Toni felt she was intruding on something special that she wasn't a part of.

"You're the hero, Brandon." She meant it. He'd been willing to take a bullet for their daughter.

"Yeah, Dad, you saved me!" Sierra lifted her head to see Brandon's expression. "And you have the bullet wound to prove it."

"It's just a graze. Nothing more." Spoken like a true hero.

He just wasn't her hero anymore, and never would be. Toni's heart was shattering into countless tiny pieces as she watched Brandon and Sierra's reunion. She was going to have to learn to live with the fact that she'd lost out on her chance with Brandon, again, for the rest of her life.

Her phone vibrated and she looked at it, desperate for a distraction from the sorry mess she'd made of her and Brandon's lives. She pressed the accept button.

Willow's smiling face filled her screen, but she saw the worry under her sister's obvious relief.

"Hi, Willow."

"Hey! I'm so proud of you, sis! You're really okay?"

"Yes, I'm completely okay, promise." And she wasn't lying. She was physically okay, despite having screwed up the chance for a romantic relationship with the one man she'd ever truly loved. "I'm worried about Aubrey and Kevin, though—"

"Stop. I just got off the phone with Kevin. Aubrey's at the same hospital and they're both okay. Kevin's going to be released by noon, and Jake's going to pick him up. Aubrey has a concussion and will probably have to spend the night, but I'll be with her. I'll be on the road as soon as all the highways are plowed. The temps are already rising, so the snow is already melting away."

"Great. That is definitely good news."

"You don't sound so happy about it." Willow let out a short laugh. "You're spent, sis. It'll take a week to recover physically from this. And the trauma of seeing your kid taken... I'm so sorry."

"Thanks." Toni didn't explain her somber tone, but instead gave Willow a summary of all that had happened since they'd last spoken, when Toni had been on the roof and Sierra still inside.

"You handled it perfectly. And wow, what a thing for Brandon to do." Willow's voice was full of awe, rare for the former Marine.

"Yeah, Brandon's a hero. Has anyone told Mom and Dad yet about any of this?" She wanted to talk to their parents, but after she had nursed her broken heart.

"I spoke to them as soon as I knew you were all okay. Mom was already cut in on the Clayton situation, because I asked her to reach out to her contacts in case they heard Toby was back in the country. If he hadn't used a false passport Mom would have found out and told me."

"So I don't need to call them until I look better?" She

didn't want to stress her parents out. They'd all been through enough these last seven months.

Willow laughed. "No, you enjoy your chance to be free of a threat. I can assure you that there's no one currently targeting an O'Malley."

"That you know of." Toni heard her name being called and looked up to see Carmela motioning for her to come back to the ambulance. "Look, I've got to go."

"Toni, wait. Whatever you think happened or didn't happen between you and Brandon over the last twenty-four hours, don't give it any weight. Let the dust settle. This isn't the time for long-term decisions."

"I'm sure you're right, Willow. Talk to you later." She disconnected. What Willow didn't realize was that it took two to make it work. Toni couldn't make Brandon forgive her for her lack of trust in him when it mattered most.

Chapter 25

One month later
O'Malley estate, Montana

Toni enjoyed her drive out to her parents' place to pick up Sierra from a week with her grandparents. Brandon had dropped Sierra off on Sunday. Their daughter had insisted she wanted to spend her spring break week in Montana and not with either parent at the various getaways they'd suggested. Toni suspected that Sierra didn't want to have to pick between her and Brandon. Because it was clear they were not all going to travel together.

She and Brandon had retreated back to their usual détente, conversing as needed for Sierra but completely avoiding anything personal to either of them. And she'd figured out that her heart was never going to heal, but she'd figure out how to keep going, for Sierra.

Work had been a welcome distraction from her inner conflict over Brandon, too. Toby Clayton remained in custody and a future trial would require her attention.

Toni had spent last night at Willow and Jay's place in Coeur d'Alene, as much to break up the long car ride to her folks' as to have time with Willow. She made the drive from Idaho to Montana in record time and pulled into the long graveled drive that led to her parents' home less than seven hours after she'd left Willow's. Rolling green hills dotted with wildflowers in Washington State had yielded to snowcapped mountains and blankets of brown soil under which spring still slept in western Montana. Patches of snow were visible whenever there was a gap in the trees that populated Mom and Dad's property.

She got out of her car and the wind immediately whipped her coat open, chilling her to the bone. "Definitely not Everett," she muttered, and went to the front double doors. Before she touched the handle, the door opened wide. But no one was standing there.

"Sierra?" She stepped into the foyer and looked around the back of the door, expecting Sierra to launch at her for a hug.

But the space was empty. The wind had probably blown the door open as she approached; her parents would have left the door unlocked knowing she was on her way.

"Sierra? Mom? Dad?" She raised her voice as she walked into the family room, noted the healthy fire in the fireplace that was the size of a medieval hearth. Where was everyone?

Probably out back, or traipsing through the woods as her mother enjoyed doing. She called it "exploring." Toni and her siblings called it "mud stomping."

The view through the wall of windows tugged at her, and she couldn't resist walking to the doors that led onto the expansive balcony. It was cold as winter but it was clear, and the panoramic vistas at once eased her heart and lightened her soul. If she lived here, she'd soak up this view any chance she could. Probably wouldn't get much work done.

She began to turn away from the beauty to continue her search for signs of life. Her gaze landed on the cocktail table outside—more specifically, the silver bucket with a bottle of her favorite champagne in it. Two flutes stood inside a wooden box next to the bucket. No crystal was going to stay put on the deck in these winds.

"I wanted to surprise you, but in a good way this time." Brandon's voice vibrated through her entire body. She turned to face him. He stood next to her and looked more vibrant, more alive, than she could ever remember. The scar on his right temple had faded to a sexy badge of honor, and there were a few more silver hairs threaded through his locks. His deep brown eyes held her gaze with determination.

And something else.

"I—I thought you were on a road trip for work." She tried to buy time, tried to keep her mind from racing ahead and convincing her heart that this wasn't what it seemed. What she hoped.

He grinned. "I was. I drove up to Calgary and came back yesterday, as planned." She knew he had clients in Alberta, other diplomats who'd traded in active service for civilian consulting.

"Where's Sierra?" She glanced over his shoulder into the kitchen. "My parents?" But she thought she might know the answer.

"They're on their way to Everett, to stay at either one of our places."

"Brandon, you have to let me talk first. If this is what I think it is—"

"Okay." He nodded, but she saw the spark of impatience in his eyes. The same look when he wanted, needed her in all ways possible. The same way she'd never stopped needing him. "Shoot."

She grimaced. "I don't think that will ever be a good euphemism after what we—what you and Sierra went through."

He grasped her hands. "We all went through it, Toni."

"Wait, let me talk." She sucked in a breath. "I'm such a fool, Brandon. I should have gone with you all those years ago. That night when we found out I was pregnant, I didn't know how to sort out what I was feeling. I made a mess of things between us and Sierra has had to bounce from me to you all these years for no reason other than my selfishness. Can you ever forgive me?"

He grasped her hands more tightly, bent his head to touch his forehead to hers. "We weren't ready to commit back then, save for our paper marriage, because we were immature. We've grown together now, as parents, as human beings. There's nothing for me to forgive you about, Toni. The question is, can you forgive me for not coming right out with my real motive for moving next door to you?"

"It wasn't for Sierra?"

"Of course it was a good move, the best move, for Sierra. But all the decisions I made to move back, to leave the service, were done with how it would affect you. Truthfully? I was making decisions based upon how they would increase my chances of changing your mind."

Tears streamed down her cheeks, and she saw his eyes glisten, too.

"We're both fools. What we want has been standing right here all along."

Brandon nodded and got down on one knee.

"Oh, no, you don't." She mirrored him, and they knelt knee to knee on the hardwood floor. Their gazes met, and she smiled through her tears. "Together?"

Brandon nodded. "Together."

"Brandon Anderson, will you make our paper marriage a real one from now until forever? I promise to love you until my dying breath."

"Toni O'Malley, I accept your proposal. Will you take me as your husband in all the ways, from today until death do us part? I've loved you forever and there will never be an end to my devotion for you."

"Yes." She barely had her affirmation out before his lips met hers, and they shared the first of many kisses of their real marriage.

* * * * *

Get up to 4 Free Books!

We'll send you 2 free books from each series you try
PLUS a free Mystery Gift.

Both the **Harlequin Intrigue®** and **Harlequin® Romantic Suspense** series feature compelling novels filled with heart-racing action-packed romance that will keep you on the edge of your seat.

YES! Please send me 2 FREE novels from the Harlequin Intrigue or Harlequin Romantic Suspense series and my FREE gift (gift is worth about $10 retail). I may cancel anytime by emailing ReaderServiceInfo@Harlequin.com or by calling 1-800-873-8635.If I don't cancel, I will receive 6 brand-new Harlequin Intrigue Larger-Print books every month and be billed just $7.19 each in the U.S. or $7.99 each in Canada, or 4 brand-new Harlequin Romantic Suspense books every month and be billed just $6.39 each in the U.S. or $7.19 each in Canada, a savings of 20% off the cover price. It's quite a bargain! Shipping and handling is just 75¢ per book in the U.S. and $1.75 per book in Canada.* I understand that accepting the free books and gift places me under no obligation to buy anything—they are mine to keep for free no matter what I decide.

Choose one:

☐ **Harlequin Intrigue Larger-Print**
(199/399 BPA G3CD)

☐ **Harlequin Romantic Suspense**
(240/340 BPA G3CD)

☐ **Or Try Both!**
(199/399 & 240/340 BPA G3CE)

____
Name (please print)

____
Address   Apt. #

____
City   State/Province   Zip/Postal Code

Email: Please check this box ☐ if you would like to receive newsletters and promotional emails from Harlequin Enterprises ULC and its affiliates. You can unsubscribe anytime.

Mail to the **Harlequin Reader Service:**
IN U.S.A.: P.O. Box 1341, Buffalo, NY 14240-8531
IN CANADA: P.O. Box 603, Fort Erie, Ontario L2A 5X3

Want to explore our other series or interested in ebooks? Visit www.ReaderService.com or call 1-800-873-8635.

HIHRS2603